CAMINOS

GUERNICA WORLD EDITIONS 4

CAMINOS

Scott Walker

GUERNICA
World
EDITIONS

TORONTO—BUFFALO—LANCASTER (U.K.)

2018

Michael Mirolla, general editor
Julie Roorda, editor
Cover design: Errol Richardson
Interior layout: Jill Ronsley, Sun Editing & Book Design
Cover Image: Letter from Mercedes González Conde
to her brother, Antonio González Conde, c. 1930
Guernica Editions Inc.
1569 Heritage Way, Oakville, (ON), Canada L6M 2Z7
2250 Military Road, Tonawanda, N.Y. 14150-6000 U.S.A.
www.guernicaeditions.com

Distributors:
University of Toronto Press Distribution,
5201 Dufferin Street, Toronto (ON), Canada M3H 5T8
Gazelle Book Services, White Cross Mills
High Town, Lancaster LA1 4XS U.K.

First edition.
Printed in Canada.

Legal Deposit—First Quarter
Library of Congress Catalog Card Number: 2017960396
Library and Archives Canada Cataloguing in Publication
Walker, Scott, 1968-, author   Caminos / Scott Walker. -- First edition.
(Guernica world editions ; 4)Issued in print and electronic formats.
ISBN 978-1-77183-312-7 (softcover).--ISBN 978-1-77183-313-4 (EPUB).--
ISBN 978-1-77183-314-1 (Kindle)
I. Title.
PS3623.A412C36
2018   813'.6   C2017-907300-1   C2017-907301-X

For Annette, who always believed.

Asturias, Spain
September 1885

CASILDA WAS JUST two hours dead, but Bernardo had already banished the baby from the farmhouse overlooking the Cantabrian Sea.

Hunched like a troll on the short stool he used every morning when dressing, Bernardo sat beside their bed, unable to look away from Casilda's face or turn loose her cool hand. The candle on the single bedside table, and another perched on the sill of the room's only window, cast a morose, yellow glow.

The big, oak bed nearly filled the little space. Bernardo had scrimped for a decade to buy it for his wife from a craftsman in the village. She had nestled for just three years among the carved triskeles, circular fans, four-pointed stars, six-petal *flor galanas*—Asturias is Celtic Spain—and the pair of griffins which stood guard from the center of the headboard. Now, Bernardo thought bitterly, that girl has killed her.

When she was young, Casilda had often dreamed of becoming a nun and joining the Order of Our Lady of Mercies—in Spanish, *la Orden de Nuestra Señora de las Mercedes*. Casilda saw the Mercederian nuns for the first time when she was four. She had gone with her parents to the nearby town of Avilés for the weekly market. As they came around a corner into the square before the hulking stone-walled convent, the nuns filed out through the dark portal into the drab street. Their white habits glowed in the sun and the wind whipped up their wimples like wings. Casilda thought they were angels. The image stuck in her mind, and she felt a strong emotional attachment to the Order, even after she had given up the idea of joining its ranks. Casilda always saved her few spare *pesetas* throughout the year to make an offering at the convent on the Virgin's feast day in September.

1

Lying on the bed at the farmhouse, Casilda had prayed for the Virgin of Mercies to watch over her daughter when she was gone. And she had named the baby Mercedes.

* * *

Ohio, USA
June 1983

The dinner dishes cleared away, Pilar came back to the kitchen table carrying a large cardboard file box. "Ahhh, the archive," her son Harry said. "This is when I go out back for a smoke." His brother-in-law Tom did not smoke, but he also had little interest in the stacks of old pictures. He followed Harry outside to continue their conversation about the US Open. They were both fanatical golfers. Pilar's niece Brenda, and Brenda's son Robert, could not wait to dig into the box.

"Oh, this is a nice one," Pilar said, "one of my favourites." She withdrew a slightly creased and faded black and white Kodak Brownie photograph and handed it to Brenda: Mercedes, gaunt and wrinkled, in a pale summer dress and an apron, her arms hanging loosely at her side; Antonio, robust and suntanned, in dark trousers, vest and a white band-collar shirt open at the neck, his hands stuffed into his pockets and a self-rolled cigarette pinched in the corner of his mouth; Pilar standing between them in a black robe and mortar-board hat, smiling shyly. "Me and Mom and Dad on the day I graduated from high school in June of 1943."

The image captivated fourteen-year-old Robert, though he thought his great-grandparents inscrutable as they stared sternly into the camera in turn of the century style. Robert wanted to know everything about these people.

Chapter 1

Bernardo's sister bundled up the newborn and started for home. Her brother's cows were bulky silhouettes in the pasture beyond the vine-covered wall beside the road. Two of the big, blonde animals, sucking at the crisp air with their moist snouts, caught her scent and came clomping toward the dirt lane. They lowed urgently. No one had thought of the cattle all day as Casilda lay dying.

"They will have to be milked," Carmen said to herself. She hoped one of her nephews would remember. She pulled the baby closer to herself, trying to block the damp, cold wind gusting off the Atlantic.

"He did what?" Carmen's husband Anselmo thundered when she came into the house with the bundle.

"Anselmo ... the baby! Keep your voice down," she ordered.

"That brother of yours is a miserable, soulless dog," Anselmo hissed.

"Anselmo, please."

Her husband loomed in the center of the squat, lime-plastered room. His head nearly brushed one of the rafters, which were fashioned from tree trunks with only the bark and branches removed. Ignoring his wife, the stocky Asturian farmer continued. "No, that's an insult to a dog. Even a bitch cares for its pups!"

"Anselmo, calm down," she pleaded again, placing her free hand lightly on the side of the baby's head to cover one of her ears while pressing the other against her chest.

"No, he's gone too far this time. Entirely too far," Anselmo insisted, his voice rising again. "We can't allow him to do this."

3

Carmen was too tired to have this argument now, and to tamp down Anselmo's flaming indignation, no matter how justified his outburst. She felt she was outside her body, spent physically and emotionally. Casilda. Dead. The day seemed like an endless, terrible dream.

"The family ... the village ... the ... the Church must stand up to him! Yes! Go get the priest!" Anselmo shouted.

Mercedes began to cry. "Oh, Anselmo," Carmen sighed. "Now you've woken the baby." She stroked Mercedes' little arm and tiny clenched fist, rhythmically rocking her up and down. "Shhh. Shhh, little one. Shhh."

Carmen returned her attention to her husband. "There's nothing to be done, not tonight anyway," she reproached. "Perhaps tomorrow, after some hours for his anger to cool, Bernardo will see the rashness of his actions."

"Your brother? Recognize the rashness of his actions? That will take centuries, not hours. I've watched him be rash, foolhardy, stupid and mean for more than forty years." Anselmo had known Bernardo all his life. The pastures of their family farms abutted. The two men grew up in these farmhouses where they were now raising their own families, as the long chain of their ancestors had for centuries.

Anselmo so loathed Bernardo that, for a while when they were young, he had even tried to harden his heart against Carmen, despite the deep affection he felt for her. He eventually surrendered to his love, though it meant that the sweetness of life with Carmen would be laced with the rancidness of Bernardo's regular presence. "The Blessed Virgin is more likely to appear in this room," Anselmo fumed, "than your worthless brother is to feel a second of remorse or show a drop of devotion to this child."

"Anselmo!" Carmen crossed herself with her free arm. "Bernardo's wretchedness doesn't justify blasphemy from you."

"I'm sorry," Anselmo said quickly, chastened by his wife's rebuke. "That was wrong." He rolled back his fury. "Here," he said, reaching out for Mercedes, "give her to me. You're still dressed for the road."

Carmen gently handed over the baby, who had fallen back to sleep as quickly as she had awoken.

Carmen removed her woolen cloak and hung it on a peg in the wall by the heavy, iron-studded oak door. Her hand lingered on the undyed homespun. It could just as easily have been a horse blanket. She closed her eyes and rubbed her forehead, trying to erase the memory of this wretched day.

Casilda's contractions had begun before sunrise. Bernardo sent one of their sons to fetch Carmen to midwife. She could tell her sister-in-law already was in distress when she arrived. The birth was arduous, the labor going on for hours. To Carmen's surprise, after a pregnancy which had been difficult from the beginning, the baby emerged healthy and strong. Casilda was overjoyed to have a daughter at last, after giving birth to four boys. Carmen nearly had to wrench the girl from her mother's arms when the hemorrhaging continued.

The baby was moved to another room. Bernardo alternately knelt and stood by the bed, clenching his wife's hand while his sister fought to save her. There was not much she could do. A bit of pressure here, a balled packing of cotton fabric there. As with new mothers for millennia, only Nature would decide whether Casilda survived the creation of this new life. Bernardo would not allow their sons to enter the bedroom, despite the women's entreaties, as his wife grew inexorably weaker. Until she drew her last, shallow breath, he insisted that God would not take Casilda from him.

As Carmen stood in her kitchen, motionless except for the rhythmic rubbing on her forehead, Anselmo cradled Mercedes in his arms and eased himself down onto one of the benches by the long dining table. He knew it was best to give his wife the time and space she needed.

As always, Anselmo was pleased with his carpentry and felt a rush of pride when the bench took his weight without the slightest groan or wobble. The chestnut tree had towered behind their shallow-roofed, limestone farmhouse for as long as anyone could recall. Anselmo loved to climb it when he was a boy. Generations of his family had roasted and feasted on its nuts every autumn. When the tree came down in a fierce spring storm, Anselmo fashioned the thick table and heavy benches from its wood.

Carmen opened her eyes. She turned and looked at her husband holding the baby in his burly arms and managed a weak smile. She gazed across the room. It was windowless, but for a small, unglazed, iron-barred and shuttered square over the washbasin. The room served as entranceway, kitchen, dining hall and cannery. Coal from the pile heaped in the adjacent dirt-floored cellar smouldered in the fire grate of the cooking chimney opposite the door. Carmen crossed the room, patting Anselmo tenderly on the shoulder as she passed, and stood before the undulating orange and gold embers to warm herself.

After a bit, Anselmo said, looking down at the sleeping child: "We'll make a place for her in our family. What did you say is her name?"

Casilda broke her gaze from the embers. "Mercedes."

"We'll make a place for little Mercedes to sleep in our bed. It's good that you're still nursing Jorge."

Carmen stepped back over to Anselmo and touched Mercedes' fat cheek. Employing an oft-used term of endearment, Carmen said: "Yes. We'll welcome this little rabbit into the world properly, and we'll sort out this absurdity with Bernardo tomorrow. Surely he'll come to his senses."

Anselmo rolled his eyes. "Yes, tomorrow," he said without additional commentary.

* * *

The mourners filled San Román Church in the village of Naveces, and they spilled out of the Neo-Romanesque building into the forecourt under the giant, old oak tree. As loathed as Bernardo was by nearly all who knew him, Casilda was beloved. But on this day, most hearts softened a little for Bernardo. He was clearly devastated by his wife's death. He sat weeping in the front pew through the entire mass.

Carmen sat near the back of the church. She still felt numb. Mercedes slept in her arms. As Anselmo expected, there had been no reasoning with Bernardo about her exile. Carmen was disobeying her brother by bringing Mercedes to her mother's funeral. His anger even stronger than his grief, Bernardo glared at his sister as he followed his wife's coffin, hoisted on the shoulders of her kinsmen, out of the church after the mass ended and the procession to the cold, wet tomb in the graveyard began.

One of the mourners, standing in the vestibule of the church and wiping away tears with the back of his hand, was a young man named Julio, though everyone always had called him Chus. The Spanish love nicknames. He was six when he first talked to Casilda, but Chus had seen her visiting his mother and working in the fields for as long as he could remember.

His parents had nine children. Chus was the youngest. Their farm near Naveces was too small to fill so many mouths; his parents and grandparents were still alive and his two older brothers with their wives and children all lived on the ancestral land. So, after he married, Chus had moved to the farm of his wife's family, on the other side of the municipal district of Castrillón. He walked all night after hearing of Casilda's death. He arrived soaked from the steady rain and covered in mud to his knees, just as the priest stepped to the altar.

One of Bernardo's typically nasty acts had brought Casilda and Chus together when he was a boy. Bernardo's farm dog had gone into heat one summer, and he locked her in an outbuilding to keep the neighboring dogs away from her. All he needed was more damned pups to drown in the stream.

Chus's dog could not resist Nature's call. One morning when Bernardo opened the door of the outbuilding, he was shocked to see two dogs inside. Bernardo grabbed a thick plank which was leaning against the wall, closed the door behind him, and in the semi-darkness beat Chus's dog to death. He dragged the bloody corpse into the woods. Chus sat up all night waiting for his dog to return home.

Bernardo made no attempt to hide his actions from his family that evening at dinner. He stood proudly in the center of the room,

7

theatrically reenacting the blows. "Bernardo, that is enough," Casilda finally said. "This is hardly a tale for the table or a good example for the boys."

"When I want your opinion, I'll ask for it," Bernardo snapped. To his sons, he added: "Listen to none of that from your mother. It's just women's weakness. You have to stand up for what is yours—every damned day." The boys nodded, their eyes cast down on their bowls of smoked pork and garbanzos, but they were unconvinced. They had experienced their father's rage and their mother's kindness enough times to learn which was preferable.

As she lay awake that night beside snoring Bernardo, Casilda remembered that she had heard of a woman in the village who was trying to give away some pups. The next morning, after the boys and Bernardo had eaten their breakfast and were hoeing in the corn crop, Casilda walked into Naveces and traded the old woman a sack of their fabes beans and a few lengths of her chorizo sausage for a wiggling, licking, female puppy.

Casilda headed back the way she came, alternately through the cool of the forest and in the sweltering sun when the road ran through the pastures and fields, past her farm, and on another mile. She saw six-year-old Chus sitting under a tree on the side of the road up ahead, forlorn and poking around in the dirt with a stick. He was slow to look up when she stopped in front of him.

"Hello, good morning," Casilda said. "You're Chus? Sara's boy?"

"Yes, ma'am, I am," Chus replied, and then he went back to his poking around with the stick.

"Look up here, Chus," Casilda said. Her voice was soft but firm. He obeyed. "I heard that your dog went missing."

Looking at the ground again, stifling his urge to cry, Chus mumbled: "Yes, ma'am. He has." He looked up at her, and his exasperation poured out. "I've looked everywhere for him for two days, everywhere, but nobody's seen him. It's not like him just to run off like that. He stays away sometimes the whole day, but he's always out there at the door before I go to bed, waiting for his dinner. I can't find him!"

For what was not the first time, Casilda thought, *How did I end up with such a man?* "Well," she said to the boy, pulling the puppy from the basket in which she had carried her beans and sausages to the old woman, "just this morning, I was down in Naveces, and I saw a lady who had some pups."

Chus's eyes widened when he saw the chocolate-brown dog struggling to escape Casilda's grasp.

"I told her I'd heard about a boy whose dog had gone missing. And she told me to give him this one." She added, after a second: "In case his has gotten lost in the woods and has to live with another boy on another farm now."

"You think that's what happened … it's for me?" Chus was having difficulty digesting these two threads of Casilda's conversation at the same time.

"Yes, this pup is for you," Casilda said. She handed him the dog, which immediately began licking Chus's face enthusiastically as he hugged it to himself with both arms. "And I do believe that is what happened to your dog. The same thing happened to me when I was a girl," she said, lying. "I had a little dog who was my constant companion, my best friend"—which was true. "And one day, she never came home"—which was not.

"Years later, after I had grown up, I was at the Monday market in Avilés, talking with a woman from all the way over in Muros de Nalón, and she told me that when she was a little girl, a dog showed up at her farm, hungry and tired. Her family knew it must have gotten lost in the woods, probably chasing a rabbit too far, but they had no way of knowing from where. So they took her in—my little dog, I know in my heart—and she lived a long, good life with those people."

Chus thought about Casilda's story for a minute. "Oh, I hope my dog found a good family too."

"I'm sure he did," Casilda said. "You know God loves the defenseless creatures and cares about them."

"That's what my mama always says," Chus mumbled, his attention on the puppy, "when she's telling me why I shouldn't throw rocks at the birds' nests."

"You should listen to your mother," Casilda ordered.

"Yes, ma'am, I will," Chus promised. "Can I go now? I want to show my dog to my mama." Chus was smiling broadly, the puppy sprawled halfway over his shoulder and chewing on his black hair.

"Of course, boy. You go on home. And tell your mother Casilda Conde gave her to you."

Chus started to run off toward his family's farm. He stopped in the middle of the narrow dirt road, dust hanging in the air around his feet, and shouted back: "Thank you, ma'am. Thank you very much. I'll call her Casilda."

The canine Casilda had lived a long, good life. She still was alive, in fact, a bit arthritic and grey around her muzzle but otherwise healthy. She was back at the farmhouse Chus shared with his wife and young daughter, as he stood in the rain watching the pall-bearers slide the box containing the body of Casilda Conde into the crypt. He noticed the inscription carved in the pediment of the marble façade on the adjoining tomb: *Tu nos dijiste que la muerte no es el final del camino.* You told us that death is not the end of the way.

Chapter 2

In the late-1800s, many industrial workers across Asturias were shedding their faith as they embraced socialism and rose up against the established powers. The centuries-long holy war to reconquer the Iberian peninsula from the Umayyad Muslims had fostered a particularly conservative brand of Catholicism in Spain. Thereafter, the Spanish Church had maintained strong ties with the monarchy and ruling classes. That relationship fueled a bilateral animosity between the Church and frustrated nineteenth-century laborers, but the farmers of Castrillón generally remained devout.

The cabildo was a fixture of the church or chapel in most Spanish villages and towns. Sometimes it was located within, at the back of the nave, sometimes under a roof off the side of the building, as it was at San Román, with stone-block benches around the perimeter. Either way, seated around the cabildo, the villagers collectively decided their community affairs. Government appointees administered the law in the district capitals, but in the thousands of tiny settlements scattered throughout the countryside, there were no regular representatives of officialdom. The parishioners essentially governed themselves by direct democracy at the cabildos.

* * *

As always for the Sunday high mass at San Román, worshippers packed every pew. The church was small, but its baroque interior was lavish. The trumpeting angels, corpulent putti and haloed saints gazed out toward the nave from the gilded altar filling the apse.

On this Sunday, two days after Casilda's funeral, Carmen and Anselmo presented Mercedes for baptism. The medieval stone font was shaped like a giant egg cup. Bernardo had elected not to attend. The parishioners, who so recently were mourners, smiled and applauded when the priest lifted the newly-christened Mercedes before the altar and then walked up the aisle, hoisting her high for them to welcome into the Church.

"That scoundrel, Bernardo," Anselmo hissed as he and Carmen stood beside the church receiving congratulations on Mercedes' baptism from their neighbors. Most of them were related in one way or another.

"Oh, Anselmo, don't taint this beautiful day with bitterness," Carmen said. She had begun to regain her sense of balance, and the joyous occasion of Mercedes' baptism further lifted the gloom which had descended with Casilda's death.

"Well, I would say," interjected an old cousin who had overheard Anselmo's comment, "that everyone else here agrees with your husband's assessment. It's a scandal for the whole village. Inexcusable."

Anselmo turned to the old man. "But what are we to do about it?" he asked. Smacking one of the church's limestone quoins with the palm of his hand, he added: "My wife's brother's heart is harder than this block on the issue. He will not take her back." Anselmo always referred to Bernardo as "my wife's brother." After twenty years of marriage, he still could not stomach calling Bernardo his brother-in-law.

"I've called a village meeting," the old man, Juan, informed them. "We'll arrange for her to live for a while with each of the families who can afford to take her in. We all know it would be a great burden for you to bear alone, given your own new baby to care for and the troubles this year at your farm."

12

It was true. They were struggling. The floods brought on by the abnormally long and heavy rains the summer before had hit their corn and hay crops particularly hard. Anselmo was forced to sell half their cattle and hogs when their low-lying pastures were swampy for weeks on end. Much of their money went to feeding the remaining livestock. Fewer cows and hogs meant less milk, butter and sausages to sell at the market in Avilés for much needed cash. Still, Anselmo began to protest, his pride bruised.

"No, no," Juan said, waving his hand in a gesture more conciliatory than dismissive. "As a village and a family, we all must share in compensating for our cousin's latest sin. Father Agustín and the others are waiting in the cabildo for us. We'll meet there now to sort out the details."

Relieved to have some assistance, Anselmo and Carmen walked with Juan around the corner of the church to the cabildo. Juan quieted their neighbors and began. "We have not gathered here to cast aspersions upon Bernardo, though we legitimately could spend the remainder of the afternoon doing so. His behavior is reprehensible. This, we all know." Pointing toward sleeping Mercedes in Carmen's arms, he added: "Now, we must focus our attention on this child and committing ourselves to providing for her."

There was murmuring and shuffling. They were all farmers with large families of their own. Most lived ten or a fifteen people to a rustic house. A six-acre farm was considered a significant patrimony. Many families subsisted on plots of an acre or two, with a couple of cows for milk, a few hens for eggs and a pen of rabbits for stewing. Grandparents, parents, children and unmarried aunts worked long days growing fruits, vegetables and greens, and making sausages and cheese for the table and to sell at the market in town. Taking on Mercedes for years would be a challenge for any of them. Bernardo had a bigger, more prosperous farm than most in the area, which fed the resentment that they were being asked to make this sacrifice.

As the discussions rumbled among the people crowded on the stone benches, a tall, bearded man stood and stepped forward into the middle of the cabildo. "God has been good to me. My animals have flourished, and I have the means to bring this girl into my household, at least for the next year. We will be the first."

"Thank you, Manolo. Thank you very much," Juan said. "I have no doubt that God will note this great kindness."

"You're a good man," Carmen said to Manolo as she handed Mercedes to his wife, Noelia. Carmen stroked Mercedes' bald little head. "I wish with all my heart that we could keep her ourselves, but … but …" She was unable to continue. It all was so unfair, Carmen thought again, as she had repeatedly over the past days. That Casilda died. That Bernardo was taking the tragedy out on this innocent child. That she and Anselmo were having so much trouble when they worked so hard and remained ardently faithful to God and the Church. At the least, they should have been able to take in her niece.

"Now, now," Noelia said. "We all understand that you would keep her if you could. We'll attend to her needs, but you always will be her mother on this Earth now that Casilda is gone."

Carmen nodded quickly. She sniffed and wiped away her tears with her fingertips. It was so unfair. Anselmo put his arm around her shoulders and pulled her close. Carmen pressed her head against his thick chest.

"Very well," Juan said. He was not much for sentiment. "Our work here today is done. I propose we meet again, in a year, to assess the circumstances and determine which household can best afford to relieve Manolo and Noelia, if need be."

The group dispersed quickly into the lane, and then home to their farms and dinners. Sunday was their one day of rest, when they could take it. Each family passed the afternoons following the mass feasting as heartily as they could manage and whiling away the hours in relaxed conversation.

Only Carmen, Anselmo, Juan and Father Agustín remained in the cabildo. "Come with me for a libation before you go home," the priest said, motioning toward the seventeenth-century rectory across the lane. The house was half as large as the church itself. They followed as the aristocratic priest strode over to the rectory, through the arched doorway and across the wide, waxed floorboards of the spacious parlour.

"I've never seen so many books in my life," Carmen whispered to Anselmo as they stood in the center of the room surveying Father Agustín's wall of walnut shelves filled with leather-bound volumes. The youngest son of a noble family which had held onto its wealth—unlike many of the impoverished titled in late-nineteenth-century Spain—the priest was an educated and cultured man.

"Please, sit," Father Agustín said as he turned from a richly-carved chestnut cabinet. Carrying a silver tray bearing a bottle of wine and four glasses, he nodded toward an upholstered settee and armchairs near the open parlour windows.

"You have comported yourselves as well as anyone, including the good Lord, could expect in this trying time," Father Agustín said as he poured them each a glass of the rich Aragonese red he preferred.

"Thank you, Father," Carmen said, taking a deep drink of the dark-purple wine. "I hope that we'll be able to take her back next year, or the next. She belongs with us."

"I know," Father Agustín assured her. "And there always is the chance that God will provide some correction to Bernardo—"

"Oh, Father," Anselmo interrupted the young priest, grimacing. "Even you'll be mouldering over there in the cemetery before my wife's brother grows any basic human decency. No, we have to be prepared for that girl to wander from family to family, an orphan with her father living fat up the road, until she's old enough to fend for herself."

Father Agustín nodded slowly and took a sip from his glass. "This may well be true. If it is, it will be as God intends. And in this world or the next, Bernardo will pay for his sins. Our part is to see that Mercedes suffers as little as possible."

They sat silently for a while, sipping their wine, feeling the breeze through the windows and listening to the birdsong. Carmen contemplated Bernardo's long list of calumnies.

Juan broke the silence. "We've made a good start," he said. "I'd hoped Manolo and Noelia would accept the duty, but I didn't want

15

to push them. They had to decide for it themselves. I'm thankful that they did." Draining off his wine and slowly rising to his feet, Juan added to Carmen: "Don't worry, Carmelita. We're all with you, and with that little girl." Glancing around the room and leaning on his cane, Juan declared: "Now, I believe there's a pot of fabada waiting for me at home, and this old body is famished."

Carmen and Anselmo also took their leave and walked the three-quarters of a mile back to their farm. Carmen appreciated their cousins' generosity, and the kind words from Juan and Father Agustín, but she was still sad and angry.

When Carmen and Anselmo arrived home, their boys were running around the barnyard, tormenting a chicken. The weather had broken not long after dawn, dark clouds and cold rain yielding to blue sky and the bright, warm autumn sun. The dusky scent from the eucalyptus trees covering the hillsides floated on the breeze as Carmen herded the boys into the house and began to lay out the family's Sunday dinner.

Mercedes was oblivious, at least consciously, to her new surroundings as she entered her third home in less than a week of life. The six children of Manolo and Noelia were intrigued and excited to suddenly have a seventh in the house, especially the three girls. As Noelia prepared a cradle for Mercedes, their oldest daughter, Covadonga, carried the baby around, talking animatedly to this living doll and pointing out items around the room.

Chapter 3

The hilltop hamlet of San Adriano was nothing more than a few small farmhouses and the twelfth-century pilgrim chapel. The Chapel of San Adriano, with its thick walls of uncut stones and little bronze bell hanging in a tiny, off-center bell tower, sat on the coastal route of the Camino de Santiago—the medieval Way of St. James. Pilgrims walking from Irún, in the Pyrenees, to Santiago de Compostela, 200 miles farther on in Galicia, had trod the dirt lane from Naveces and passed through the village for eight centuries. Each year on September 8, the feast day of San Adriano, people from across Castrillón made their own small pilgrimages to the chapel for the fiesta to honour the district's patron saint.

Don Pelayo and the Moors was one of the boys' favourite games. In 722, a Visigoth chieftain named Pelayo ambushed a Muslim expeditionary force in the Cantabrian mountains near a place called Covadonga. According to the legend, the Virgin Mary appeared before Pelayo and his men as they cowered up in a hillside cave. She assured them victory if he rallied his fighters and led them into battle carrying their priest's wooden cross. Divine visitation or not, Pelayo and his pack of armed Asturian farmers found the courage to descend on the foraging Muslim soldiers, killing many and forcing the survivors' retreat back into León, south of the mountains. The Battle of Covadonga marked the birth of the Kingdom of Asturias—the only part of the Iberian Peninsula not incorporated into the Umayyad Caliphate—and the beginning of the Reconquista. "Asturias is Spain," the Asturians still like to say, "and the rest is just reconquered territory."

* * *

San Adriano, Asturias
September 1891

"José! José!" Mercedes shouted at her brother when she saw him horsing around with some village boys in a small pasture on the hillside below the church. She had walked with Manolo, Noelia and their children along the winding, unpaved roads from their farm on this Tuesday morning to attend the annual festival of San Adriano, for whom the church and the village were named.

Luck had remained with Manolo and Noelia since that Sunday afternoon six years before, and Mercedes had as well. Anselmo and Carmen's fortunes had slowly improved. However, they never felt confident enough about the next growing season to bring their niece back to live with them, and though neither of them would admit it aloud, relations with Bernardo were less complicated without Mercedes under their roof.

Bernardo still acted as if his only daughter did not exist. He never permitted her to visit the family farm called *Las Cepas*. But Carmen made sure Mercedes knew her brother José who still lived at the farm with their father. Her brothers Antonio, Ramón and Manuel were only characters in stories for Mercedes. They had gone to the Spanish colony of Cuba to seek their fortunes before she was born.

"José! José!" Mercedes cried more urgently as he kept playing with the boys. When they stopped to catch their breath, sweating profusely on the clear, sunny day, José saw Mercedes waving her arms and jumping up and down. He ran over to her.

"Hi, little rabbit!" José said, returning her tight embrace. He always used the moniker their Aunt Carmen gave Mercedes on the day she was born. "That's a very pretty dress!"

"Noelia made it for me, for the fiesta!" she exclaimed, twirling around for her brother. It was the first new garment she had received in her life. Noelia made such a traditional dress for each of her daughters when they turned five. Mercedes' fifth birthday, and then her sixth, passed without one, and it reinforced the sense of displacement she frequently experienced. When Noelia surprised her with the dress that morning, Mercedes stood for ten minutes in front of the mirror, admiring the dark green, deeply pleated skirt, the white, puffy-sleeved blouse, and the black pinafore which covered her shoulders and tied in a bow around her waist. She finally felt like a member of the family.

"It's the prettiest I've seen all year," José said.

Mercedes twirled again and beamed.

"So, they're still being nice to you? Manuel and Noelia?" José asked.

"Oh, yes," Mercedes said, patting her skirt straight and adjusting the bow of the pinafore. "I have my own bed off the kitchen, and I get all I want to eat. Noelia's teaching me to read and write, and she made me this beautiful dress."

"And the kids?" José asked. He had heard some stories.

"Mostly," Mercedes replied. "Covadonga isn't very nice to me anymore, but the others are, and I just stay away from her as much as I can." Mercedes could tell how Covadonga's behavior irritated her brother. She was not eager to stoke his quick anger, but she did wish he would find her tormenter and throw her into the nearest manure pile.

"You should tell Aunt Carmen next time you see her," José said. "She'll talk to Noelia about it."

"Oh, no, I couldn't do that," Mercedes said. "I don't want Noelia and Manuel to make me leave. I like it there with them."

José grunted and looked around the increasingly crowded festival. Everyone they knew was there, most of them wearing the best articles of clothing they owned to honour San Adriano.

"Have you seen the cows yet?" he asked, turning his attention back to his sister. "There are some beauties up there at the fair." He pointed up the hill toward the cluster of houses. "Papa has entered one of ours in the competition, and I'm sure she'll win!"

The mention of Bernardo doused Mercedes' bright mood. "Is he here, too?" she whispered, her eyes darting over the crowd along the far side of the churchyard where the boys had been playing. She hoped to catch a glimpse of her father, and she hoped not to at the same time.

"Oh, he's around somewhere," José said. "Probably on his fifth bottle of cider by know. You know how he is."

She did not, actually. Not in the first person.

"Hey, why don't you come down to the stream with us," José said, trying to lighten her mood again. "Munch thinks he's found an old stone fortress in the woods, and we're going to play Don Pelayo and the Moors."

"No," the dejected Mercedes said. "If I go to the woods, I may ruin my new dress."

"Oh, come on," José insisted. "Ramón just sent me this shirt from Havana, and I've already torn it!"

The mention of one of the brothers she had never known—and one who sent gifts, but not to her—only made Mercedes feel worse. "Thanks, José, but I'd better go find Noelia. She'll be cross if I miss the mass."

"Hey, José! Are you coming?" Munch shouted from the edge of the woods. "Or are you just going to stand there yakking with your orphan baby sister all day?"

"Shut your mouth," José yelled back.

"Why don't you come over here and shut it for me?" Munch taunted.

José turned to Mercedes, who was stricken by the succinct verbalization of her familial circumstances. Her face was crinkling up to cry. José turned his burning eyes to Munch, who was laughing and stoking on the other boys. He looked back to his sister.

"You pay that loudmouth no mind, Mercedes," José said. He hugged her stiff, skinny body.

She loved that he cared about her, but at that moment, José's embrace did not make Mercedes feel any better. And his eruptions of anger, though never unleashed on her, always frightened Mercedes. The summer before, she had seen him beat a boy bloody over a practical joke he played on José.

"Look at him now!" Munch laughed to the boys, shouting loudly enough for José to hear. "Maybe he should just go play with the girls."

"You're going to pay!" José shouted back over his shoulder. To Mercedes he said, as calmly as possible: "Go on now and find Noelia and the kids, and have some fun at the fiesta. Mrs. Álvarez is selling her almond pastries, and I'm sure she'll give you one if you ask." The rich, almond paste pastries called *carbayones* were one of his sister's favourites. "You know how much she liked mama," he added.

"Okay, José," Mercedes mumbled, her eyes downcast. She was disappointed that her happy day had soured so quickly, and that her time with José was clipped short. "See you later."

"Yes, see you soon, little rabbit," José said, giving her one last quick hug before sprinting across the pasture to pummel Munch, who had already taken flight into the trees.

Mercedes climbed the hill to the chapel forecourt, which was enclosed by a semi-circular stone wall, and threaded through the worshippers chatting and lingering outside. She entered the chapel and sat on the top stone step, leaning back against the opened door. Mercedes again smoothed the pleats of her green skirt. She stared hard at the resplendent statue of the Virgin of Covadonga, the patron saint of Asturias, adorned in a red and white cloak and bejewelled crown. The painted wooden Madonna stood on a platform at the altar rail, its base wreathed in freshly-cut white and yellow flowers. Mercedes' anguish eased. Sitting in a church and marveling at the saints always comforted her.

The live Covadonga, Manolo and Noelia's oldest daughter, came rushing in after a while and saw Mercedes sitting on the cool, grey slab of stone. "Mercedes!" she said sharply. "We've been looking all over for you. Mama is terrified we'd lost you!" Grabbing her firmly by the upper arm, Covadonga pulled Mercedes to her feet.

"Ow!" Mercedes cried. "That hurts!"

"Stop whining, you little brat," Covadonga barked. "You come with me this instant, and stop making trouble!" Covadonga dragged her outside and up the hill toward the village.

When Mercedes saw Mrs. Álvarez and her pastry stand, she tried to pull away from Covadonga. "I want to get a *carbayon*," she squealed.

"And what do you plan to pay for it with?" Covadonga asked. She tightened her grip on Mercedes' arm. "Or did my mother give you some pesetas to go with that new dress?"

"I won't have to pay anything for it!" Mercedes yelled, thrashing around trying to free herself. "She was friends with my mama, and she'll give me one."

"Oh, your mama! I'm sick and tired of hearing about your dead mama, and about poor, abandoned little Mercedes!"

At that, her hatred of Covadonga leaping to a new level of intensity, Mercedes bit the girl hard on the wrist. Covadonga recoiled and turned her loose. "You little viper!" she shouted as Mercedes ran off down the hill.

Mercedes tore across the pasture as quickly as she could run and disappeared into the woods, looking for her brother José.

* * *

In 1895, when he was fifteen years old, José boarded a ship in the Asturian port town of Gijón and followed his brothers to Cuba. Two years later he was dead, killed in a fight with three other Asturian migrants over a dispute about money. Though José had fled Bernardo, he could not so easily leave the rage behind. He went to his Caribbean grave with raw knuckles and a knife wound to his heart.

Twelve-year-old Mercedes was living in Naveces, working as a house maiden for a different family. She wept for three days when word arrived that the only brother she'd known was gone.

* * *

West Virginia, USA
July 1976

Robert was terrified. As he lay flat in the center of his bed, he felt as if an icy electric current was racing through his eight-year-old body, down his back and legs, up his arms and through his shoulders, and back down again.

Robert loved his new bedroom in the daytime. His parents let him choose the scarlet carpet and navy blue colour for the walls, as well as the ceiling light with its baseball globe and three miniature Louisville Slugger bats at the top. He liked the big window looking out at the woods near ground level, through which he could watch the birds flutter and squirrels scurry. He even liked the windowless storage room through the door on the wall opposite the window, into which he could retreat. He would close the door, and sit in the silence to read by the light of the single bulb mounted on the wall beneath the staircase.

But at night, his bedroom became a chamber of imaginary horrors. He thought over and over of how easily someone could look in the window at him, or break in and carry him off into the dark woods. He worried that vampires lurked in the storage room and that some terrible creature skulked under the bed, waiting to grab him if a hand or foot broke the vertical plane of the sides of the mattress.

Two nights before, he had braved the creature's grasp as he leapt from the bed and went down the hall to tell his parents he was scared. His father had come back with him to the room and turned on the light, showing him that there was nothing under the bed or in the storage room and that the window was locked. Robert could not go back into their room again tonight. He felt they would be angry and disappointed, and he feared that worse than abduction or vampires.

So there he lay: flat because he could not bear to turn his back either to the window on his left or the door to the storage room on his right, and in the center of the bed so the creature below could not reach up with its scaly, clawed hand and grab him. He tucked the blanket tightly up to his ears so the vampires could not get to his neck. Somehow, he managed to sleep.

He woke to the scent of bacon frying and the sound of *The Today Show* on the television in the kitchen upstairs. The summer morning sunlight was greenish filtering through the trees out the window. He loved his room.

"Hey, mammaw," Robert said as he climbed onto the stool at the breakfast bar in the kitchen.

"Hey, Robby," his grandmother Virginia said, flipping the bacon sizzling in the pan. There had not been a case of trichinosis in West Virginia in decades, but she still fried all pork until it was the consistency of chalk. It was just as Virginia's mother did on the farm before she died, when Virginia was Robert's age. "I thought you were going to sleep all morning," she said to her grandson. "You want some bacon and eggs?"

"Yes, please," Robert said enthusiastically, "with toast and jelly." He watched the little television on the kitchen counter as his grandmother prepared his breakfast. His parents, Brenda and Tom, both worked full-time. Virginia had taken care of him every weekday since he was a baby. She had never learned to drive, so her husband Sam brought her to Tom and Brenda's house in the mornings and collected her in the evenings after Brenda arrived home.

In addition to caring for Robert, Virginia cleaned the house, did the laundry and ironing, and often started preparing the family's dinner. During the school year, she also packed his lunchbox, but now it was summer break. Usually, they ate sandwiches together for lunch while watching the first of Virginia's afternoon soap operas.

After Robert finished his breakfast, he changed from his pyjamas and bounded outside. At the bottom of the big, sloping back yard stood a soaring, old, oak tree. Its thick roots spread out from the base of its fat trunk along the ground. The tree was one of his favourite places. Even the hottest August day seemed to be cool under its thick canopy.

Robert unpacked his Matchbox cars from their vinyl valise and went to the woods to collect as much moss as he could carry. Then he went back for twigs. He spent the morning digging tunnels under the tree's roots and constructing a town from the twigs and moss. He drove the cars along the roads he had built and imagined all manner of activities in the settlement. Robert did not want to come inside when Virginia called him to lunch, so she brought his sandwich and cherry Kool-Aid to him.

At four o'clock, she came back down from the house. "Look! Look, mammaw!" Robert shouted when she was halfway across the yard.

"Look at my town!" He pushed around some of the cars for her, demonstrating every tunnel and bridge and explaining the functions of all the stick-and-moss buildings.

"That's very nice, Robby. You've built some place there," Virginia said. She adored the boy and loved the summers when he was around every day. "But it's time to come in and get cleaned up. Your mommy'll be home soon. You can play down here again tomorrow."

Robert packed up his cars and followed Virginia up the hill to the house. He rarely complained or disobeyed his parents. "You are such a good boy, I love you very much," they had told him frequently all his life. They did not intentionally link the two—being good and being loved—but that was the message which Robert unconsciously internalized.

After his bath, Robert lay on his belly on the family room floor and watched reruns of *Gilligan's Island* and *The Munsters* as he waited for Brenda and Tom to return from work and for Sam to come for Virginia.

Chapter 4

Hundreds of thousands of Asturians sailed to the Americas during the nineteenth century, looking for work and dreaming of wealth. They could find neither at home. Most of the Indianos, as they were called in the north of Spain, went to Cuba. Some ventured to countries throughout Latin America. Thousands of Indianos realized their ambitions and returned to Asturias with cash enough for them and their extended families to live comfortably for the rest of their lives.

The stereotypical Indiano came back and built the biggest, most elaborately-decorated house he could afford. The preferred location was atop a hill overlooking the ancestral village, but one of the new Indiano neighborhoods on the edges of the principality's primary cities of Oviedo, Gijón and Avilés also sufficed.

Antonio González Conde went to Cuba, by himself, when he was fourteen years old. Mercedes' oldest brother was industrious and hard working, but his conservatism and good nature mostly sabotaged his aspiration to wealth. A staunch Spanish nationalist, Antonio volunteered for the colonial army when the Cubans began their armed struggle for independence. The required purchase of his own weapon and uniform were only the first economic costs of his patriotism. His dry-goods shop suffered during his absences campaigning with the army against the revolutionaries. Then his trusted partner swindled him out of what was left of the business while Antonio was being held a prisoner of war by the U.S. Army in 1898.

Along with other captured colonial troops, the U.S. repatriated Antonio after Spain's defeat. He went home empty handed, the bitterness of his country's loss multiplied by his failed dreams and so many years of toil wasted. He tired quickly of Bernardo's ridicule and tyrannical reign back on the farm in Asturias. In the spring of 1900, Antonio took a job as a deckhand on a cargo steamer in exchange for passage to Cuba. He started anew, just as he had when he was fourteen, hauling for hire anything that would fit in his burro-drawn wagon.

Antonio arrived this second time in a Havana to which he took an immediate dislike. The Cubans overflowed with triumphal nationalism, and he deeply resented the implication that 400 years of Spanish rule had been some sort of imprisonment. Thus, he was not too troubled to leave—though his quest for an Indiano fortune again remained unfulfilled—after a little over a year. One morning, a telegram came to the boarding house where Antonio was living. It announced that he was the new patriarch of the family and the farm across the Atlantic. Bernardo was dead.

* * *

Naveces, Asturias
June 1901

Antonio knocked at the door of the tidy little house which sat high on the hill above San Román Church. When it opened, he said to the middle-aged woman who stood wiping her hands on her apron: "Good morning. I have come to take my sister home."

A bit flustered by his unannounced visit and his pronouncement, Anna Carbajal stammered after a moment: "Mr. González ... hello ... good morning ... welcome. I wasn't ... we weren't expecting you. I wasn't aware you'd even returned home from Cuba."

Antonio stuck a hand into the jacket pocket of the new hopsack suit he'd had made in Havana for his return. "I sailed into Gijón yesterday and arrived in Avilés only late this morning. And my first order of business is to see that my sister spends not one more night in the servitude to which my father sentenced her sixteen years ago."

"Well, Mr. González," Anna said, pushing her shoulders and elbows back and standing a little taller, "I don't believe it's fair to call it servitude. We and the other families took Mercedes in for all these years, at our own expense. I'd expect a little gratitude from you."

Antonio nodded and smiled, replying quickly: "I apologize, Mrs. Carbajal, for any offense. I did not intend any criticism of you or our kindhearted neighbors and relations," although he did. Mercedes had written him often in Cuba in recent years. She lamented her semi-servant status in most of the families with whom she'd lived after Manolo and Noelia urgently summoned Juan and Father Agustín on the day of the San Adriano festival ten years before and insisted that they had done more than their fair share. "Any negative emotion I feel is directed squarely at my late father," Antonio added.

"Of course, of course, Mr. González," Anna said, relaxing her stance again. "It's been a heavy cross for her to bear, what your father did." She turned back into the house and shouted: "Mercedes! Come!"

For God's sake, Antonio thought, she's not a dog.

Mercedes appeared in the entranceway behind Anna. She was lean and muscular from much scrubbing of floors and pots and hoisting of Naveces babies and toddlers since she was scarcely more than a child herself. Mercedes burst into tears at the sight of Antonio and pushed past Anna to embrace her brother, kissing him once on each cheek. "You've come! Oh, you've come, Antonio, just as you promised!"

Before he departed for Cuba that second time the year before, Antonio had visited Mercedes at the Carbajal house and assured her that when Bernardo died—"the old goat can't live forever," he told his sister—he would return and liberate her from exile.

Mercedes' nickname had also stuck with Antonio. "Yes, rabbit. I've come to take you home to Las Cepas."

"Oh, Antonio, you have no idea how I've longed for this day!" Mercedes said, her arms still around his neck. She had wanted to believe her brother, both about Bernardo's mortality and Antonio's good intentions, but she had experienced so much disappointment in her life. Until that moment, when Antonio appeared, she did not feel that she could trust much of anything.

"I know, Mercedes," Antonio said. He pried her arms from around him. "Go, now, and collect your things."

She ran back into the house and placed her meagre belongings into a burlap sack. Antonio had politely demurred when Anna Carbajal invited him inside. He waited for his sister outside in the sun, smoking one of his Cuban cigars and gazing out at the cerulean sea, a froth of white curling along where the distant crag met the water.

Antonio had missed this vista, and his homeland, every day during those nineteen years in Cuba. As a boy, he often wandered up this hill after Sunday mass and sat looking at the sea. Sometimes the surf slid in gently, like today. Sometimes it pounded in, leaping high and white as it raked the bluffs. Always, he found its endless churning landward and its flat expanse to the horizon reassuring. It had been there for millennia and would be there for millennia to come. Whatever troubles or joys he experienced were momentary and insignificant compared to this physical manifestation of geologic and universal time.

* * *

A month later, Antonio, Mercedes and their Uncle Anselmo walked the two miles to the Castrillón municipal hall in Piedras Blancas to appear before the chief councillor of the district. Mercedes was still a minor, and with Bernardo dead, the law required two men be named her guardians. They would have to concur on any legal question concerning her, such as marriage or the percentage of the farm she inherited, until she reached the majority age of eighteen.

The two-storey, three-bay neoclassical Ayuntamiento, constructed a half-century before, was the only building of any significance among the dozen structures in the otherwise unremarkable village. Mercedes, Antonio and Anselmo had arrived early for the appointment, so they drank a coffee in the four-table café across the road and then sat for an hour outside the councillor's office on a long wooden bench.

The clerk who called them into the high-ceilinged office had prepared the guardianship papers. All three copies were written in a clear, tight hand on official government paper: heavy cotton-rag stock with two ultramarine stamps embossed at the top of the cream-coloured page. A typewriter would not have produced more legible documents. The clerk handed them to Antonio and Anselmo to review as Mercedes sat in a chair by the door.

The councillor came sauntering in a few minutes later from his siesta and introduced himself as he adjusted his black frock coat. It had been purchased when he was twenty pounds lighter, and he frequently tugged at it as if one more shift in the heavy woolen fabric would make it fit as pleasantly as it did when he bought it in the provincial capital of Oviedo the week he was elevated to his current position.

Picking their names from the first page, the councillor said: "Mr. González, Mr. Cueto, you understand the responsibilities and requirements set forth in these documents?"

"We do," they replied.

"And you will uphold and fulfill them honestly until the young woman achieves majority age or is wed?" he asked.

"We will."

"Very well," the counselor said. "Mr. Goméz here will show you where to affix your signatures, and I will add mine. When you have paid the registration fee, all will be complete and in order."

Everyone present, except Mercedes, signed the copies of the documents, and the clerk pasted on an additional stamp after they paid the fee.

As they walked back the way they had come, along the dirt road toward Naveces, Mercedes felt relieved. She believed Antonio and Anselmo would be compassionate guardians. In a different time and place, such a transaction and legally-mandated subjugation to her brother and uncle would have chafed. After all, she was two years older than Antonio had been when he went off to Cuba, and she had been fending for herself her entire life. But Mercedes was a daughter of a nineteenth-century Spanish village. Though her upbringing was unconventional in a country where the immediate family was the most sacred and fundamental element of the society, she absorbed its culture and mores as thoroughly as anyone else.

Chapter 5

Catholic feast-day processions were as much a natural part of life as the changing of the seasons. In the villages, the parishioners followed the priest and four of their fellows toting the two- or three-foot tall statue of a saint up the main dusty lane for a hundred yards or so, and then they made their way back to the church. The people were the procession. It reinforced the ties of the community and inspired devotion for the saint, even among the children, but spectacle it was not.

The cities were a different story. There, onlookers packed the cobblestone streets and crowded the balconies and open windows along the procession route. Costumed penitents marched to the steady pounding of drum corps, and the tiered wooden platforms bearing the life-sized statues were so large they took twelve men—always only men—to carry.

When he was in Cuba, Antonio González Conde became friends with two brothers from the fishing village of Sabugo. It was nearly as old as Avilés and lay less than two hundred yards from the city, across a small river and inlet used as a harbour. Sabugo maintained its separate identity through the centuries and had lain outside Avilés' medieval defensive walls.

The younger of the brothers, José María Iglesias Ruíz, shared Antonio's nationalism and misplaced pride in Spain's rapidly-waning military might. They volunteered together to fight the Cuban revolutionaries. The older brother, Javiér, thought them foolish for distracting themselves with that nonsense. "We didn't come here to save the scraps of the old the empire," Javiér told José María when his brother enlisted. "We came here to get rich and go home." Javiér had no sympathy for the rebels, rather all his energies remained focused on the dreams which had propelled them to the Caribbean colony.

Accordingly, José María was repatriated penniless to Spain alongside Antonio, following their stint as U.S. prisoners of war. Javiér had grown rich despite the turmoil and stayed on in Havana for another five years after the war, further fattening his fortune. He built a grand house on a hill behind Sabugo, which had become a barrio of Avilés when the little river and inlet were filled and a fashionable park constructed while the three men were away in Cuba.

When Javiér returned to Asturias, he invested in enterprises all over growing Avilés. He bankrolled fishing boats and built warehouses at the busy port. He owned a quarter interest in the Grand Hotel and opened a café on bustling Calle La Cámera, which José María operated. Both brothers were yet to marry. They lived and entertained lavishly together in Javiér's sprawling, sky-blue mansion.

* * *

Naveces, Asturias
April 1908

It was José María's idea to invite their old friend Antonio and his family to spend Easter with them; Javiér was delighted by the plan and quickly agreed. They stopped at Las Cepas to extend the invitation personally one afternoon as they returned from surveying some farmland Javiér was thinking of purchasing nearby. At first Antonio demurred, telling the Iglesias Ruíz brothers: "It's a kind and generous offer, but I can't imagine not celebrating Easter down there at San Román with our family and neighbors."

However, Antonio noticed the jolt of excitement which shot through his wife, sister and children when the brothers proposed the visit. After a bit of Antonio's apple cider—the fundamental libation of Asturias, the brothers' Cuban cigars and a long, easy chat by the fireplace in the little parlour, Antonio was transported back to their most pleasant times in Havana, and he accepted their invitation. Antonio and María's children were uncontrollably giddy, and Mercedes only slightly less so, for the intervening two weeks. No village family they knew had spent the entire holiday—from Good Friday until Easter Monday—in Avilés.

"Come along children," María called to their sons Ramón and Pepe and their daughter Pilar. The children were scurrying around in the bushes beside the country road. "If we don't hurry, we'll miss the procession of the saints, and you don't want that, do you?"

"No, ma'am," they shouted enthusiastically and in unison. The prospect of seeing the statues of the saints paraded high on the shoulders of the penitents was electrifying. They had only seen the small processions on holy days in Naveces and San Adriano, and occasionally in other nearby villages. They loved them, but they had heard stories of the cities' grand processions. They were wild with anticipation.

"Oh, María," Mercedes sighed as she and her sister-in-law walked side by side down the lane through the undulating countryside. They clipped along at the steady, rapid pace of people accustomed to traveling long distances regularly on foot. "How lucky we are that the months of rain ended just as the Holy Week—*Semana Santa*—began."

It was indeed a glorious day. The sun dappled the mostly dry ground. An ocean breeze rushed through the skinny leaves of the eucalyptus trees, sounding like a swiftly flowing stream. Mercedes breathed in deeply through her nose. She did not feel that she could take in enough of the rich scent of the eucalyptus. "I can't tell you how happy it makes me to be here with you and the children, coming to the fiesta. Thank you, thank you, María, for taking me in."

"For the thousandth time, Mercedes," María admonished, "you don't have to thank me—or Antonio." She stopped and took Mercedes by the arm, turning her sister-in-law to look her in the face. "You living with us isn't some act of charity. Those days are over for you. You're not our servant. You're our sister, and Las Cepas is your home."

Mercedes broke María's gaze and looked down at the ground. A silvery-brown lizard raced across the road between their feet. María reached out and gently lifted Mercedes' face by the chin, looking again into her black eyes. She placed her hand on the side of Mercedes' head and softly stroked her long hair. "For Heaven's sake, you own a share of the farm, thanks to the inheritance laws. It's yours as much as ours, no matter how much Bernardo tried to thwart it."

"I suppose it still seems like one of those dreams I used to have," Mercedes said, looking up into the treetops, "when my bed was a pallet in the kitchen of one of the houses where I worked. In my sleep, I was sitting in the sun, surrounded by geraniums, on the steps of the granary at Las Cepas. I never had lived there, but somehow it always felt like home. Then I would wake, and I was alone in the cold and dark."

Seven years had slipped by since Antonio collected Mercedes from Anna Carbajal's house. Now, several weeks at a time often would pass before she jolted awake in the night, usually without any particular trigger during the day, her chest so stuffed with anxiety that she could hardly breathe. Her life felt comfortable and satisfying to a degree she had not imagined possible for her, but that only intensified the sudden, overwhelming fear that she would lose it all.

"Well, this is no dream," María said. She pulled Mercedes closer. "And you'll never be alone and suffering again."

Noticing the quiet around them, broken only by the breeze pressing through the eucalyptus and the squawk of a seagull, María looked back over her shoulder and shouted down the road. "Children! Don't make me come there and drag you from the woods, or you'll pay a penance that makes carrying a saint through the streets of Avilés look mild!"

Ramón, Pepe and Pilar came running from the trees and up to their aunt and mother. The boys each blamed the other for their foray. Pilar, who was the youngest of the three, took Mercedes' hand and hugged it. They all hurried off together. In the distance, they finally could see the five-story stone bell tower of San Nicolás de Bari Church in Avilés.

Mercedes, María and the children pressed through the crowd to a spot on the street at the edge of the stone-pillared arcade covering the sidewalk on Calle San Francisco, directly across from the church. The throng silenced as the priest—dressed in a white alb and chasuble and a crimson cope elaborately embroidered in gold—delivered a benediction from the seventeenth-century portico which sheltered the main entrance to San Nicolás de Bari. After what seemed an eternity to Ramón, Pilar and Pepe, the two bronze bells hanging in the arched portals at the top of the austere tower began to swing, and then to roll end over end. Each bell was a yard wide at the base. The clanging echoed across the town. The saint was coming.

The priest who gave the benediction, four other priests and three altar servers—one hoisting the processional crucifix and the other two holding candle-topped silver staffs ramrod straight—had stepped to the foot of the broad stone steps leading up to the church from the street. The bells tolled. The drummers assembled in the forecourt began vigorously beating out a dirge-like march.

The tiered, wooden platform—the *paso*—slowly emerged from the shadow of the portico through the center of its five Gothic arches into the sunny afternoon. Atop the paso stood St. John the Evangelist, six feet tall and with a placid visage. He was haloed and dressed in a dark-blue velvet tunic and maroon velvet cloak. A carpet of red and white carnations ascended to his feet, and the rows of tall white candles ringing the statue's base flickered in the breeze.

Mercedes gasped and nearly laughed with delight. She crossed herself three times at the first sight of the saint, as did all the others in the dense mass.

The twelve, barefoot penitents wore the full medieval raiment called *nazerones*: royal blue tunics; scarlet capes; bone-white gloves on their hands and tall, conical hats—called *capirotes*—on their heads. The fabric of the capirotes draped over their faces and shoulders, with holes cut out for their eyes. Each man was identically attired and anonymous—all the penitents were men. They braced the long, thick poles attached to the sides of the paso on their shoulders, one arm wrapped around for a secure hold. In his free hand, each held a wooden staff with a U-shaped iron crook at the top for supporting the paso when they rested briefly during the two-mile-long procession.

The drum corps filed ahead of the saint from the side of the fore-court and descended the stairs, positioning themselves behind the altar servers and priests. The paso followed with great effort by the penitents. Mercedes put her hand to her mouth, worried he would topple over, when St. John angled forward precariously as the plat-form nosed down the stairs. Safely again on level ground, the paso took its place after the drummers. The penitents rested their burden on the crook-topped staffs.

More blue-, red- and white-clad penitents filed out of the church and down the stairs two abreast, carrying staffs and lanterns, and lined up behind the paso. When all were in place, a penitent rang the brass bell hanging from an ornate iron hook on back of the paso. The men hefted the platform up off the crooks and onto their shoulders, and the slow procession began its route down Calle San Francisco toward the Plaza de España. The paso rocked gently from side to side with each step, and the penitents smacked the pavement with their staffs in rhythm with the beating drums.

Mercedes was mesmerized. The crushing crowd. The deafening bells. The pounding drums. The majestic penitents. The enormous paso. The towering saint. It was nearly too much to take in, but it transported a visceral power and peacefulness. "Gracias," Mercedes whispered as she watched the procession trail off, the drums fading in the distance.

* * *

The walled town of Avilés—thriving on salt production, fishing, and trade with the British Isles—all but burned to the ground in 1497. That September, the devastated merchants, traders and local officials appealed to the Catholic Monarchs—Queen Isabella I of Castile and King Ferdinand II of Aragon—for the right to hold a weekly street market in hopes of resurrecting the town. The royals assented, and Avilés has held the market on Mondays for more than five hundred years.

As the town expanded and the regional population grew over the centuries, so did the market. By the mid 1800s, the wagons and makeshift stalls of the vendors—who ventured there from all over the neighboring rural districts of Castrillón and Gozón—stretched all the way down Calle Galiano from the livestock market at the Plaza de Carbayedo and filled the Plaza de España. It was chaos, and a waterlogged mess when the frequent rains came.

This weekly rustic, medieval vignette clashed with the modern, urbane image which Avilés' leaders—public and private—were working earnestly to cultivate. The solution came in 1873, with the construction of the Plaza Nuevo: a square block of uniformly fashionable, three-storey neoclassical buildings housing shops and apartments surrounding a flagstone-paved plaza with arcades on all four sides and a covered market in it center. Plaza Nuevo filled the vacant lowland between the southern edge of medieval Avilés, where the thirteenth-century stone defensive wall had been removed a few years before, and the old fishing village of Sabugo.

* * *

Avilés, Aturias
September 1909

Every week, Mercedes, Antonio and one of the older children departed Las Cepas before sunrise for the Monday market in Avilés. María usually remained at home, tending to the younger children and the livestock. Mercedes and Antonio took their milk, butter, onions, greens and sausages—both spicy chorizo and the blood sausages called *morcillas*—in big woven saddlebags slung over the back of their horse. They walked the five miles. The animal was for hauling. Only the wealthy could afford the luxury of horses to ride.

They always set up in the same spot under the high, wrought-iron arcade at Plaza Nuevo. After a few frenetic hours, the market would wind down at around two o'clock, when the last of the shoppers headed home for their daily siesta. Mercedes and Antonio would pack whatever they had failed to sell into the woven saddlebags, eat the lunch María had packed for them that morning, and take a rest themselves in the quiet of the afternoon.

When the shops reopened at four, Antonio and Mercedes would make the round of shops up Calle La Cámera and Calle Rivero to purchase the necessities they could not produce on the farm. Mostly, they bought coffee, sugar, salt and tobacco. Occasionally, they got fabric from the shops on Calle La Fruta, but good fabric was expensive and cash always scarce.

This Monday, Antonio had a surprise for Mercedes.

As they crossed the main square, Plaza de España, and walked up Calle Rivero, Antonio took Mercedes by the elbow and pulled her over to the window of the pastry shop called Polledo. The bakers at Polledo were wizards of confection, though the price of the creations matched their quality. Pausing at the window to gawk was the closest the weekly visitors from the countryside generally came to sampling Polledo's offerings.

"What do you think of that chocolate-pistachio cake over there?" Antonio asked, pointing toward a perfect torte sitting high on a metallic cake plate at the back of the display.

"I think it would cost most of what we earned today," Mercedes replied. She turned away from the window to continue on their way to buy coffee. Antonio took great pleasure in window-shopping as they sauntered along the sixteenth- and seventeenth-century streets, but Mercedes had little interest in such frivolities. What was the purpose, she reasoned, if they could not afford to buy anything?

"No," Antonio cried and pulled her back to the window. "How do you think it would be to savour an enormous piece of that cake? Though it looks nearly too tasty to desecrate by cutting."

"Oh, brother," Mercedes sighed, "sometimes I wonder who is older, you or your boys. We're not the Marquis and Marquess down there at the Palacio de Ferrera, you know. Why waste time thinking about such things?"

"But you like chocolate, do you not?"

"I like it very much. You know that."

"And pistachios?"

"They're my favourites, as you also know."

"And what is today?"

"Oh, Antonio, what's this game?"

Farmers in rough, hand-made clothes and townspeople dressed in the latest fashions squeezed by on the narrow sidewalk, pressing them closer to the window.

"What is today?" Antonio asked more insistently.

"It's Monday." Mercedes paused to think what Monday it could be. It was not a saint's day. It was not the first day of any month or season. She shrugged her shoulders.

"For Heaven's sake, Mercedes," Antonio said. "It is your birthday!"

Mercedes never made a point of remembering her birthday, let alone celebrating it. For most of her life, she tried to forget it. On that day, she had killed her mother.

"You wait here," Antonio ordered. He left her side and entered the shop. Mercedes was shocked, and a bit annoyed, as she watched her brother point to the chocolate-pistachio cake. It does look delicious, she thought. She was dumbfounded when the shop assistant did not cut a slice, but put the entire torte into a box and wrapped it for the road.

Antonio was beaming when he emerged from the confitería. A cigar clenched in his teeth, he said: "Happy Birthday, Mercedes," handing her the box. "We may not be the Marquis and Marquess, but they will not eat a finer dessert this evening!"

For the remainder of their shopping excursion in Avilés, and all the way home to Las Cepas, Mercedes clutched the cake box as if she had been entrusted with a holy relic.

As they walked the dusty roads, flanking the plodding horse, with the sea popping into view when they crested the hills and then disappearing when they descended into the forest, Mercedes felt deeply content. Her brother was such a good man, and Las Cepas had become home in a way that she long believed she would never know. She enjoyed the rhythm of her life: the farm work, caring for her niece and nephews, helping María prepare the meals, the weekly journey to Avilés.

Still, her life felt incomplete. The desire for a home and family of her own lurked around the periphery of her thoughts and her sense of satisfaction. She shook it off and focused on appreciating the life she had, this day, and the magnificent cake she cradled in her arms.

Chapter 6

The daily lives of most Asturians in 1800 were not dramatically different at their core from those of their ancient ancestors. Families clustered on individual farms and in small farming villages. They tilled their fields with plows nearly identical to the ones the Romans had with them when Caesar Augustus finally brought the Celtic Astures to heel in 19 B.C. The Asturians survived on what they could grow from the ground or haul from the rivers and sea.

This agrarian world endured for nearly two millennia, but its end came swiftly in the mid-nineteenth century. Coal mining turned farmers into industrial laborers. Generations of inheritance had reduced many individual farm plots to patches of ground insufficient to feed the large families who lived on them, and tens of thousands of men and boys welcomed the chance to earn a wage, however meagre and whatever the physical toll. Most families who had farms maintained them. The women and children worked the land, and the men joined them whenever they were free.

In 1815, the Real Compañía Asturiana de Minas de Carbón sunk Spain's first vertical coal mine on a high bluff above the Cantabrian sea. Rather than dig horizontally into a hillside coal seam as the companies did at the mines proliferating in the Asturian interior, the Real Compañía dug a shaft down to the coal, lowered the miners in a lift, and sent them burrowing out under the seabed. It was magnificently successful, even attracting the approving eye of the King. They called their new village Arnao. The Real Compañía vaulted into international trade forty years later, when it added a smelter in Arnao and began making zinc out of calamite ore from northeastern Spain and the coal mined a few hundred yards away.

The conditions for workers at Arnao were harsh, but one of the Real Compañía's founders, a Belgian named Nicolás Maximilien Lesoinne, had infused the operation with the paternalistic ideal embraced by industrialists in his homeland. Real Compañía workers enjoyed a higher quality of life than many other industrial workers, though the corporate generosity came at a price.

The workers' lives were completely intertwined with their employer's. They lived in the company's houses and shopped at the company's store. The company doctor treated them when they were ill, and their children received their high quality, free education at the company school—as long as their father kept his job with the Real Compañía. There was no public school for them to attend if he did not. The company organized entertainment for the workers and their families and sports for the employees' children.

Still, the Real Compañía was battered by the same labor unrest which festered and erupted in the early twentieth century. Workers across Asturias launched strikes regularly starting in 1900, with varying degrees of intensity. The most serious began in 1910 and lasted until 1912. So many of the Asturian workers participated during those two years that the Real Compañía recruited strike breakers from the neighboring province of Galicia to keep the coal coming out of the ground and the zinc pouring from the smelter's retorts.

The Gallegos—as people from Galicia are called—had suffered a difficult few centuries since the heyday of the Way of St. James during the Middle Ages. Then, hundreds of thousands of pilgrims from every corner of Europe clambered across Galicia each year to venerate the purported remains of the saint at Santiago de Compostela in the far west of the province. The pilgrims had been good business, but they were centuries gone.

Galicia remained rich in natural beauty, with lichen covered granite farmhouses and villages and magnificent medieval churches dotting the lush countryside. But the economy ground weaker and weaker with each generation. Hundreds of thousands of Gallegos emigrated to Argentina alone in the nineteenth and early-twentieth centuries, so many that Argentinians began to call anyone who came from Spain "Gallegos." The Asturian strikes provided an opportunity for survival closer to home.

* * *

Arnao, Asturias
December 1910

Antonio González Conde and his brother Manuel together owned eight acres of land. On such a small holding, they could not feed their families and produce enough to sell for cash at the Avilés market. In 1902, a few months after his return from Cuba, Antonio took a job with the Real Compañía at the zinc smelter in Arnao to earn hard cash. Manuel joined him later that year. They were paid a *peseta* a day, about 30 modern eurocents.

Laboring among the smelter's furnaces was brutally hard and hot. The smelter men typically got every other day off. It took that long to recover from the heat, fumes and shoveling. Working the mines, which stretched out for more than a mile under the seabed from the village, was worse. Antonio always said a prayer for those poor wretches he saw trudging toward the *castillete de la mina*, the structure containing the lift which lowered them into the dark, dank galleries. The castillete's tall, zinc-clad wheelhouse, Antonio often thought, looked perversely like the bell tower of an industrialized chapel.

Like the others, Antonio chafed under the working conditions. However, he could not abide the communism many of his compatriots were embracing and the labor radicals' antipathy toward the King and the Church. Antonio earnestly believed that those two institutions had been the only civilizing forces on the Iberian penninsula for centuries. For him, the communists offered only anarchy and destruction, cloaked in the promise of better pay and shorter hours.

"Those bastards," Antonio said to Manuel as they passed the ragged cluster of strikers outside the smelter gate on a day shortly after the big strike began. "They will dynamite every church, burn down every business, take every farm and rape our wives and daughters if they ever get their way." To him, all strikers and labor organizers were communists, anarchists and atheists, whether they declared such tendencies or not.

One frigid morning, when Antonio and Manuel arrived for their shift, there were several new faces in the room where they donned their work clothes and prepared to smelt that day's quota of zinc. "Gallegos," Antonio said to Manuel, "brought in to fill the jobs our hungry Asturians choose to forego."

Relishing the final deep breaths of crisp December air, before entering the poisonous atmosphere of the sweltering smelter, the fresh crew walked from the changing house toward the smelter's open door. Antonio spied the hand-pushed railcar waiting for them inside. It was heaped with the first of many loads of yellow calamite ore they would spend the next four hours shoveling into the clay retorts which ran the length of the long furnace. Antonio stuck out his hand to a new man. "Antonio González Conde, of Las Cepas."

The Gallego eyed him warily. He grasped Antonio's outstretched hand firmly and replied: "Antonio Rivas, of nowhere you'd know." He took a drag on his self-rolled cigarette and sauntered on in silence.

Antonio Rivas' taciturn response merely spurred Antonio González Conde's curiosity, which had not been the Gallego's intention.

"There are not too many places I would not care to know, Mr. Rivas, so you should try me," the Asturian said. "From where do you come? I presume some place in Galicia."

The cigarette dangling from the corner of his mouth, Antonio Rivas said only: "Portomarín."

"Portomarín!" Antonio González Conde exclaimed. "Why, that is in the heart of the French Way, on the Camino de Santiago." Four hundred years had passed since anyone thought much about, let alone walked, the Camino. But Antonio was deeply devout, and his love for the traditions and history of the medieval Church ran deep. He turned to Manuel and added as they tromped into the smelter: "I have not seen it myself, but I hear there is an impressive fortress church there, built by Templar knights in the twelfth century!"

"Yes, there's a church," Antonio Rivas said. "There's a lot of them in Galicia. If we could eat church stones, none of us would be here working in Asturian smelters and mines."

Antonio González Conde laughed heartily. Antonio Rivas was not joking.

"You stick with us, Gallego, and we will make you glad the good Lord brought you to our fair Asturias, the land of sidra and fabada. They will make you turn your back forever on your native octopus and grape-mash liquor!"

Antonio Rivas had heard all his life that the Asturians took an almost obsessive pride in their *sidra*—fermented apple cider—and *fabada*—faba bean stew with sausages, bacon and ham. He curled up one corner of his mouth, a typically furtive Gallego smile, picked up his shovel, jammed it into the rail car's heap of coal, and started the long morning of feeding the retorts.

Their job was the first and most physically demanding step in the smelting process. For loading the calamite, the bulbous retorts were pulled away from the fifty-yard-long furnace, exposing the men to the three-thousand-degree heat as they shoveled. When they emptied a car, boys would push it back down the rails and bring up another, over and over. Behind them as they progressed up the line, the men called *embuchadores* would affix the conical cap on the filled retorts, pack them with the pulverized coal that helped fuel the roasting of the ore, and attach the condensing coils. The retorts then could be pushed into place against the furnaces for the ore to melt and release the gaseous zinc. The workers called *tiradores* took over on the later shift, scooping out the molten zinc from the water-filled condensation trays beneath the retorts. With long-handled spoons, they carefully poured the liquid metal into racks of waiting moulds.

* * *

"So, will you go home to Portomarín to visit your family for the Christmas holy days, Antonio Segundo?" Antonio González Conde asked Antonio Rivas two weeks later as they shoveled, stripped to the waist and slathered in sweat despite the icy temperature outside. Their black moustaches were coated yellow from the calamite dust.

They had quickly tired of the confusion caused by two Antonios working side by side and agreed on referring to the Asturian Antonio González Conde as "Antonio Primero" and the Gallego Antonio Rivas as "Antonio Segundo." Already, the entire smelter had started using the shorthand.

"I don't have any family in Portomarín to visit," Antonio Segundo said, "or anyplace else for that matter. I'm an orphan."

"You mean to say you have no family at all?" Antonio Primero asked. He was mystified. Everybody he knew had enormous families, with most of the relatives living clustered on the same patch of ground. "Surely you must know of some relation somewhere in Galicia?"

"Not really."

"Why ... why, I find that hard to believe ... hard to believe," Antonio Primero sputtered, and he was not one for sputtering.

"Well, believe what you want, but it's the truth," Antonio Segundo said. He chucked another heaping shovel-load of calamite into the retort.

"No family at all?"

"None I have any contact with."

"You have no wife or children. What do you do at Christmas and Easter? Where do you go?" Primero asked as he scraped his shovel along the bottom of the rail car.

"I don't go anywhere," Segundo replied languidly.

"You do not go anywhere? How do you celebrate the major feasts of our Lord?"

"I don't."

"You do not!" Primero nearly shouted. "I thought you said were a Christian?"

"Well, I am," Segundo said. "I was baptized and confirmed, like everybody else, and I go to the masses when I have to. But I don't have any family, and I live in the room they rent me wherever I'm working at the time. So, I don't make the kind of big fiesta like I guess you do."

"That we do indeed," Primero declared, excited by the recollection of fiestas past. "For Christmas and Easter, my house at Las Cepas is packed to the rafters with family, from babes in arms to my ninety-six-year-old spinster aunt."

Antonio Segundo nodded and dug his shovel into the yellow pile filling the fresh car the boys had pushed up beside them.

"And this year," Antonio Primero added, "the revelers will include a Gallego orphan. I insist that you join us." The idea had only occurred to him at that moment, but that did not diminish his fervor. "There is no way under Heaven that I will allow you to spend the festival of the birth of our Savior sitting alone in that room over there at the company boarding house."

Antonio Segundo considered protesting. He treasured his quiet holidays alone. He knew, however, after these two weeks of acquaintance, the futility of attempting to dissuade Antonio González Conde when he had set his mind.

"Thanks, Primero," Segundo said. "It'll be good to have some hot food and company for a change."

"Very good!" the Asturian said, putting his shovel on the ground for long enough to tap the Gallego lightly on the back. "That is the spirit! I promise you, it will be a Christmas you will remember."

* * *

The house was packed with Christmas revelers as Antonio Primero had promised, though filling it did not require many visitors. His was a basic little Asturian farmhouse, nearly a perfect cube with its two stories of plastered stone and shallow, red barrel-tiled roof. An *hórreo*—the ubiquitous elevated Asturian granary—sat directly beside it. A low, stone wall ran along the upper side of the house and granary, separating them from a pasture sloping gradually up the hill to the forest of oak pine trees. The chattering crowd spilled out of the house and filled the modest courtyard enclosed by the wall. It was a balmy Christmas Eve with no wind and a clear black sky full of winking stars.

Antonio the host introduced Antonio the guest to all his relatives who had gathered for the evening. There were at least four dozen people. Antonio Segundo struggled to remember a third of their names. It helped, or did not, that several each were called Antonio, Manuel, José, María or Marina. There were two Covadongas. The one name and face he did not have difficulty remembering was that of Antonio Primero's sister. To each person he met, Segundo gave the traditional introductory greeting of *Encantado*—enchanted—but to Mercedes, he meant it.

Mercedes stood nearly a head taller than the compact Antonio Rivas. She was not beautiful. Mercedes was lean as a greyhound, and her twenty-five-year-old skin was weathered from the long days of farm work in the sun. But her black eyes were like velvet, and in them Antonio saw a blend of melancholy and resilience he understood well. He had a hard time moving on to the next introduction. Casting about for glimpses of her over the course of the evening, Antonio got the sense that Mercedes lived mostly within herself, separate from the crowd even when crushed within it, which appealed to the solitary Gallego.

Arroz con leche—creamy, sweet rice pudding, with a crust of caramelized cinnamon sugar—capped the hours-long Christmas feast at four o'clock in the morning. After the dessert, the guests began shuffling home. More than a few focused diligently to put one foot ahead of the other, their balance challenged by the endless green bottles of hard cider the revelers had consumed. While they departed, Antonio Segundo took the opportunity to venture out into the deserted courtyard for a smoke.

As he pulled a portion of tobacco from his leather pouch and began working it expertly into a cigarette paper, Mercedes said from where she was sitting in the dark on the top step of the hórreo: "Feliz Navidad."

She so startled Antonio that he dropped his cigarette and tobacco pouch to the limestone pavers. Mercedes giggled lightly and said: "I'm sorry, Antonio. I didn't realize you hadn't seen me sitting here."

Sweeping together his scattered tobacco with one hand and

recovering the cigarette with the other, Antonio mumbled: "No matter, no matter. I have it all." Standing up, he added: "It's, ah, a nice surprise to find you here."

"And you," the disembodied voice said from the darkness.

Antonio stood there stiffly, pouch in one hand and unlit cigarette in the other.

"Why don't you light that, and take a seat here on the step, and roll one for me?" Mercedes said.

Antonio fumbled for a match. His heavily moustached face was illuminated for an instant in the flash of the yellow flame. Then—just the orange glow of the cigarette tip in the black night—Mercedes scooted over to one side of the step, and he sat beside her. Antonio fished out a paper and another portion of tobacco.

"I don't smoke much," Mercedes said, "but I figure, it's Christmas. Why not indulge?"

"I'm happy to take this little gift from the Americas frequently," Antonio said. He handed the cigarette to Mercedes and proffered a light. "For a poor man like me, it's one of the few pleasures at hand every day."

Mercedes exhaled a cloud of smoke and leaned forward, elbows on her knees. "I'm satisfied to make it a bit of an event. And I thank you for sharing your American treat with me."

"You're welcome," Antonio said.

When Antonio added nothing further, Mercedes asked: "Did you enjoy your González family Christmas?"

"I did, very much." He paused, then added: "It was kind of your brother to invite me."

"If I may ask, Antonio," Mercedes said somewhat reluctantly, "why didn't you go home to Galicia for the fiesta?"

"As I told your brother, I have no home to go to in Galicia."

"You have no family there?"

"None I care to visit." Antonio took a long drag from his cigarette.

"I know how lonely that feels," Mercedes said, sighing.

"You?" Antonio said, turning toward her. "How could you, with such a gang of relatives?"

She looked toward the ground. "For a long time, I wasn't surrounded by such a loving family." Mercedes told Antonio the story of Bernardo's wrath and her exile from Las Cepas, and of her years toiling in house after house in the village.

"Your father sounds like he was as much of an ass as my own," Antonio said. "My mother also died after giving birth to my brother, when I was five years old." Antonio never had spoken to anyone about his family or his childhood, but with Mercedes it flowed naturally. "He tried to send my brother away, too, but the priest told him he would burn in hell if he did it. Still, he made life so miserable for my poor brother that I think he would've been better off being sent away immediately."

"Trust me, nothing is worse than that," Mercedes said. She crushed out the butt of her cigarette with the heel of her shoe. "It's terrible beyond imagination to be cast away like a deformed calf and forced to live on the charity of others as your father goes on about his life as if you don't exist."

Antonio had never considered that possibility.

"Of course," Mercedes continued, "I saw my father and one of my brothers often. They were at every festival, in the church in Naveces and at the market in Avilés, which just made it worse. My brother José—Antonio, Ramón and Manuel were off in Cuba—always came to me, sometimes bringing me little presents, but only when my father wasn't around. He'd forbidden him to talk to me."

"I'm sorry, Mercedes," Antonio said. It was an inadequate response, but it was all he could think to say.

She turned and smiled at him in the darkness. "Thank you, Antonio." She also never spoke of the past, but she felt unencumbered with him. "Fortunately, that's all over now, thanks to my dear brother. And helping bring the babies into the world comforts me more than I can say."

"You're a midwife?" Antonio asked.

"I am," Mercedes said. "I'd often helped the midwives prepare for the births in the houses where I was working when I was a girl, and the first time one let me stay in the room—I must have been about ten—I knew it was what I was supposed to do. Not long after I came to live here, I mentioned it to Antonio, and he arranged for me to apprentice with a midwife over in Santiago del Monte."

"That's important work," Antonio said. "The road to our farm was flooded when my mother had my brother, so the midwife didn't arrive in time. I've always believed that's why she died."

"Well, we're not miracle workers," Mercedes said, "and every midwife I know has lost at least one mother." She remembered the three young women she had been unable to save. Each of their faces appeared clearly before her. When they died, and every time she recalled those three awful days, the thought of her own mother's death intensified her agony and sense of failure.

Mercedes pressed down the feelings of sadness and guilt, as she always did when they flared, and continued. "But usually it is beautiful beyond description, Antonio, to see that new life emerge into the world and experience the new mother's joy. And every woman I help get through the birth alive makes me feel that I've compensated a little for killing my mother."

"Oh, Mercedes," Antonio said softly. "You shouldn't say that. You didn't kill your mother any more than my brother killed mine. Nature is hard, and it can be cruel. It wasn't your fault."

"Well," Mercedes muttered, unconvinced, "enough prattling on about me. What about you? How did you end up here in Asturias?" Her mood and voice brightened again as quickly as they had darkened. "And you could make another of those cigarettes for me as you tell me, if you don't mind."

Antonio rolled one for each of them as he began. "My father died when I was twelve. Slipped and fell while repairing the barn roof. There were eight of us kids, and the land had already been divided between my grandfather and his brothers, and then my father and his. So, split eight more ways, there wasn't much of a farm left. We agreed to let my oldest brother take it over and try to feed his family. The rest of us made our way however we could. My younger brother, who was seven then, went to live with some relations of my mother down in León." He paused for half a minute, staring out into the dark.

"I haven't seen him, or much of the others, since. I spent the next ten years or so working on farms all around Galicia, and then on the docks in A Coruña, until I came here to work in the smelter. I lied and told them in Arnao that I'd worked the furnaces before. Otherwise, they'd have stuck me down in that terrible mine. I could never do that, no matter how hungry I got."

They sat quietly for a while, each enjoying the surprise of meeting a person with whom they could unburden themselves freely. Neither of them had appreciated until then, until they had spoken it aloud, the weight of carrying their stories around all by themselves. It was like lugging an invisible steamer trunk full of stones strapped to their backs.

Mercedes broke the silence. "I think your life's been even harder than mine, Antonio. I was often unhappy and confused when I was a girl, but at least I always felt I was at home here in these little valleys around Naveces."

"I don't think of it much, but I suppose I do wish I could feel again that someplace is home," Antonio said. "I haven't felt that since the day I left the farm, eighteen years ago. I just figure wherever I lay my head is home, but it really isn't the same."

"Here you are!" Antonio Primero said loudly, and tipsily, as he strode into the courtyard from the house. "I did not bring you here to disgrace my sister, Gallego!"

Antonio Segundo leapt to his feet. "I ... I ... I didn't ... I know ... I apologize, Antonio, for any—"

"Oh, sit down, Segundo," Primero said, laughing hard. "I am pleased you two had some time alone to chat. I hoped you would get on well tonight. I do not want my sister to live out her life as a spinster—we have enough of those in the family—and we could use another strong back on the farm."

"Well, I ... uh ... we ... uh," Segundo stammered.

Mercedes rescued him. "Oh, brother. I believe you've gotten a little deeply into the anis bottle tonight. Leave our poor guest alone."

"Fair enough! Fair enough!" Antonio Primero howled, throwing up his arms in mock surrender. "I merely will bid you both a Happy Christmas!"

Chapter 7

It was a good year for onions. They needed every able-bodied member of the family to dig the fat, coppery-skinned bulbs from the ground. Even Antonio Segundo had volunteered to contribute this Sunday off from the smelter to help. Seven months had passed since that Christmas chat on the hórreo step, and Mercedes and Antonio were thankful for every encounter. This one necessitated donning the wooden clogs Asturians had worn for centuries to keep from sinking ankle-deep into their muddy fields. Now it was abnormally rainy, after the dry and sunny May and June which had produced the bumper onion crop. The saturated soil and cool days made a quick harvest essential.

Sitting in the stout wooden chairs brought from the house into the little courtyard at Las Cepas, two unmarried aunts well into their eighties skillfully wove the onion stalks into long strands. The teenage boys came occasionally from the field, happy for a few moments of standing upright, to hoist the braided onions up onto pegs in the outer walls of the hórreo, sheltering them beneath the wide eaves.

Mercedes and Antonio worked as a team in the field, with him hauling the big woven basket to the end of the row and pouring the onions into the burro-drawn wooden cart. "This is harder work than the smelter," Antonio said to Mercedes as he returned with the empty basket. He wiped his brow with his shirtsleeve, stretched his back and rolled a cigarette.

"In my brother's imagination," Mercedes said laughing, on her knees in the mud and caked nearly to the waist, "you'll be doing a lot more of this one day."

"With the most respect for your brother, and all my fondness for you, I hated farm work when I was a boy, and it hasn't grown on me over the years."

"Oh, Antonio," Mercedes scoffed. "You can't honestly say that you prefer being cooped up in that reeking, hot building in Arnao to this. Smell the fertile earth and the fresh air and the eucalyptus. Look up at the wide sky. Feel the cool breeze blowing away every care. This is as good as a workday can be!"

Antonio had heard this paean to the farming life from Mercedes before. Many times. "There's no mud in the smelter," Antonio said, drawing on the cigarette pinched at the corner of his mouth as he knelt down and squishing his hands into the muck. "Asturias is as dry as La Mancha compared to Galicia, and I got enough mud there to last me a lifetime. Give me a furnace any day over this."

Mercedes shook her head. She had heard this paean to industrial work from Antonio before. Many times.

"Mercedes! Segundo! Dinner is ready," her brother shouted from the edge of the field. "We need to fortify ourselves or we will not survive the rest of the afternoon!"

María had placed long planks across the tops of upright wine casks to serve as tables in the courtyard. The boards were covered with platters of cured meats and sausages, cheeses, loaves of warm bread and pots of fabada.

Everyone ate lustfully as Antonio Primero held court at the head of the ersatz table. Antonio Segundo sat to his immediate right and Mercedes directly across. "I tell you, nothing good can come from this naval competition between England and Germany. Nothing good. They keep building more battleships and producing more armaments. And, from what I read in the papers, France is just itching for a war with Germany."

"What do you think, Segundo?" he asked, turning to Antonio Rivas and taking a deep drink of his red wine, cool from the cellar.

"I don't read the papers."

"Do not read the papers!" Antonio Primero exclaimed. "How? I could not live without them."

"Well, for one thing," Antonio Segundo said flatly, without any shame, "I never learned to read. And if I had, I still don't think I'd bother with the papers. I don't see how all that has much to do with me." He tucked into his bean stew. "Now, this fabada, María, if I had to learn to read to get a bowl of it, I'd race to the first teacher I could find and stay up nights learning. I don't know what England, France and Germany are all worked up about, but they can have it, as long as I can keep coming here to your table every now and then for your cooking. All of it is the best I've ever eaten."

"Thank you, Antonio," María said, embarrassed by the praise. "You're welcome in this house whenever you can come." Looking at her husband, and then leaning toward Antonio Segundo, she added: "We hope that one day, if I may be so forward, you'll be more of a regular fixture around here."

Antonio Segundo simply nodded and said: "Many thanks, María. You and Primero—and Mercedes, of course—have been better to me than anybody in all my life."

"You are a good man, Segundo," Primero said. He clasped Antonio Rivas' hand, which was resting on the table, and squeezed it. "Solid. The kind of man I wish I'd had as a partner in Cuba, instead of that snake Paco. We could make this farm the best in Castrillón. Maybe buy up enough land and cattle to get out of that smelter. And the good Lord only knows what our sons could do with the place!"

Now it was Mercedes' turn to be embarrassed. She and Antonio had seen much of each other, and they knew well her brother's plans for them. However, the Gallego always changed the topic when any conversation ventured to marriage and children. Mercedes, for so long the abandoned daughter and now twenty-six years old, was hungry for both. She would lie in her bed at night and imagine marrying Antonio at San Román Church in Naveces. She would picture building a little house at the bottom of the field, near the rushing stream she loved, up against the fragrant eucalyptus grove. Her brother had told her the spot was hers if she wished. Antonio Rivas was sweet and kind, in his unemotive way, but his reticence about marriage and children troubled her greatly.

"Okay, okay, you two," Mercedes said to her brother and sister-in-law in a playful tone which masked her deeper angst. "That's enough matchmaking. I believe it's time for the rice pudding, and then back to the fields to get our onions out of the ground before they rot."

"My sister," Antonio Primero said. "She ever is the practical one. María, do please bring out your divine arroz con leche."

María excused herself from the table. Antonio Primero turned back to Antonio Segundo. "Now, on this reading matter. It is not that difficult. Children can do it, for Heaven's sake. I know you never had the chance to learn when you were a boy, but she and María would be happy to guide you."

Segundo teased out some tobacco from his leather pouch. "Well, I don't—"

Primero interrupted him, his enthusiasm swelling. "When I left for Cuba, I was an ignorant farm boy—not to suggest that you are ignorant, of course—but I was. So was nearly every other Asturian I knew who went there. But the atmosphere of Havana was unlike anything any of us had experienced. It inspired us to improve ourselves, to learn and absorb all we could. We became educated, cultured people. I discovered the great works of history and literature and philosophy there, and I became addicted to the newspapers. I may be a simple Asturian farmer again now, but those things are a permanent part of me. I still can be a man of the world thanks to them." He downed the rest of his wine, plunked the empty cup on the table, and surveyed the dozen faces locked on his.

"That's certainly an inspiring story, Primero," Segundo said, "and your offer to help me with the reading is very generous. But, honestly, I still don't see any need for it, for me. I'm content as I am."

Antonio González Conde was disappointed by the response, but he did not wish to bully his friend about the issue. "Understood,

understood," he said. He poured a last splash of wine into both their cups. "But if you ever change your mind, the proposal stands. I cannot have my nieces and nephews outpacing their father—"

"Antonio!" Mercedes nearly shouted. "Enough!"

* * *

The first thing Antonio Segundo noticed when he entered the Avilés market square was the cacophony of farmers calling out to the shoppers. "Hola, Señor!" shouted a stout, elderly woman with thick ankles and meaty, strong hands. "Las fabes! Las fabes!" she added, gesticulating alternately toward Antonio and the open burlap sack of fat, white beans at her feet. Each seller tried his best to entice the milling buyers to purchase his fruits, vegetables, garlic heads, onions, dairy products, sausages and beans, which were identical to those being proffered by the farmer to the left and right.

The second thing he noticed was that the builders of Plaza Nuevo had copied the style popular in the Galician city of A Coruña on the inward-facing façades. An uninterrupted band of tall, slightly arched paned windows ran around all four sides of the square on the single storey above the high arcade. The window frames were painted a bright white, as were the recessed panels below each window and the wide, dentilled entablature beneath the red-tiled roof sloping up to the blue sky.

In such a square, fourteen years before, on such a brilliantly clear day with the white façades and panes of glass blindingly bright in the midday sun, Antonio's heart was broken. She was the only person, prior to Mercedes, with whom he felt he could be himself without reservation. She was the daughter of a Madrid merchant who had tired of the capital and taken his money and his family to Galicia. He purchased a large farm from a group of Gallego brothers who could not agree on how to manage their patrimony together.

The merchant-turned-cattleman hired Antonio to work on the farm. He thought highly of Antonio as an employee but would never have accepted him as a son-in-law. The daughter knew her father well, and on that summer day at a market square in A Coruña, she told Antonio that the affection they shared had no future. Antonio quit his job a week later, and he never set foot on a farm again, until Las Cepas on Christmas Eve 1910.

Antonio had not recalled that day in a long time. He quickly crammed the memory back into its box at the rear of his mind.

"Antonio!" Mercedes shouted, waving her arms. "Over here!"

The Real Compañía had closed the smelter for three weeks to clean and repair the zinc furnaces and retorts. Most of the Gallego workers took the opportunity to go home and visit their families. Antonio generally passed the time sleeping late, prowling the trails along the coastal bluffs around Arnao, and helping with the farm work at Las Cepas. Today was a Monday market day, and Antonio Primero had invited him to come along. Segundo was not keen on rising before dawn to go to work in the market, but he was happy for the chance to meander around in Avilés with Mercedes after their goods were sold.

"Segundo!" Primero said as if he had not seen him in a month and firmly shook Antonio's hand. "I am pleased you finally arrived. We were afraid you had fallen off the cliffs and been washed out to sea."

"No, no. Just a nice late morning in my quiet little room, and then a slow stroll here. It's a magnificent day."

"It's better now that you've come," Mercedes said. Despite the often intense inner turmoil she felt over the uncertainty about their future, every absence and new meeting deepened Mercedes' love for Antonio.

"You two go off and enjoy the town together," Antonio Primero ordered. "We are almost finished here, and Pepe and I can tend to the shopping. Try to have my sister home before dark, Segundo. You know how the provincials are. Those old women in Naveces, who have never been more than 50 kilometers from home, will have old Father Agustín reprimanding me as if I am some dastardly communist atheist because I allowed Mercedes out with you unchaperoned."

The social strictures for unmarried women still were rigid in rural Spain. Custom dictated that at least one mature female relative trail along, guarding the honour of the unwed sister, niece or daughter. In Avilés, the tradition extended even to the sunny weekend perambulations of young men and women around the new Parque de Muelle, the former cruising counterclockwise and the latter strolling in the opposite direction.

Antonio Primero rarely met a conservative notion or tradition he did not tightly embrace, but his attitude was more liberal on matters concerning his sister. She had been so badly treated by their father; she had survived on her own all those years he was in Cuba; and she was not some blushing, irresponsible girl. Mercedes was twenty-six and as capable of managing her own affairs as well as any man he knew, and more so than several.

"Don't worry, Primero. I'll protect both your reputations," Antonio Segundo said and gave his Gallego half-grin. He was always amused, and a bit perplexed, when Antonio Primero ranted to him about the "provincials." He had never ventured outside Galicia and Asturias himself.

"This is your town, Mercedes, so you lead the way," Antonio said, rolling a cigarette as they walked through the market arch into Calle Muralla. "I was only here once, on the train from A Coruña when I came to Arnao. I'm guessing you've planned a grand tour."

"You know me well," Mercedes said. She took his arm. It was a bold gesture, with them unchaperoned, but today she felt free and light and did not care what anybody other than Antonio Rivas thought. "I've prepared all week, pestering Antonio to tell me everything he knows about the Avilés buildings and history."

They paused by the Café Colón, one of the town's newest and most popular, on the corner facing the park. They watched the men taking their afternoon red vermouths or *cafes con leche*—the traditional shot of espresso with an equal amount of hot milk—al fresco and competing to see who could toss the most small, wooden rings into the open mouth of the big, cast iron frog which sat near the café door.

"Twenty years ago," Mercedes said, "we would have been standing in the harbour. Ships sailed up the estuary and moored at the docks which stood right here, outside the old city walls, and unloaded their cargo." Antonio agreed that the park—built on the filled-in portion of the estuary—with its palm trees, dome roofed bandstand, statuary and gurgling fountain, was a pleasant addition to the booming town.

"But our first stop," Mercedes continued, "is the oldest building in Avilés, from the twelfth century, and my favourite. The Franciscan Brothers' church, just up there at the edge of the medieval town, when it was called only La Villa."

"I should've expected you'd start with a church," Antonio said, chuckling. Other than protecting his baby brother from his father's attempt at banishment, he had not seen much of value from priests and the Church. To the contrary, Mercedes' travails had strengthened her religious sentiment. For many years, God was her only reliable companion and the mass her primary source of inner peace.

"You know, it wouldn't kill you to visit one a little more regularly," she quipped.

"Here we go," Antonio said, shaking his head and smiling at Mercedes.

"I'm not lecturing! At least not today," Mercedes said. "You can treat it like it's one of those hillsides you never tire of exploring."

As they turned up Calle La Ferrería, the principal street in medieval Avilés, the church popped into view. Antonio said: "Well, it used to be part of a hillside, anyway." It was constructed from cut sandstone blocks of various sizes, now rounded unevenly at the edges and ridged horizontally, like a seaside escarpment, by the centuries of buffeting from ocean winds and rain.

"I adore it," Mercedes said. "Don't you?"

Even Antonio had to admit it was beautiful in its Romanesque simplicity. "It's a lovely church," he replied. "I understand why it's the first place you brought me. If I was of a mind to go to a church regularly, I'd want to come here."

Mercedes was giddy, for the second of many times on this day. The first was when she glanced up from her last three links of chorizo lying in the basket and saw Antonio standing perfectly still amid the chaos of the market, looking at the sparkling white façades. She had wondered then, and wondered again now, what had so transfixed him. But she did not ask.

They entered the church through its carved, rounded-arch main portal, and Mercedes knelt to say a brief, silent prayer: "Thank you for this. For this day and this man. Please keep us healthy and happy. And please keep me strong." She eased back from the kneeler and onto the pew beside Antonio. They sat in the placid silence of the empty church, until Antonio began to fidget. Mercedes touched him on the forearm and pointed toward the door.

Directly across from the church, Mercedes led Antonio up the narrow Calle San Bernardo—she always winced when she saw the sign: her father certainly had not honoured his saint's name—which entered a small square after about 20 paces. Mercedes turned and pointed back at an irregularly windowed, two-storey stone and plastered house which fronted on the plaza. It was not a palace, but would have been a prominent dwelling in the walled town of the sixteenth century. "The most famous Avilesino was born there the early 1500s. Admiral General Pedro Menéndez, the founder of the city of San Agustín in La Florida, in the United States of America."

Antonio never had heard of Pedro Menéndez or San Agustín in La Florida, but he had thought often about the United States of America, especially since hearing Antonio Primero's stories about their brother Ramón, who was living there in some city called San Luís.

Mercedes continued, relating the history her brother had told her. "Don Pedro had a boat built with the money from his inheritance when he was not much more than a boy, and he defeated three French cruisers in a battle just off the coast. He went on to become one of King Felipe's most able and successful commanders in the New World, and he is still the pride of Avilés."

Antonio's mind was stuck on America. More than a million Gallegos had gone to Argentina over the past century, and now thousands more were sailing off to the United States. He was so tired of struggling to keep himself housed, clothed and fed.

Mercedes noticed the distant look in his eyes. "Have you ever thought of going to America?" she asked, though it was a question she would rather not ask when they were having such an enjoyable day.

Antonio was slow to respond. "I've thought of it as an alternative, if anything ever happens with my job in Arnao."

A dark cloud sank over Mercedes.

"Antonio says that your brother Ramón is doing very well over there. Making good money. Bought his own house."

"Mmmn, yes, that's true. He has," Mercedes said.

"But look here," Antonio added quickly. He placed a calloused hand on her arm. "I'm not eager to go. For one thing, I'd guess you can't get a decent chorizo or slice of Spanish ham in the whole country."

The cloud dissipated as quickly as it came.

They went back the way they had come from the church and meandered up Calla La Ferrería, which looked for the most part as it had for 700 years: three- and four-storey sandstone buildings on either side of the narrow street, with stone arcades covering the pink, black and blonde limestone slab sidewalk pavers worn wavy by centuries of pedestrians. The medieval blacksmiths had their shops along this street, and the arcades allowed them to work outside during the gloomy, rainy days of the long Asturian winter.

At Plaza de España, the town's main square, they paused to admire the neoclassical municipal hall, with its eleven-arched arcade, pedimented clock face and central tower crowned with a fat bronze bell suspended in what looked like a Victorian iron birdcage.

They crossed the square, and Mercedes pointed to a residential palace with a giant carved escutcheon on its façade and a trapezoidal corner tower topped by a green copper cupola. "That," Mercedes said, "is the residence of the Marqueses of Ferrera. The first one, who had it built in the middle of the seventeenth century, was a descendant of Don Pedro Menéndez."

"That's quite a house," Antonio marveled. "I don't think I'll ever be able to afford one of those for you."

Mercedes turned to face him and took both his hands in hers. "I don't care if we lived in my brother's granary, Antonio, as long as we could marry and have a family of our own. You must believe that."

Antonio's shoulders stiffened, almost imperceptibly. The face of the girl in A Coruña flashed before him, which he quickly beat back into the recesses of his consciousness. Impossible to so easily dispatch was the tightness in his stomach and throat he always felt when Mercedes talked about children. Every time she mentioned it, a despair so cold suffused him that he felt chilly and his hands numb. Antonio could not escape the conviction that he was unable to care properly for children or give them the attention they deserved. He knew what it was like to be a child under such circumstances, and Antonio was determined never to inflict such pain himself.

This fear and anxiety sprung from two sources, one practical and one existential. He owned nothing, except a small suitcase of clothes, and he had no real trade. Since he was twelve years old, Antonio had survived by manual labor, exchanging a lot of sweat for a little money. How was a man with no land and no marketable skill, who lived at the mercy of employers who could dispatch him at any time they no longer required his toil, to maintain a wife and family?

Worse than the economic uncertainty, however, was the restlessness. It lived within him, like some virus or parasite or possessing demon. It had been there for as long as he could remember. It was not constant, and often it would quiet to a point and for such a duration that he thought it had migrated to a different host. But it always returned. And the harder he tried to ignore it, the more intensely it berated him.

Occasionally, he thought it a positive force, pushing him toward that unknown place where he would find the contentment which seemed to lie eternally over the next hill, in the next town, out beyond the horizon on the wide sea. But most of the time, he saw it only as a tormenting spectre which had decided he would never know peace. Either way, when the restlessness came, it felt like eels were wrestling in his chest. Temporary relief came only when he yielded to it and moved on to yet another life in yet another place. As long as the restlessness plagued him, he knew, he could not shoulder the burden of children.

"What is it, Antonio? Where are you?" Mercedes asked.

"It's nothing," he said. Antonio looked up Calle San Francisco, which ran away from the square to the right of the Palacio de Ferrera. "And what's that one?" he asked, pointing toward the Gothic church of San Nicolás de Bari, where Mercedes, María and the children had watched the Easter procession two years before. "I'm sure you know the history of that church, too."

Mercedes had grown accustomed to his evasions. She knew not to press. "That, ah," she said, "used to be the Franciscan Brothers' church and monastery. But they were driven from the city when the First Republic disbanded the monasteries in 1836. When the Franciscans returned, after the monarchy was restored, they settled in the other church." She focused on the history and pushed away her prickling apprehensions, determined not to let them spoil this outing.

Beyond the church, they stood on gently sloping Calle Galiano and watched an Indiano supervise the workers wrangling a tall palm tree into the freshly dug hole beside his immense new home. Two well-nourished gulls sat squawking loudly in the gutter concealed behind the Doric entablature. The five-bay neoclassical mansion, painted a vivid ochre, was the latest display of Indiano ostentation constructed on this street which for two hundred fifty years had housed only workers and the poor. "No! No! More to the left!" the portly man shouted, stamping around impatiently in his dove-coloured tailored suit and spats, a bright blue cravat around his neck.

Though they used their recent riches to affect the lifestyle of aristocrats, the Indianos generally had begun their lives as struggling farmers and laborers, and they knew how a job should be done. And whether they built grand palacios like this one, or only a modest new farmhouse, the Indianos shared that one new tradition: planting the biggest palm tree they could afford in the garden. It was the proud emblem of an Asturian successfully back in his homeland to stay.

As the man relished the sight of his erected palm. Mercedes and Antonio continued their stroll. Arm in arm, they explored every street and park in Avilés until the bells at San Nicolás began to announce the evening mass. It was an afternoon Mercedes often would recall for the remainder of her life: a gentle, lovely, effortless day shared by two troubled people finding a little joy in life where they could.

Chapter 8

Las Cepas, Asturias
April 1912

The rain poured and poured. Mercedes had not seen the sun in more than a week, nor Antonio for nearly a month. She despised this season of the deluges. This year the Semana Santa penitents got no respite from the raw weather. Spring refused to arrive. The cold, soggy, windy days stretched on and on. Mercedes' mood matched the heavy skies.

There had been much discussion recently that the strike could be settled soon. She worried what that would mean for Antonio Rivas. The Real Compañía brought the Gallegos in to replace the striking Asturians. What would happen when the Asturian workers came back to the smelter? Neither her brother, nor anyone else she asked, seemed to know. Antonio Segundo would just shrug his shoulders and roll a cigarette when she asked his opinion. She loved him, but he could be a difficult man.

"Why are you sitting here, staring out the window?" María asked as she came into the little parlour. "You know it doesn't help to ruminate when that darkness comes over you."

"I know, María."

"So why do you sit there, your hands unoccupied but your mind and spirit clearly burdened?" her sister-in-law asked.

"I'm just ready for the sun, and the blossoms of spring. This winter has dragged on for long enough."

"It's far better," María said, placing a hand lightly on Mercedes' shoulder, "to take each day as it is, and be thankful for it."

"Mmmn," Mercedes grunted.

"So what, other than the rain, is troubling you?"

"I don't want to lose Antonio," Mercedes said without shifting her gaze from the rain.

"Why should you lose him, rabbit? I know that he often keeps to himself, but why would you lose him?"

"It's all this talk about the strike being settled," Mercedes said. She turned from the window. "I can feel it, in my heart and in my stomach, that he'll lose his job in the smelter, and then he'll leave and go to America."

"Or, perhaps, he'll be glad, at last, to be rid of that miserable toiling at the retorts every day and join us here at Las Cepas. We could use a man around full time."

"You know he'll never do that," Mercedes said dismissively.

María suspected this was true, though she did not want to admit it to herself, her always enthusiastic husband or her frequently melancholy sister-in-law.

"He hates farm life," Mercedes continued, exasperated. "I can't understand why he prefers the smelter work, and why he doesn't want me or a family. But he doesn't, and I should just accept it."

"Oh, Mercedes, that's putting it a bit strongly, don't you think?" María said. "It's simply part of the Gallego character. You know how they are, God love them. Constantly keeping one eye open for the chance they may miss and agonizingly slow ever to make a definitive decision about anything."

Mercedes considered María's observation. "Yes, I suppose," she said. The cold rain beat against the window in waves with the gusts of wind. "It's just so frustrating. After all these years alone, I have to go and fall in love with such a man."

"But he's a good man!" María insisted. "He is one of the gentlest, kindest men I've ever known. He's been so much help around here when we needed him, and he's such a pleasure to have at our table. And clearly, he is smitten with you."

"But what good does that do me, if he never proposes marriage and is always looking out to the sea, as if something is out there waiting for him?"

For those questions, María had no good answer. "I believe Antonio came here for a reason, Mercedes. We may not comprehend at the moment what it is, but the two of you meeting when you did was not mere coincidence. Of that I'm certain. Have some faith, rabbit. It all will be clear in good time."

"But I don't want it to be clear in good time!" Mercedes said, rising in her chair. "I want to know it now! If Antonio is going, then I just want him to go. I'm tired of waiting and wishing!"

"I know, dear. I know," María said. She reached over and patted Mercedes on the forearm. "But be patient for a short time longer. Antonio will have to make up his mind soon. All the women are saying the strike will end in a matter of months, and I suspect the result will not be good for the Gallegos."

Mercedes frowned and looked back out the window. The oak trees across the pasture sagged under the weight of the downpour.

"It's terribly unfair," María continued. "Except for us and a few—very few—of your brother's friends, there's no sympathy for them, even though the smelter and mine have stayed open only thanks to their labor. Most people despise them for replacing the striking workers, and the Real Compañía always has considered them temporary help. Their fates are in the wind."

* * *

Arnao, Asturias
August 1912

As Mercedes crested the high bluff on the footpath from the village of Santa María del Mar, she saw Antonio Rivas standing motionless up ahead, his back toward her. He was looking across the small bay toward Arnao. The wind blew steadily and hard off the Atlantic.

Antonio put his arm around Mercedes' narrow waist when she stepped close beside him. "Windy today," he said.

"Yes. And it smells like rain."

"Yes."

They were silent for a long while, watching the waves crash against the cape where the smelter stood and roll into the pebble covered beach. A group of miners slowly trudged toward the castillete below them.

"You know I can't go down there," Antonio said. His eyes were fixed on the miners. "Now that the strike is settled, all the Gallegos they're not firing are being transferred to the mine."

"I know," Mercedes said. Her voice was flat and cold. "My brother told me yesterday."

"I don't mind the smelter work," Antonio said distantly. "I even enjoy it sometimes. And it's always warm and dry in the winter. Those poor men," he added as he waved a hand toward the miners, who now were filing into the castillete. "They spend ten hours a day down there in the coal dust and wet and cold of those tunnels under the sea. It's a death sentence."

"I know, Antonio," Mercedes replied. Irritation and empathy mixed in her voice.

He rolled a cigarette for each of them, and they stood silent again, smoking and staring. Antonio was in agony. From the moment his affection for Mercedes had slid into love, he knew he would be confronted with this choice. He viewed his options as equally bad. He could stay in Asturias and become a farmer, slopping around in the muck, living on

Mercedes' land for the remainder of his life. He would wrestle with the restlessness every day and blame her and the children for his inability to leave and quiet it. Or he could return to his completely solitary life, this time in faraway America, in hopes that steady work and a house of his own would free him from the restlessness, once and for all.

"So, what will you do?" Mercedes finally asked. As on that afternoon in Avilés, it was a question to which she actually did not want an answer.

"For now, I'll go down to Oviedo," Antonio said. He took a last deep drag on the cigarette and flicked the butt into the wind. "I have a cousin who works in one of the factories there, and he'll try to get me on. But there are so many of us looking for jobs now. And most of my experience is working with the zinc, and they only do that here."

"And in America."

After a lengthy pause, Antonio added: "Yes, and in America."

Mercedes was unable to restrain her emotions any longer. She cried out: "Oh, Antonio!" Tears streamed down her face. "I don't want you to go to America. You can't go. You must stay here with us, with me." She grasped him tightly on both his arms. "Please, please, Antonio. Come to Las Cepas. Work with us on the farm. Make a life with me here. It'll be a good life, I promise. I know you don't like the farm work, but we'll be happy. You'll see."

Antonio's body was rigid and his expression opaque. The old chill which had nothing to do with the wind surged through him, as if he had been injected with Arctic seawater. "For now, I'll go to Oviedo. I'm sorry, Mercedes. But that's what I must do."

Mercedes whipped from weeping to fury. "Damn, you, Antonio Rivas! And damn your stupid, Gallego pig-headedness! You can have a good life and home with my family and me. Why? Why, do you persist in this ceaseless drifting, like some ship out there in the sea with tattered sails and a broken rudder?"

"I'm sorry, Mercedes," he said, barely above a whisper. His throat suddenly was thick and dry. "I don't understand it fully myself. But I know I have to find stable work and some solution for this restlessness.

And I know I can't stay here now and live on the farm. I just can't. I feel suffocated when I even think about it."

"Suffocated? Suffocated?" she yelled. Mercedes had stepped away from him. She towered over him as she stood fully erect, clenched fists on her hips. "You feel suffocated by people who love you and value you and want you to be happy?"

Antonio shrugged his shoulders and shook his head, but he did not know what more to say.

"You and your damned Gallego shrug. I'm sick of it, Antonio. I'm sick of waiting and hoping. Fine. If you want to go, then go. Go and slave away in whatever factory will take you, and live alone in those company boarding house rooms. I've had enough!" She turned and stormed off down the footpath toward Santa María del Mar without a single glance back in his direction.

Antonio sat down on a rock. He pulled a rolling paper and bit of tobacco from his leather pouch, and watched her go.

* * *

In a month, Antonio was gone to America. As he suspected, there was no job for him in Oviedo. Though he was nearly as disappointed as Mercedes by Antonio's decision not to join them at Las Cepas, Antonio González Conde had wished his friend well and telegrammed his brother Ramón in St. Louis.

There were zinc smelters in more than twenty towns and cities across the northeast and mid-west United States, with clusters around St. Louis, Pittsburgh and Clarksburg, West Virginia. Ramón had advanced to the most senior floor position in the smelter where he worked in St. Louis. He maintained the fires and managed the crews which shoveled the ore, prepared the retorts and collected the zinc for an entire seventy-five-yard-long furnace.

The U.S. companies were hungry for Asturians and Gallegos. They performed in the terrible conditions better than any other workers, immigrant or domestic. It was easy for Ramón to arrange a position

71

for Antonio with the Grasselli Chemical Company's zinc smelter in Grasselli, West Virginia.

Mercedes could not bear to see Antonio when he came to Las Cepas for a farewell feast on the eve of his departure from Asturias. She spent the evening with the pair of spinster aunts who lived in a cottage down the road. Antonio was sad she was not there, but he understood and was a bit relieved. The decision to emigrate had been excruciating, and feeling her fury and watching her march away that afternoon on the bluff above Arnao was the worst moment in his life. Mercedes' presence would have drained every ounce of pleasure from the dinner. Antonio already felt apprehensive enough about going. America was so far away and so alien. He did not need another emotional blow.

"Be well, my friend," Antonio González Conde told him, embracing Antonio Rivas and kissing him once on each cheek. "Go with God. And know that you always are welcome here when you tire of the furnaces and America. I fully appreciate why you must go. I had my own nineteen years in Cuba, as you know. There is something irresistible about that tug of the New World. But, I assure you, life here in the old one is better. Do not hesitate to return when this American fever has run its course."

After a short sail to Liverpool, Antonio Rivas boarded the Cunard steamer *Carmania* for New York. Like more than twenty million other immigrants between 1892 and 1924, Antonio was processed into the United States through the crowded Great Hall at Ellis Island on October 2, 1912. As he slowly advanced through the long line under the high, arched ceiling of the vast room, Antonio felt mostly numb.

He was surrounded by a Babel of languages and the smells of hundreds of wool-clad people emerging from a week packed in the poorly ventilated lower decks of transatlantic liners. When he finally stepped to one of the tall, wooden registration desks, the uniformed immigration officer changed the spelling of his last name to "Ribas," because that was how Antonio pronounced it.

An agent for the Grasselli Company met him at the ferry dock in lower Manhattan and guided him through streets nearly as crowded as third-class steerage on the *Carmania* had been. Antonio would not have believed that such a city could exist had he not seen it with his own eyes. It was a different universe from any place he knew. With his one small suitcase and fourteen dollars in his pocket, Antonio caught a train at Penn Station and headed off to his new life in the hills of northern West Virginia.

Mercedes sat in her room at Las Cepas. She wept harder and longer than she had at any time since her brother José was killed in Cuba when she was a girl.

Chapter 9

As nature slept through the bone chilling, rainy winter, Mercedes felt less burdened by Antonio's absence, little by little. Still, seven months after his departure, a sight or scent or slant of the sunlight would cause the tears to come unexpectedly. A day or two would grind by before she recovered from the feelings of loss and abandonment.

On this spring market Monday, María accompanied Mercedes and Antonio to Avilés. She needed a break from the farm and wanted to replenish her sewing basket. She was also worried about Mercedes and hoped that the two of them spending a relaxed afternoon in the town might help improve her sister-in-law's mood. Nothing else María had tried over the past seven months had given Mercedes much relief.

As they strolled up Calle San Francisco, Mercedes was morose and lost in the memory of walking there with Antonio Rivas the summer before. A cluster of nuns in snow-white habits emerged from the cloister at San Nicolás de Bari. They passed Mercedes and María and walked briskly down toward the Plaza de España.

"Maybe I should take holy orders," Mercedes said as she watched them go.

"Perhaps you should, rabbit," María said. "But not now. Not in your current frame of mind. You want to marry Antonio, not the Church. Christ can't be reduced to the role of default suitor."

Mercedes sighed. She knew she no more wanted to be a nun than a laborer in the smelter at Arnao. "As always, you're right, María."

Fat raindrops, driven by a sudden stiff wind, began to smack against them, and the two women took shelter under the arcade along Calle Galiana. It was the longest covered walkway in Avilés, ascending and bending toward the livestock market at Plaza de Carbayedo. Mercedes adored this street.

The wending line of narrow, two- and three-storey houses had changed little since they were built three hundred years before. Mercedes always wondered about the lives of the generations of families who had lived out their days there, more on this street than any other in town. The floor of houses' extended upper storey façades—supported on the street side by weathered, battered sandstone columns, some Doric, some Ionic and most looking as if they had been feasted upon by stone-eating termites—formed the ceiling of the arcade. The structural arrangement created a feeling of intimacy with the people who resided above the pedestrians' heads. And Mercedes was always amused by the arcade's pavement: granite slabs on the inner half for the people, bulbous beach-rock cobbles on the outer half for the cows headed up to the market.

"Why does everything have to be so hard for me, María?" Mercedes asked as they neared the end of the arcade, the momentary distraction of her favourite street ended.

"I have no answer for that, dear," María said. "Life certainly has given you more than your share of troubles. Perhaps it will be that you've paid in advance for a long time of happiness to come. You're only twenty-eight, and we all seem to live well into our nineties in this family. You're still just getting started."

Mercedes was skeptical. "Oh, María, I'm nearly a spinster, and you know it," she said. "How many women in all of Castrillón have you known to get an offer of marriage and start a family at my age?

My mother was twenty when she married my father. And you? You were, what? Nineteen?"

"Eighteen," María replied reluctantly.

"Eighteen," Mercedes repeated to emphasize her point. "I'm a twenty-eight-year-old woman with no money and a quarter-interest in a small farm that I never would sell even if I could. I'm not beautiful. Midwifery is not a skill men appreciate thirty seconds after they see their wife has given them a healthy baby. And with my dark moods, I don't even like being around myself half the time. It's no wonder Antonio left. No man could want me."

"Oh, Mercedes," María huffed. "Don't always look at everything so blackly." She softened her tone and added: "All I can say is that you must have faith. We don't know where our paths will lead. All those years on your own, you never expected to be with us at Las Cepas, did you?"

"No," Mercedes said, still sullen.

"Nor to meet Antonio Rivas, and fall in love?"

"No. But that may not be the best example you could've chosen," Mercedes said, cracking a smile.

"I couldn't disagree more," María said. "Have you fallen in love with another since he left?"

"No."

"And has he, with someone else, in America?"

"Not that I've heard, no."

"I would say, then, that your paths are clear to merge again," María said.

"He could come back," Mercedes admitted, though she did not feel it to be true. "I suppose it's not impossible."

"It certainly is not," María insisted. "How can he not get enough of that smelter in America, so far from the sea and Spain, no matter how much money he is earning?"

"But if he doesn't?" Mercedes asked.

"Well, then he's more foolish than I imagined," María said, waving a hand as if she were shooing away gnats. "But if he does decide to stay, for whatever reason, why could you not join him in America?"

In her months of suffering, Mercedes had never considered that option. She pondered it and felt a flicker of possibility. "I suppose I could," she said. She pursed her lips and nodded slowly. She had stopped walking without realizing it. "Yes, I could. I could." Then her thoughts skipped immediately to what such a move would mean. "But, María, to leave you and my brother and the children, and Las Cepas, and Asturias?" That was nearly too painful to contemplate, perhaps worse than losing the man she loved. "I'm not some wandering soul like Antonio. This land is my home. It's part of me, and I'm part of it. I can't even imagine leaving here."

María had faced that same dilemma once. She and Antonio González Conde had known each other as children, and they corresponded frequently during his years in Cuba. When he was repatriated in 1899, they decided to marry. María believed he was home for good. They were wed in San Román Church just before Antonio went back to Havana.

She stayed in Asturias, hoping that Antonio's new Cuban adventure would be short. He left hoping that his absence would cause María to reconsider and join him. But she only grew more determined never to leave her homeland. One of the many blessings which came from Bernardo's death was her husband's swift and permanent return.

If Mercedes were forced to make such a choice, it would be much more difficult. She would not be going to Cuba, which had been a distant piece of Spain for four centuries. She would be going to that strange, Anglo land of the United States.

Chapter 10

Graselli, West Virginia
May 1913

In Graselli, Antonio was surprised to learn that good chorizo and Spanish ham actually were available, as was just about every other taste of the peninsula he desired. So many Spanish workers had settled there that other enterprising Iberian immigrants opened shops and imported goods from Spain, catering to the culinary longings of their fellow expatriates. He heard Spanish being spoken in the streets more frequently than English, and he met several men from Avilés and Castrillón who knew Las Cepas and Antonio González Conde. These encounters made Antonio miss Mercedes intensely and to question the wisdom of his decision to leave. It was not much of an improvement to replace restlessness with self-doubt.

The spring after he arrived, Antonio recognized three men sitting outside a café, sipping beers and playing dominoes. They were Asturians, striking workers who had returned to the Arnao smelter shortly before he quit. For his two years in Arnao, Antonio spent little time with the other workers. He preferred his solitude, and he had presumed from the day he arrived at the Real Compañía that when the strike ended he would be dismissed. He saw no reason to get close to men with whom he could part company forever at any time.

The returning Asturians were even less inclined to associate with Antonio and the other strike-breakers than Antonio was with them.

They had cursed the replacement workers every day, blaming them—not without some justification—for the strike's two-year duration. Antonio nodded at the three men outside the café in Graselli as he strolled by. They nodded back, unenthusiastically. "I see Grasselli has no qualms about hiring Gallego scabs here," one grumbled to the others.

Other than missing Mercedes, Graselli was Spanish enough to inoculate Antonio against any homesickness. He had not felt at home anywhere since he was a boy in Portomarín anyway, so this town was as good as any other. Here, at least, Antonio believed he had the chance to make a real life for himself and that he was adequately compensated for the back-breaking work. These West Virginia hills had not become home, he thought, but perhaps they could be one day.

* * *

Las Cepas, Asturias
August 1913

Mercedes had not received a letter since she was a girl, when her brother would write her from Cuba. The West Virginia return address confused and concerned her, because she knew Antonio could neither read nor write.

"Dear Ms. González Conde," the letter began, in the handwriting of an unschooled person. "I am writing you for my friend, Antonio Ribas." Mercedes did not understand why Antonio's supposed friend had misspelled his last name. "He sends his fondest greetings and hopes that you are healthy and well." A wave of emotion crashed over her. She nearly had given up hope of hearing from Antonio.

"He is well here in West Virginia," the letter continued, "and Antonio says he misses you very much. His work has been good, and he can buy one of the houses in Graselli that the company has built for the workers. But he says that he does not need a house just to live alone, and he would be happiest if he could share it with you. Antonio apologizes for doing this by mail and through me, but he asks you if you would consider marrying him and moving to live with him here. He waits for your response and hopes you will accept his proposal. Sincerely yours, Jávier Gómez Díaz."

Without a word, Mercedes handed the letter to María, who was sewing in a chair across from her in the little parlour. María read the letter and said: "Well, my dear rabbit, it appears you have a difficult decision to make. But at least, for once, your fate rests in your own hands. How do you feel about it?"

"I ... I ... I don't know. I don't know what I feel." For so long, Mercedes had prayed that she could make a life with Antonio. The year and a half since he left had been the most difficult of her life, and she was no stranger to angst and disappointment. But was this an answer to prayer? To choose between Antonio and her homeland and family? "I feel ... overwhelmed. Overwhelmed by joy and sadness. In equal parts."

María understood in the way that only one who had faced the same stark choice could understand.

"How can I say no?" Mercedes said, then added: "But how can I go?"

"Yes," María said. She kneaded absently at the fabric in her hands. "These men always subject us to such painful dilemmas." Again, she did not tell Mercedes of her own struggle when Antonio González Conde wanted to stay in Cuba.

"I'll take a walk," Mercedes said abruptly. "I always think clearer out in the fresh air, among the eucalyptus trees."

"You do that, rabbit. Nature is a good advisor. And you may want to go down to Naveces, to San Román, and talk to God about it as well."

"Yes, yes. That's a good suggestion," Mercedes said, brimming with nervous excitement. "Thank you, María. Oh, my. I certainly didn't expect the day held this when I woke this morning and went out to milk the cows!"

María watched Mercedes through the window as she started across the pasture toward the woods. She walked quickly, erect and with a purpose. Then she stopped suddenly, pulled the letter from her apron pocket and read it again. A cow wandered up and nudged her. Mercedes stroked its muzzle lightly as she read. She dropped the hand clutching the letter to her side and looked up at the sky. Then Mercedes looked at the cow, for what seemed like an eternity to María as she observed from her seat in the parlour, before patting the animal lovingly on its jowl and marching off toward the eucalyptus grove.

* * *

A fit old Asturian man, dressed in a well-worn vested suit and Asturian beret called a *boina,* with the stub of a cigar clenched in the corner of his mouth, tugged a reluctant calf by a chain lead into the Avilés live-stock market at the Plaza de Carbayedo.

"That one appears to have a lively spirit," Antonio González Conde said to Mercedes when he noticed the man with the calf. Their milk and sausages had sold well at the Monday markets all spring and into the summer, and Antonio had decided to invest the proceeds in more livestock.

"I don't know that's such a desirable quality in a milk cow," Mercedes said, "especially if we have to drag it all the way home."

"You make a valid point, sister. But I always have a soft spot for an animal with some spunk!"

Mercedes smiled and shook her head. She adored her brother for the world he had given her. He and María had made her feel loved, wanted and accepted for the first time in her life. With them and the children, for thirteen years now, she'd had a home. She felt rooted at Las Cepas, as if she were one of the apple trees or the camellias, reaching deep into the soil and rising from it, drawing strength and sustenance from the Asturian ground.

Her stomach went hollow and her chest filled with anxiety when she thought of leaving her family and land. But she also longed for a home and children of her own with Antonio Ribas. This desire had multiplied exponentially since she received his letter. His proposal overpowered the sense of security and joy she had derived from her life at Las Cepas.

"It is awfully hot today, even for August," Antonio said. The Asturians loved to complain about the weather, and the turbulent climate provided them with many opportunities. He removed his straw hat and said, patting his forehead dry with a linen handkerchief: "They seem to be selling cool drinks at that house over there by the arcade. What say we refresh ourselves and survey the field from up on the sidewalk."

The compact, two-storey house from which the refreshments were being sold resembled a small fortress with its thick walls of uncut stones, small windows and narrow wooden door. It was one of the first houses constructed on the Plaza de Carbayedo in the late-sixteenth century. From the beginning, it had been the residence of the family which ran the livestock market. On sweltering days like this one, the single sidewalk-level window was perfect for selling beer and cider from the perpetually dark and cool interior of the house's ground floor.

"That would be delightful," Mercedes said. They each took a small glass of beer and stood in the shadow of the house examining the cattle out in the marketplace.

Mercedes was so ambivalent about the declaration she was about to make, and the unknown path down which it would lead, that she could hardly breathe. Her heart felt constricted, and there was a constant high-pitched ringing in her right ear. She had to tell him, now, and make her decision concrete. "Antonio," Mercedes said. She could not organize the words to continue.

"What is it, Mercedes?" Antonio asked. "Do you feel ill from the heat?"

"No, no." Mercedes took a small sip from her glass. "I … I have something important to tell you." María had agreed to keep the letter from Antonio Ribas between them until Mercedes made her choice and told her brother herself.

"What? What?" Antonio pressed.

After another long pause, Mercedes said: "Nearly a month ago, I received a letter from Antonio. Well, a letter from a friend of Antonio's in West Virginia, writing to me for him."

"I told that man he needed to learn to read and write," Antonio started, then caught himself before he ran off on the tangent. "Sorry. Sorry. That is very good news Mercedes. Very good." When she continued to look more pained than happy, he asked: "It is, is it not, good news? He is not having some sort of difficulty, is he?" Referring again to his dishonest business partner in Cuba, Antonio added: "There do seem to be an inordinate number of swindlers over on that side of the Atlantic."

"No, he's well. Very well, in fact. He's even getting a mortgage from the company to buy one of the houses they've built for the workers."

"And he has asked you to marry him and go to the United States," Antonio surmised.

"That he has," Mercedes said. Now it was real, and she was again doused with doubt.

"And you will accept his proposal and go," Antonio said evenly.

Mercedes did not know whether it was a question or an order. She scrutinized the barns and little houses running up the other two sides of the tree-canopied square, and at the hilly countryside beyond. *How can I leave this?* she thought for the hundredth time. After another long pause, she looked again at her brother and said: "I believe I will, yes."

Antonio drank the remainder of his beer and wiped his moustache with his handkerchief.

"What do you think, Antonio?" Mercedes asked. "Do you believe that's the right decision?"

"Well, you know I have very mixed feelings about the United States," Antonio said. "Clearly, it has been good to Ramón, and now to Segundo. But I cannot ever forgive them for taking Cuba and the rest of the empire from us, or for the friends I lost in the war. But for you? Yes. Absolutely, I will support your decision if you wish to marry Antonio and go to him there."

With her brother's unhesitating endorsement, the anxiety ebbed and excitement rushed in. Mercedes hugged him tightly, her face brightened by an enthusiastic smile. "Oh, Antonio, thank you. You always have been so kind to me."

Patting her lightly on the back, Antonio said: "Of course I have. You are my only sister, and I love you. And I want you to be happy, rabbit, especially after what our father put you through."

"You can't know how happy you've made me, Antonio," Mercedes said. "You and María and the children ..." Out washed the excitement and in surged an excruciating sense of loss. Her smile twisted into a grimace and her brow furrowed. "But how can I leave, Antonio? I never could feel at home any place else."

"It does not have to be forever, you know," Antonio said tenderly. "There are thousands of Indianos here who stayed over there just long enough to make their fortunes and then came home. Ramón seems to have become permanently rooted in San Luís, but he always had that tendency. Had the United States not stolen Cuba, he still would be in Havana instead. But Segundo? You know how that Gallego is. Once he has filled the poor orphan's need to make enough money to feel secure, he will tire of life among the *Yanquis* and begin to pine for home."

Mercedes was not so sure. "Do you really believe it, Antonio? That he could want to come back?"

"Perhaps not to Las Cepas, especially if he has enough money of his own. But certainly to Galicia," he said. "A person does not need much of a fortune to buy a large piece of land and house there, the times are so difficult in Galicia, and that would be close enough. We could see each other every year at Christmas and Easter, and you would feel at home there as much as you do here. Particularly after a few years in that United States."

Mercedes felt herself righting, like a boat that has been rolled sail to water by a fierce sea. "I'll do it, then, Antonio. I'll marry Antonio Ribas and go to West Virginia and start a family of my own. You know how much I love Ramón, Pilar and Pepe ..."

"Of course I do, rabbit. And they you. Sometimes, I think they love you more than they do María and me."

"... but I have wanted children of my own for so long," Mercedes continued. "Every time I help bring a new baby into the world, every time I sit at your table with your happy family, I want my own little ones, my own happy family, even more desperately."

"And now you shall have it, my dear rabbit." He then returned his attention to the purpose of their visit to the Plaza de Carbayedo. "Let's buy one of those fine animals out there and get ourselves back to Las Cepas. We have a bit of celebrating to do!"

Despite Mercedes' renewed protests, Antonio could not help himself. He found the old man in the boina and bought the strong willed calf. It was a long walk back to the farm.

* * *

Long before the Romans came, Celts settled in Asturias. Celtic artistic and cultural traditions remain a fundamental part of Asturian culture, and like other Celtic places, bagpipes are deeply rooted in Asturian life. Many towns even maintain municipal bagpipe corps to this day. Their high pitched tunes—the Asturian instrument has only two pipes, so its sound is less robust than the better-known Scottish bagpipes—accompany nearly every public event of any significance. Weddings are no exception. The gaiteros, as they are called, greet the bride and groom as they arrive at the church, and then pipe them off to the marriage feast after the mass.

* * *

Naveces, Asturias
August 1914

María made a final adjustment to the simple white dress. It was her own creation. "You look beautiful," she said to Mercedes. "Absolutely beautiful. Radiant. It is such a pity that Antonio cannot be here to see you."

"Well, I can't have everything, I suppose," Mercedes said. "I know he's here in spirit, and that's what matters most."

There was a knock at the bedroom door. "I know I am supposed to wait downstairs," Antonio González Conde shouted through the closed door from out in the hallway. "But I have never been skilled at waiting."

"You may enter," María told her husband. "The bride is ready for viewing."

"Glorious!" he bellowed. "I have not seen such a vision of beauty since María on our wedding day."

"Thank you," Mercedes said. "It still doesn't seem real that I'll marry Antonio today." As the two months had passed, and the anticipation of this day grew more intense, Mercedes' apprehension and sadness about leaving diminished bit by bit, and a glowing optimism rose in their place. She still could not imagine living so far away from her family, but the fact that she would soon be making a family of her own eased the pain of contemplating her separation from them and from Asturias. And she clung tightly to the hope that she, Antonio Ribas and their children would return to Spain one day.

"Well, we must move along," María said, making two more minor adjustments to Mercedes' dress, "or you will be late for your own wedding!"

They rounded up the children and hurriedly walked the three-quarters of a mile to Naveces. As they appeared around the corner of the medieval rectory across the lane from San Román Church, the five bagpipers—dressed in black knee pants, white shirts and bright-green vests, with wide, gold sashes tied around their waists—began to play.

The rotund parish priest, Father José Lama, was waiting for them just inside the door of the church. The two witnesses, both neighbors and old friends of Antonio González Conde, also stood there, as did the Castrillón district court secretary, Don Justo Álvarez y Álvarez, sent by the judge at the municipal hall in Piedras Blancas to record the details of the proceedings for the civil record.

María and the children took a seat in the front pew. They exchanged quiet greetings with Bernardo's sister Carmen and her husband Manuel, who were among the handful of guests. "What a beautiful day," Carmen said, "and what a blessing that the path which began here with such sadness and pain returns to this place with such jubilation."

"Yes," María said, "at last, I believe Mercedes is able to put that dreadful chapter of her life behind her."

At the rear of the church, Father José welcomed Mercedes as he sorted through the paperwork with the lithe, black-suited Álvarez y Álvarez. "This is a blissful afternoon, Miss González. And given the important role he his has played in your life, it is appropriate and fortuitous that your brother can stand in for your fiancé today."

Antonio Ribas was 4,500 miles away, working at the zinc smelter in West Virginia. Antonio González Conde had insisted, on the day he and Mercedes bought the calf, that they stop at the telegraph office in Avilés so she could wire her acceptance of Antonio Ribas' marriage proposal. Antonio Segundo had gone to a notary public in Clarksburg the next day to have proxy documents drafted for Antonio Primero to represent him at the ceremony.

"Yes," Mercedes told Father José, "I'm very lucky that God has given me these two Antonios." All morning, as she prepared for the wedding, her mind reeled through images of the many days she had spent with Antonio Ribas, and the many without him, good and bad. But now she stood in this church where nearly every person she knew had been baptized and nearly every couple she knew had married, and her mind was filled only with this moment and her heart with joy.

After Álvarez y Álvarez read through the proxy document and gave his assent, he and the witnesses took their seats, and the ceremony began. Mercedes processed up the aisle behind Don José and the altar boys. Despite the groom's absence, the priest celebrated the full marriage mass before the Baroque altar, under the silent gaze of the solemn saints and the corpulent putti.

As Mercedes and the guests emerged from the church after the mass, the bagpipers broke into "Asturias, Patria Querida," the hymn of the principality. Every person stood tall and sang with pride:

Asturias, my beloved fatherland,
My loved one Asturias,
Ah, lucky he who could be in Asturias
For all times ...

The sun shone, and swallows fluttered from the massive old oak tree whose branches spread over the forecourt. Mercedes felt born anew.

Chapter 11

Asturias

October 1914

Mercedes and ten-year-old Pilar shared a love of chestnuts. In the autumn, the spiny pods covered the Asturian hillsides. Their favourite spot was about a thirty-minute walk from Las Cepas, where the chestnuts piled a foot deep under the boughs of two grand old trees. Two weeks before she departed for the U.S., Mercedes took Pilar on one last expedition.

"So, you're really leaving us, Aunt Mercedes?" Pilar asked as they carefully pried open the pods and added another handful of the mahogany coloured chestnuts to their bulging bag. The girl had been quiet and withdrawn all day.

"You shouldn't think of it that way, Pilar," Mercedes replied. She had wondered whether her niece would open up about how she felt. She did not want to force it from her like a chestnut from its thorny husk. Pilar had not said a word about Mercedes leaving since she sat the children down in the kitchen and told them, as if not verbalizing it would make it go away.

"How else can I think of it?" Pilar said without looking up from her pile of pods. "You're going to America, and we'll be here."

"That's true. But when you say I'm 'leaving' you, that makes it sound like it's against you, and it's not."

Pilar plunked another chestnut into the sack.

"I've married Antonio," Mercedes said, "as your mother married your father. But his work is in America, so I have to go there to be with him. I wish so much that I could stay here, but I can't right now."

Pilar shrugged her shoulders and shucked another chestnut. "Do you love Antonio more than you do us?" she asked eventually.

"Oh, of course, not, Pilar." Mercedes put her hand on the girl's back and nudged her around to face her. "I love you and your brothers and your parents more than any other people on this Earth. You especially. If I have a daughter, I want her to be just like you."

Mercedes was not exaggerating or saying this only to comfort her niece. She loved Antonio Ribas, but it was different. Their relationship contained an element of necessity. They were like two castaways washed up on a beach who had only each other for building a new life. With her brother and his family, Mercedes felt only unconditional, abiding love and acceptance. It was not possible, she imagined, that she could love and care about her own daughter any more deeply than she did Pilar.

"But you have me!" Pilar said. She threw the chestnut burr in her hand to the ground. "We have each other. Why do you have to leave and go have a daughter and live on the other side of the ocean?" Tears filling her eyes, Pilar cried: "I'll never see you again!" She jumped up and started running into the woods.

"Pilar! Pilar!" Mercedes shouted, leaping to her feet and taking after her. She quickly overtook her niece. "Pilar, stop!" she said, more sharply than she intended, when the girl kept flailing and trying to escape Mercedes' grasp.

Pilar was not listening. The suffocating panic had seized her. The repressed frustration and fear, now uncoiled, overwhelmed her consciousness. The more Mercedes tried to restrain her, the harder she struggled and the louder she squealed. It was like trying to subdue a terrified deer.

Mercedes finally took Pilar by the shoulders, pushed her to the ground and lay on top of her. Pilar kicked and beat the ground and her aunt with her fists. But Mercedes pressed herself more firmly on

Pilar's slender body, limiting as much of her movement as possible. She said softly, over and over: "Come back, my sweet girl. Come back, my sweet girl. Come back, my sweet girl."

Slowly, Pilar began to relax. The crazed look faded from her eyes. She lay still with Mercedes in the dry leaves on the forest floor, breathing deeply.

"There, there, my sweet girl," Mercedes said. She released Pilar's shoulders and stroked her hair. "It's okay. You're safe."

Pilar had been tumbling into these fits with greater frequency and severity over the past two years. Mercedes was the only person who could calm her and bring her back. As they lay quietly on the ground, Mercedes wondered what would happen when the storm came over Pilar, and she was no longer here.

María knew her only daughter was troubled, but she was so swamped by her work on the farm and tending to the other children— a fourth had come the year before—that she did not have the time or patience Pilar needed. And empathy for what he saw as a weakness of character was not among Antonio González Conde's many admirable qualities. He possessed a surfeit of compassion for his sister because she had been treated so poorly. But he could not comprehend why his daughter was so often glum and difficult, when all she had known was affection.

That left Mercedes as Pilar's only anchor. It had loomed over her decision about whether to marry Antonio Ribas and go to the United States. She believed that the move would not be permanent, that they would return one day to Spain. But when? For how many years would she stay over there? And how could fragile Pilar manage alone? In the end, Mercedes' need for a family of her own trumped the responsibility she felt for her niece, but just barely.

Once, during one of their long walks along the coastal bluffs, Antonio Ribas had led Mercedes down a steep trail, through thick tufts of straw-coloured grass and thorn bushes, to a little cove. There were hundreds of similar spots along the ragged Asturian coast, but this one had seemed to call out to him the first time he saw it from high up on the trail.

Antonio told Mercedes it was one of his favourite places to sit and think, surrounded on three sides by the towering crags and with the ceaseless churning of the surf at his feet. As each wave receded, the tumbling beach stones rattled like marbles being rolled down a hill in a tin.

Antonio had gone down to the water's edge and examined the stones. He dug around, picked one up, looked at it, discarded it, picked up another. Over and over. After several minutes, he returned to where Mercedes was sitting. He handed her a smooth, thin oblong stone about three-quarters of an inch long. It was black with a narrow vein of white running around its center from side to side. She had never been without it since. Every time she squeezed it tightly in her hand, she immediately felt a sense of calm and peace fill her chest, as if some vast, universal spirit was flowing into her from the stone.

Mercedes sat up beside Pilar and reached into the pocket of her dress. She withdrew the pebble and gave it to the girl. "This stone has great power, Pilar. Whenever I think that I can't go on, I hold it, and it gives me strength. You keep it." It pained Mercedes to give it away, but she believed her niece would need the talisman more than she. "Keep it with you all the time. When you feel yourself sliding into that terrible place, or feel the dark fog coming over you, take it out and squeeze it tight in your hand, and think of me and how much I love you."

Pilar took the black stone and looked at it closely. "Where does it come from?" she asked.

"From the sea. Many centuries of being tumbled by the waves wore it smooth and round. And just like you, there's no other in the world exactly like it."

Pilar clasped the stone in her fist as she threw her arms around Mercedes' neck and hugged her tightly. "Thank you, Aunt Mercedes. Thank you. I'll always carry it with me, and I'll give it back to you when you come home."

"Yes," Mercedes said. "You do that. You keep it safe for me, and one day, I promise, I'll come and get it from you."

Mercedes stood and pulled Pilar up from the ground. She whirled her around by the wrists until the girl was laughing uncontrollably. Setting Pilar on her feet, Mercedes said: "Now, we still have room in that bag for at least another half-kilo of chestnuts!"

"Chestnuts!" Pilar howled as they ran, hand in hand, back down the hill to the pile of prickly pods.

* * *

Mercedes had no money to pay her passage to the United States. Her husband Antonio could almost cover it if he sent her all his savings and borrowed the remainder from his friend. But she did not want to begin their life together that way. The only meagre asset she owned was her quarter interest in the farm.

Mercedes asked her brother Antonio if he would buy her out. He agreed, reluctantly. He was uncomfortable with the idea of his sister selling her patrimony, even if it was to him. After they had signed the documents, and he gave her the cash, Antonio said: "You should consider this an interest-free loan, with your land as collateral. When you come back, if you wish to return here and make your home with Antonio on Las Cepas, I will sell it back to you for exactly this amount."

With all her belongings packed in a leather suitcase her brother bought her for a wedding gift, Mercedes began her journey to her new life across the Atlantic: a rickety train along the coast to A Coruña; an old side-wheel steamer from A Coruña to Liverpool; Liverpool to Ellis Island aboard the White Star liner *Adriatic*. She arrived in New York Harbor on November 14, 1914. Mercedes had never been so happy, and so sad, in her life.

* * *

Clarksburg
24 December 1914

My dear brother and sister-in-law,

I have arrived safe and sound and am happier than I can say to be spending this first Christmas with Antonio. Still, as I sit here in our little apartment waiting for him to return from work, my head is full of images from my thirteen Christmases with you at Las Cepas. I miss you and the children fiercely.

I am not certain how I can balance these competing feelings of elation and loss. They sweep over me in succession. One hour I feel that I can sprout wings and soar. The next, I feel as if I am lying under a slab of stone and cannot lift an arm without great effort. Somehow I will manage it, and I am sure it will improve after I have been here for a while.

What a journey! After banging along in the train for two days to A Coruña, it was a relief to be rocking gently on the sea as I sailed up to England. The weather was perfect, and I was even able to go out on the deck to sit in the sun and gaze at the endless expanse of blue water. I was not as afraid as I expected to be, because it was just so intoxicatingly beautiful.

The Atlantic crossing was not as nice, and I was thankful that my first experience at sea had been so pleasant. We were packed in like livestock on a busy day at Carbayedo, down in the bowels of the ship, and on two of the days and nights the ship was heaved and tossed by awful storms. I spent a lot of time on my knees with my rosary, wondering if I would set foot on land again. It reminded me of the stories you often told us, Antonio, about your passages to Cuba. I pray that when we come back, we will have clear skies the whole way.

It took a full day for me to get processed through Ellis Island. The crowds for Semana Santa in Avilés are nothing compared to the throngs of people disgorging from the ships and filling the yards and quays and the cavernous hall where we were questioned by the immigration agents. I had never felt so small and insignificant or as far away from everything I knew and loved.

And then, New York. It still does not seem real. I do not know how people live there, like ants in a hill or bees in a hive. But it also vibrates with strength and vitality, a giant engine driving an immensely powerful land. I am glad I could see it, but more glad I could leave. Clarksburg is bigger than Avilés, but it feels like a four-house village after New York. Much more to my liking.

Antonio took me down to Graselli last week to see the house he is buying for us. It is only about 20 minutes away on the streetcar. I am happy we will have our own home, and it is a nice, new little house. The town is smoky like Arnao, with the smelter at its center, but it is full of Asturians and Gallegos. That makes me both less homesick and more so. An Avilesino named Daniel—he says he knows you, Antonio—has even opened a place called Belmonte's Café modeled on Café Colon in Avilés, right down to the big iron frog out front for the ring-toss game.

I will close for now. I did not expect to write so much when I sat down here, and I have to get back to preparing our Christmas dinner! Kisses and hugs to you both and the children, dear Pilar especially. I will eagerly await a letter from you about all that is happening there.

Mercedes González Conde

Chapter 12

There were no eucalyptus trees in the woods around Anmoore—as the town of Grasselli had recently been re-named—nor any twelfth-century churches in the town with clanging ancient bells and costumed penitents. It was all clapboard houses and shops, none more than 30 years old, nor any apparently constructed to last for longer than a single lifetime. The acrid smoke of the zinc furnaces hung constantly in the air. None of that mattered to Mercedes.

"Okay, ma'am, a half-step closer to your husband, and chin up," the photographer instructed Mercedes. He had grown up in Gijón, the big port city fifteen miles to the east of Avilés. With the steady influx of immigrants, his photography studio in Clarksburg was thriving more than he had dreamt possible. The photographer came around from behind the camera, pulled Antonio's hands from his trouser pockets and squared Antonio's shoulders. "There, sir, hold that pose, please." Antonio and Mercedes stood perfectly still as the photographer crossed back to the camera perched atop its heavy tripod, and his ever-smiling face disappeared behind the large wooden box. "Ahhh, perfect," he cooed. "You look like their majesties."

Click. The aperture in the large lens on the front of the camera snapped open, paused for a long second, and then slammed shut.

"Please hold your poses," the photographer ordered as he carefully withdrew the photo plate and inserted a fresh one. "Photograph once for disaster, twice for perfection my dear father, God bless his soul, always told me," he said with a hearty chuckle.

Click. The photographer reappeared, still smiling, from beneath the black cloth which covered the back of the camera. He smoothed his silvery shock of hair. "Okay, okay, very good, I believe you will have a lovely portrait. Just lovely."

Mercedes and Antonio continued to stand as stiff as sentinels on the intricately patterned Arabian carpet in the cramped studio. It was the first photo either had taken in their lives. "You can move!" the photographer exclaimed.

Antonio tugged at his shirt collar and then shoved his hands back in his pockets. Mercedes smiled giddily, released from the forced seriousness of a proper studio portrait. "You think it will be nice?" she asked the photographer.

He gently pressed her on the back, urging her toward the door—he had four other couples waiting outside—and said: "Absolutely perfect, I assure you. You'll be delighted you chose to memorialize this moment with me."

They paused on the sidewalk outside the studio in the unusually warm and sunny February afternoon, and Antonio grumbled to Mercedes as he rolled a cigarette, "For what he's charging, that picture should sing and dance on command."

"Oh, Antonio, don't be so Gallego for once," she said, giggling. "We didn't have a real wedding, so we should indulge ourselves a little for our portrait."

"Hmph," Antonio grunted, though the truth was that he always did whatever necessary to give Mercedes anything she wanted. He had worked overtime for a month to afford this trip to the photographer.

"Oh, I can't wait 'til it's ready!" she said. "I know exactly where I will hang it in the parlour. In our parlour!" Mercedes luxuriated in hearing herself say it. "Our parlour," she repeated, squeezing his arm which was interlocked with hers as they strolled toward the streetcar stop. "I still can't believe we have our own parlour."

Antonio half grinned. "And kitchen, two bedrooms and bath-room," he added.

"Yes!" Mercedes said so loudly and enthusiastically that a grey-bearded man in a top hat and expensive suit passing them from the opposite direction jerked up his walking stick reflexively and whipped his head to look at them, as if Mercedes had reached out and smacked him on the shoulder.

She composed herself and said as casually as possible: "And it's good you bought the two-bedroom house instead of the smaller one, because we'll be needing that other room soon."

"Is somebody already coming to visit?" Antonio asked.

"Well, you could put it that way. But it will be a long visit," she said.

Antonio stopped in the middle of the sidewalk, cocked his head and looked Mercedes in the face. "What exactly are you talking about? Who's coming?"

Mercedes smiled radiantly. "Our baby, Antonio. Our baby!"

Antonio remained dumbstruck for the entire streetcar ride back to Anmoore. Mercedes sat, beaming. He stood above her, his knees pressed against hers in the crowded car. He stared out the big window as Clarksburg slipped by. First the storefronts with their plate glass windows and striped awnings, then the joyless brick tenements, then the small clapboard houses like theirs, then the soot covered steel mills and glass factories, then a bit of green countryside, and then their hamlet of Anmoore.

Antonio's reaction to Mercedes' announcement surprised him. No distress. No tightness in his stomach. No slithering coldness in his veins. He had proposed to Mercedes not because he felt any less angst about children, despite his improved financial condition, but because he missed her so much that he could not stand being separated from her any longer. All through those months since she had arrived, he always felt a deep ambivalence about their marriage and the children who would inevitably come: they desired each other physically, and acted on it with a frequency that would be expected by two people who have discovered sex for the first time in their thirties.

Antonio was not rapturously happy about the revelation, but he was okay. That alone felt like a miracle to him. "Oh, Mercedes," he said as they stepped to the pavement from the streetcar, "what wonderful news."

Mercedes had been terrified to tell him, and his reaction so far had not been particularly reassuring, but she was so ecstatic about it—especially after she had said it aloud to Antonio—that she felt only a tinge of the old darkness. "You know, you can't be that surprised about it." She blushed.

Antonio laughed heartily, a rare occurrence, and took her hand in his. "Yes, well, I suppose you're right about that."

* * *

Their little house was furnished mostly with hand-me-downs from Antonio's coworkers who had been friends of Antonio González Conde. They never seemed to sit on the tufted settee. Mercedes preferred the richly carved, high backed Castilian-style chair with the burgundy velvet cushions. Antonio always plopped down in the well used overstuffed armchair.

After dinner in the kitchen, at the wooden table and chairs Antonio was proud to have purchased himself, they had taken their usual spots and listened to the evening Spanish-language news broadcast on the radio.

"Primero must feel like a prophet," Antonio said as he reached over and turned off the radio. The war was flaming higher and wider every week. Today, the German government had announced it would begin a naval blockade of Great Britain. "Even I can see where that can lead," Antonio said.

"At least the King has had the good sense to keep Spain out of it," Mercedes said.

"A little evidence that he's not a complete idiot, anyway," Antonio added. "But enough of that ridiculousness. What should we call the baby?"

Mercedes was delighted by how much interest Antonio had taken in the baby over the days since her announcement. "If it's a girl, I'd like to call her Julia."

"Julia," Antonio said noncommittally.

"Yes. One of the books my brother used to teach me to read was *The Lives of the Saints*—"

"Of course," Antonio interjected.

"Don't be mean," Mercedes said.

"I'm not being mean," Antonio said, laughing, "just making a logical observation. Primero would approve."

"Anyway," Mercedes said. "I read about St. Julia of Corsica in the book, and I've always felt close to her because she was a slave girl, and I know how that feels."

"Julia it should be, then," Antonio said.

"And you, if it's a boy?" Mercedes asked.

"I'd like to call him Luís, after my uncle," he said after a minute. "He treated me better than anybody I knew after my mother died. And whenever my father was drunk and looking for somebody to beat, I always could slip out the window and run down to his farm, and he would feed me and let me sleep there for the night. He was a good man."

"As you are, Antonio," Mercedes said. "I honestly don't know how you managed to be, after all you went through."

He shrugged his shoulders. "Gallegos are as tough as the bark of an old tree. That can cut either way, I suppose. I was lucky I had my mother around until I was five." Antonio fell silent, a distant look in his eyes. "I wish you could have known her, and she could've known you," he added after a bit.

"I wish that too, Antonio."

Chapter 13

Although the United States is "a nation of immigrants"—as every elementary school pupil learns—new arrivals have always suffered a degree of hostility from those who migrated earlier. Even Thomas Jefferson expressed concern about the Germans coming to the new generally-Anglo country because they hailed from places which did not inculcate democratic mores.

The Asturian Indianos were an exception—with their desire to make their fortunes in the New World and return to their homeland—but generally, the tens of millions of people who crossed the Atlantic in the nineteenth and early-twentieth centuries came to stay and build new lives. The discrimination they faced affected where and how they lived and the nature of their integration into American society.

The Irish and Italians, for example, came in enormous numbers: 3.6 million Irish between 1840 and 1900, 4 million Italians between 1880 and 1924. Often they settled in nearly homogeneous neighborhoods and towns, as the "Little Italys" in major eastern US cities still attest. As they slowly integrated, many also maintained their hyphenated identities, and for Irish-Americans such as former Vice President Joe Biden, it remains an important cultural dichotomy to this day.

However, many later immigrants such as Antonio and Mercedes found themselves living in different circumstances. Shunted inland from the great coastal cities to new industrial towns, they still experienced discrimination and lived in municipalities whose residents were primarily immigrants—or the decendants of former slaves—but they were not exclusively of one national origin. Anmoore had a large population of

Asturians, but also many Italians, Poles and African-Americans. This mixing—as well as the tectonic cultural effects of the Great Depression, New Deal, and Second World War—more rapidly diminished the emotional connection to their nations of origin and hastened their adoption of American identity.

* * *

Anmoore, West Virginia
April 1927

Thirteen years. As many as Mercedes had lived with her brother and his family at Las Cepas. Thirteen years since she had arrived in America. Months vanished barely without notice. The seasons came and went. Years melted away. She still missed Asturias. But her love for Antonio had ripened, and she was grateful for their home, even if it was just this little wooden house across the street from the smelter.

Luis was born in September 1915, and Julia came along in January 1918. She was followed two Januaries later by another son, Manuel, and by Antonio Jr. in the spring of 1922. Though the midwife trade was brisk among the immigrant families, Mercedes sometimes felt during those years that she was having as many babies as she was delivering.

The demands of their expanding family made her often wish that she had a Mercedes of her own to lend an extra hand. She thought several times about bringing Pilar over, but her brother Antonio was always cool—or non-responsive—to the idea when Mercedes mentioned it in her letters.

She wrote often to her brother. It made her feel as if her life in the US was not so far removed from theirs at Las Cepas. Antonio González Conde's responses were voluminous and filled with detail, but his commentary about her niece generally went no further than some version of "that girl is a mystery to me." In truth, Pilar was increasingly unwell. The panic attacks worsened the older she got, as did the duration and depth of her depression. But she still clutched Mercedes' stone every day and waited hopefully for her aunt's return.

Antonio Ribas, on the other hand, was doing very well with the Grasselli Chemical Company. The conditions and labor troubles of the American zinc industry were not significantly better than in Asturias. Only the pay was, and then, only for the workers willing to endure their neighbors' ire and break the frequent strikes.

Without a family to feed, Antonio would have felt no more solidarity than he did with the strikers in Arnao. With a wife and children to support, he had even less of an inclination to respect the picket lines. He never was absent from his post at the retorts. "A scab's always a scab," another of the Asturians who remembered him from Arnao once sneered as they passed in the street, loudly enough for Antonio to hear. Antonio merely nodded and sauntered on.

The Ribases had become the picture of a prosperous immigrant family, and Antonio was putting every spare dollar into the booming stock market. He still could neither read nor write, but Luis and Julia had taught him to sign his name. That was enough for him to join the national frenzy of stock buying. He understood absolutely nothing about it, other than the fact it was making him wealthier than he ever dreamed he would become. At least once a month, Mercedes would tell her brother in a letter that she hoped their swelling account with the stockbroker would hasten their return to Spain. When she broached the topic with her husband, he would shrug his Gallego shrug and roll a cigarette.

On this morning, Mercedes was wrangling the children and getting them dressed in their best clothes to sit for the family's third studio photograph. Twelve-year-old Luis, complaining, had donned his charcoal grey confirmation suit. Nine-year-old Julia—protesting only slightly less than Luis—was in her new cream coloured linen dress with lace around the neck and hem.

"And put on that necklace your father gave you for Christmas," Mercedes shouted into the bedroom. Julia did like the gold necklace, with its little filigreed locket, very much. It was worth the aggravation of wearing the dress and the uncomfortable patent leather shoes for the chance to put the glittering chain around her neck. She was allowed to wear it only on special occasions.

As Mercedes buttoned the black suede ankle boots on her squirming youngest child, three year-old Pilar, she heard a crash from the dining room. Manuel and Antonio Jr. were wrestling on the floor, in their matching white sailor suits with navy blue piping.

"Don't make me come in there!" Mercedes yelled at them. "Stop that right now!"

Her husband came strolling out of their bedroom, struggling to fasten the button of his high collar. "Is this really necessary?" he said to Mercedes. "It feels like we're at the photographer's every other month."

"We haven't been in five years," Mercedes scoffed, "and we don't have a portrait that includes little Pilar here. Don't you want one with her?"

Antonio grunted and continued to fumble with the collar button. "You know how much I dislike putting on this stuff."

"Oh, Antonio," she said, setting the successfully shoed Pilar on the living room carpet. "You look dashing in your suit. I don't know why you complain about it so much."

"I look like an undertaker. And I never can get this fastened around my neck. What's the sense of these impractical clothes? Only the lazy upper class could create such a thing."

"Yes, yes," Mercedes said. She fastened his collar button for him and then tied his necktie. "There. If we were in Avilés, people in the street would confuse you for the Marquis of Ferrera."

"If we were in Avilés," he retorted, "I wouldn't have two pennies to rub together, let alone this suit."

"You are living proof that some things never change," Mercedes said with a smile and went off to gather the children to catch the streetcar for their appointment with the photographer in Clarksburg.

* * *

"It'll be okay," Antonio assured Mercedes, though he did not sound so convinced himself. "I can sell some of the stocks, and we can live off that until I find another job."

Five months after they sat for the photograph—which was framed in mahogany and hanging prominently in the parlour alongside their wedding portrait and their first family picture—the Grasselli Chemical Company closed its smelter in Anmoore. Some of the workers were moved to the nearby Grasselli smelter in the town of Spelter, but Antonio was let go. He had worked through every strike, but the reticent Gallego never became close to any of the furnace bosses, who recommended their friends and relatives for the few positions in the other smelter.

"Factories are booming all over the place here," Antonio said. He slurped his café con leche and rolled a cigarette at the kitchen table he had purchased when they moved into the house. "I'm only forty-eight, and I have a good reputation with the company, even if they didn't take me on at Spelter. I'll get something before too long."

"But what if you don't?" Mercedes asked. Desperation sucked at her like a strong undertow trying to pull her out to sea. "We have five children to feed."

"Don't you think I know that?" Antonio snapped. He never snapped at anybody. "I'm sorry, Mercedes. I'm sorry," he added quickly. He took her hand. "I promise, it'll be okay. I've always taken care of you and the children, haven't I?"

"Yes, you have, Antonio." Mercedes forced a thin smile despite her agonizing apprehension. "I know you'll find something." They sat in silence and finished their coffees. Antonio could not believe he was facing yawning uncertainty again, after all these years of stability.

As usual, Mercedes broke the silence. "Why don't we sell all the stock, and the house, and go back to Asturias? Or to Galicia?"

Antonio sighed. "First, who would buy the house now, with the smelter closing? And, second, what would I do for work in Spain? It's not as if we can move in with your brother on the farm."

"Why can't we?" Mercedes asked, exasperation seeping into her voice. "Why can't we go back to Las Cepas? We have enough money to buy back my share of the farm, purchase some additional land and build a house there."

"That's really no solution. We can't live off what we could grow on the farm, and I won't have a job there."

"You don't have a job here anymore, Antonio! And you don't know that you can't find one there. It's not 1912 anymore. Even Asturias has changed. And, besides, we could live off what we could raise on the land we could afford to buy."

Antonio's face was a frozen mask.

"It's just your damned Gallego pig-headedness that keeps us from going." She was on her feet, slamming coffee cups and saucers into the sink. "You haven't changed a single bit in all these years. You make me crazy, Antonio! Why must you always be like this? How is it better to be here struggling to find some other stupid factory job than to go home?"

"This is home," Antonio said without emotion.

"This is home? This is home?" Mercedes was fuming. "No, Antonio, this is an American company town where they don't care if you live or die. Why can't you see that? Home is in Spain, with our families, where people care about us."

"I don't have any family there, Mercedes."

"And enough of that orphan garbage, Antonio!" She returned to where he was sitting at the table and towered over him. "You have family there, but you choose not to recognize it. And my family—Antonio and María especially—love you as if you were our own flesh and blood! They'd be overjoyed if we returned. My brother still wants nothing more than to build up the farm with you and the boys."

"That's your dream," Antonio shouted, rising to his feet. "Yours, Mercedes, and Primero's. It's not mine, and it certainly isn't our boys'. For God's sake, Mercedes, they're Americans, not Asturian villagers! They speak English, and they've lived their whole lives here. How can we drag them off to some country they don't know and drop them into farm life?"

"They speak Spanish, too, Antonio," Mercedes shouted. She was shocked by his outburst—Antonio never raised his voice—but his anger also fed her own. "You know I only allow them to speak English at school and in the street."

"That's because you just don't want them saying things you don't understand," Antonio said, forcing himself back down to a less confrontational volume. He had learned passable English at the smelter, but Mercedes had defiantly refused to learn a word of it. It was bad enough that she had to go by "Martha" all these years with their Anglo neighbors because they could not understand the pronunciation of Mercedes, with its Castilian "c" said like "th".

"Damn you, Antonio Ribas!" His moderated tone did not lessen the sting of his comment. "That's completely unfair. You know I never bothered with English because I always believed we'd go home."

"America is home now, Mercedes," Antonio said slowly and firmly. "You must accept that. We are not going back. Ever."

Mercedes sank into the hard kitchen chair, put her face into her hands, and wept. When Antonio came over to her and put his hand on her shoulder, she threw it off. "I never wanted this, Antonio," she said in a fierce, rasping whisper. "I came here because I loved you, and because I wanted to make a family with you. But I never wanted to live here. I never wanted to stay here. I keep it to myself, but I still miss Asturias every day. I miss my family every day. I want to go home every day. This place may be home to you, but it never will be for me."

"I'm sorry, Mercedes," Antonio said. It was all the comfort he could give.

* * *

Mercedes wrote to Antonio and María a month after that soul crushing conversation with her husband. She could not bring herself to write earlier. It was a struggle even now.

Anmoore
November 1927

My dear brother and sister-in-law,

I hope you and the children are healthy and happy, and that your sales at the market have continued to be good. I miss working the market with you and our afternoons in Avilés.

Unfortunately, I write with bad news. The smelter here in Anmoore has closed, and Antonio lost his job. Do not worry. We are fine, because he has sold some of the stocks, but I hope we will not be forced to deplete all our savings before he finds a new position. But it is not easy with so many of the other workers also searching.

I told Antonio we should sell all the stocks and return to Las Cepas, but he will not hear of it. He will not leave America. He says that it would be too hard on the children. I understand his concern. It would be a hard adjustment for them, because they are so American. However, I believe Antonio uses it mostly as an excuse. He simply does not want to leave. He says this is home now, but it never will feel that way for me. Home will always be there in Asturias with you. I do not know how I will live the remainder of my life here. But it appears that may well be the case now.

All is not doom and gloom. The children are well. School started this week, and most of them are happy about it. It is so good to see them growing big and strong and smart and being happy with their lives. Julia is difficult about school, as she is with everything else. Sometimes, she is like having a wild animal loose in the house. I do not know what to do with her. Antonio says she will grow out of it, but I am not so confident. Still, she has a good heart and is very loving—when she is not a complete terror—and I hope that part of her will come to rule the other.

I am sorry to trouble you with my burdens. Perhaps I will be able to write with better news soon. If Antonio gets desperate enough, maybe he will reconsider and agree to come home. I doubt it, but I still cling to the chance. Please give my love to the children, dear Pilar especially.

Mercedes González Conde.

* * *

Las Cepas, Asturias
June 1928

María realized, as the sun dropped behind the hill across the valley, that she had not seen Pilar since before noon. Antonio and the boys were at a neighboring farm to help renovate a granary, and she was certain their daughter had not gone with them. Pilar often took long walks in the woods alone—even more frequently over the months since they had received Mercedes' letter—but she always told María before going out. María checked every room in the house. Perhaps Pilar was sitting somewhere in the twilight. She had also been doing that more than usual.

There was no sign of Pilar inside, so María went out into the courtyard and called to her. Nothing. She checked in the granary and in the cellar. Nothing. She crossed the lane to the field and walked down to the barn. She could not imagine that Pilar had gone there, but she was running out of places to look.

María unlatched the door, pushed it open and called into the near darkness, "Pilar? Pilar, dear, are you in there?" Nothing. She was getting frustrated. "Pilar, if you are in there, you need to come out this minute. I don't like this hiding." Nothing.

Dusk was deepening by the minute, and María had not thought to bring a lantern. She opened both barn doors wide, went inside, and opened the shutters of the two, small, west-facing windows. When she turned, María jumped and a chill raced down her back and arms. For an instant, she thought she saw a ghost in the back of the barn. Then she realized it was some kind of light-coloured fabric catching the faint light. *It must be a feed sack hanging back there*, she thought. María chuckled that it had given her such a fright.

"Pilar? Are you in here somewhere dear?" she asked again. María looked in the livestock stalls and behind the hay bales as she made her way toward the back of the barn. She stood only a few feet away from the dangling fabric when she finally recognized what it was, but it took a moment for the horror to hit her. It was not possible that what she saw was real. It could not be Pilar hanging there, the perfectly knotted noose tied to a rafter.

Returning from the neighbor's, Antonio and the boys dropped their tools in the lane and ran as hard as they could across the dark field when they heard the long, terrible screams coming from the barn.

* * *

As the months became a year, Antonio did not find another job. He also did not change his mind about returning to Spain. When the stock market crashed in November 1929, leaving them with nothing but the unsellable house in Anmoore, that door was closed forever.

Mercedes had slogged around in a grim fog every day since the news came of Pilar's suicide. She blamed herself. She blamed Antonio. She managed to function only for the sake of their children. They had become the only source of satisfaction in her life. Her body had gone from lean to gaunt. Mercedes was forty-nine. She looked twenty years older.

She sat down at the kitchen table and took out a sheet of thin, faintly lined writing paper.

Anmoore
21 December

My dear sister-in-law and brother,

I have just received your letter in which I read that you are all well, which makes me very happy. That we all have work is everything, otherwise our lives will be as hard as the people who are suffering without relief from this endless Depression. It is as you used to say, Antonio. If I want to eat, I have to work, and God provides plenty where the people are not afraid of labor.

María, when your neighbor Tomás comes to Anmoore, please have him bring me the Asturian cabbage seeds and the jeans buttons you bought. Thank you very much for always sending me the things I need. These have been lean years.

Give my regards to all those who have asked about me, especially to Aunt Carmen and her family at La Siega. I send a tight hug to you and my nephews, and when you write to Ramón, tell him his aunt is thinking of him.

No more for today.

She stopped before signing the letter and added:

And the same wishes from your brother-in-law.

Mercedes González Conde

She called her husband into the kitchen from the living room. "I've just written to Antonio and Maria, and I included your regards. Do you want to sign it?"

Antonio clenched the pen awkwardly in his thick hand and wrote below her signature, slowly and with great concentration:

A Ribas

Chapter 14

"No, Julia. For the last time, you can't go. I won't permit it," Mercedes said. She was angry but too weary to raise her voice.

"I'd like to see you try to stop me!" her daughter shouted. She started down the steps in front of the house. "I'm eighteen, and I can do what I want, and go where I want, when I want!"

"Antonio, please," Mercedes pleaded, "say something about this."

Antonio was sitting in a porch chair, with a café con leche and a cigarette, staring across the road at the shuttered smelter. He passed many afternoons that way. He and the boys did a little odd job here and there, which brought in some occasional money, but the family mostly survived on the produce from the garden in their back yard for food and barter.

"Antonio!" Mercedes snapped. "I'm talking to you."

He slowly turned his head to look in her direction. Julia stood defiantly on the gravel walk leading out to the street. One hand clutched the pillowcase into which she had stuffed some clothes and tied closed with garden twine. The other hand was planted firmly on her hip. An unemployed son of one of the unemployed smelter workers sat on an old motorcycle at the curb.

"There's no reason to fight with her, Mercedes," Antonio said, sighing. "She's right. She's old enough to do as she pleases, and there's really not a thing we can do about it."

"As long as she lives in our house, and eats our food—" Mercedes started, but Antonio cut her off.

"Oh, Mercedes, it's not like she and Luis and Manuel are children, living here because they want to. They live with us because there's not a job in the whole damned country. Where are they supposed to go?"

"But I—" Mercedes started again.

"But nothing," Antonio interjected, quickly growing irritated. He wanted to be left alone. "Why shouldn't she get out and see some of the country? And what good does it do any of us to have her sitting around here sulking?" He looked out to Julia. "Go on, girl. Go. Don't just stand there."

Mercedes stormed back into the house. The screen door smacked shut behind her. Julia laughed and ran out to the young man on the motorcycle. He crammed her pillowcase luggage into a saddlebag and mounted the bike. Julia climbed on behind him, wrapped her arms tightly around his waist, and pressed her pelvis hard against his lower back. Antonio looked blankly at the smelter as she waved a quick goodbye and they sped off down the street.

Mercedes slowly lowered her bony frame into the kitchen chair. She opened her letterbox and filled her forty-year-old fountain pen. Her brother Antonio had sent her the bottle of black ink so she could keep writing to him. She muttered under her breath, consumed by frustration: "Such a girl! The boys all are growing into such fine young men, but that girl! Poor, sweet Pilar dead in her grave all these years. She never had a chance after I left, and Julia behaves like such a demon. And Antonio. Just useless. I don't know, Lord. I don't know. Why does my path always circle back to pain and disappointment?"

She stared at the blank sheet of writing paper. Her thoughts refused to be contained or organized. After writing, "My dear brother and sister-in-law," she could add no more. Mercedes slipped the sheet and her pen back into the box, stood up from the table, got her change purse, and went out to the porch.

Antonio sat gazing absently across the street, a cigarette burned nearly down to the fingertips in which he pinched it.

Mercedes' feelings about her husband were such a jumble, and she ricocheted from one to the other. They seemed to have a life of their own, separate from her will. The anger and frustration had abated as she attempted to write the letter. As she saw Antonio sitting there, broken and lost, she felt more sad for him than she did for herself. She stopped and put a hand on his shoulder. "How are you, Segundo?" she asked.

He chuckled twice, and a hint of his Gallego half-grin crept into the corner of his mouth as he looked up at her. "I'm still here. Don't know whether that's a good thing or bad."

"That's the truth," Mercedes said. She patted him on the shoulder and managed a melancholy smile down at him. "I'm going to post this letter, and then I'll stop to buy a bag of flour. Do you need tobacco? We have money enough for both at the moment."

"No," Antonio said as he poked around in the same leather pouch he had on that Christmas Eve in the courtyard at Las Cepas. "Better save what you can. I have enough tobacco here for another day or two, and I don't know whether that fencing job down at the Rodríguez place will come through this week or next."

"Until later, then," Mercedes said. She plodded down the stairs and out to the street. Antonio watched her until she disappeared around the corner, two blocks away.

A good woman, he thought. *The best I ever knew. I should've taken her home when I still could.*

* * *

"Mama! Mama!" twelve-year-old Pilar shouted as she ran into the house. "I got another postcard from Julia!" Mercedes shared none of her daughter's enthusiasm as the girl handed her the card. "Look where she is she now!"

Mercedes studied the water-coloured photograph of a square and cathedral on the front of the postcard. It looked like some place in Castile. "In Mexico City, or she was anyway. Constitution Square and the Cathedral," Mercedes said languidly.

"It's very pretty!" Pilar exclaimed.

"Dear Pilar," Mercedes read. Julia always addressed her postcards only to Pilar, but she wrote in Spanish so Mercedes could read them as well. "We crossed into Mexico a week ago and now are in Mexico City. It is a beautiful city and a beautiful country. I am glad I speak Spanish because almost nobody speaks English here, but it is hard to understand them. They use lots of different words for things, and they pronounce all their c's and z's like s's. I really don't like how it sounds. But I like the people here. They all are very warm and welcoming, especially when I tell them mama and papa came from Spain. They do not much like Americans, and they think of me as Spanish. I am running out of room on this card, so I will stop. We are going to see the Pacific Ocean! *Un abrazo fuerte*"—a strong hug, which was the usual Asturian farewell—"Julia."

"I want to go to Mexico!" Pilar howled. "Can we go? You and me and papa? Can we, please?"

"Maybe one day, Pilar," Mercedes said, sighing. "But today, we need to pick all those tomatoes and beans out there and start canning them for winter."

"Oh, mama, I don't like picking beans and tomatoes," Pilar pouted. "It's hot, and those vines make me itch."

"Well, somebody has to make sure we have food to eat this winter," Mercedes said. "We can't all sit on the porch or go sightseeing across the continent."

"Oh, mama," Pilar whined. She sank to the kitchen floor like a rag doll.

Mercedes took her by the wrist and pulled Pilar back to her feet. "Now go in there and change into your work dress. I don't have time for your foolishness."

* * *

The enormous disk of the orange-red sun sinking into the Pacific Ocean was the most magnificent thing Julia had seen in her life. She and the young man with the motorcycle had almost no money, so they were sleeping on the beach. They had spread one of their wool blankets on the sand. A cluster of bushes and scrubby trees sheltered them somewhat from passers-by.

"You love me, don't you, Rico?" Julia asked as they entwined themselves under the other blanket. "You really love me and want to marry me, don't you?"

"Uh, yeah, sure, Julia," Rico said as he struggled with the clasps on her bra. "But, you know how it is. I don't have any work, and we both live with our parents."

"I know all that, but some day, right?" Julia asked. She shifted her body to restrict his fumbling with the bra. "When the Depression is over? It can't last forever. Then we'll get married and move out on our own? Won't we?" She had given herself to him whenever and wherever he wanted, from the first time he answered affirmatively when she asked if he loved her. That had been somewhere in Indiana, two days out of Anmoore. Julia wanted desperately to believe him, about the love and the future, despite his obvious reluctance. Her life with her parents felt like a prison, and a man and marriage the only tunnel under the wall.

"Sure, Julia," Rico said. He shoved his free hand down the front of her underwear. "Sure we will."

She placed a hand on his between her legs and looked into his eyes. "I love you, Rico."

He glanced away quickly. "I know, Julia. Me too." This dry crumb was enough to sustain her hope. And she knew for a fact that none of Rico's previous girlfriends had given him sex. She figured that had to count for something.

After they finished, or Rico did anyway, they cuddled beneath the blanket on the sand. The low, rhythmic crash of the surf whisked Julia quickly off to sleep, and she slept so soundly that she was surprised to see morning had arrived when she next opened her eyes.

Rico snorted, rolled onto his other side, and tucked the upper blanket around his neck as Julia slipped from their makeshift bed.

Julia stood and stretched, and savoured the cool breeze against her body. She looked around and saw no one, so she walked naked down to the blue sea. The water was cold as it washed over her feet, but she felt giddy as a child to be so far from Anmoore, so free, and standing alone on a beach looking at the Pacific.

She waded out to her knees, and then to her waist, laughing aloud each time the new surge of waves crashed into her. When she was chest deep, Julia dove into the next white-cresting wave. She swam under the water for as long as she could hold her breath, cocooned in the silence of the sea. When her head popped to the surface, she could no longer touch the bottom with her feet. She was beyond the breaking waves, bobbing among the swells rolling with determination toward the beach. Julia treaded water and watched the swells slide past and the long, broad leaves of the palm trees along the shore waving slowly in the morning breeze.

When her arms and legs began to tire, Julia rode the swells, and then the waves, into the beach. She sat in the sand with the last cool bit of each dying wave creeping around her. She could not breathe in enough of the salty air and the clean, white sunlight to satisfy her. Her head and heart felt cleansed and buoyant. Her life felt light and carefree to a degree it never did when she was at home. There, she was always enveloped by her parents' suffocating despair and the sense that she would never escape to a life of her own.

When her suntanned skin was dried by the breeze and the sun, Julia ambled back to the still-sleeping Rico, put on the colourful cotton skirt and billowy-sleeved white blouse she had bought at the market in Mexico City for thirty US cents, and strolled along the path at the back of the beach beneath the palm trees.

After a few minutes, Julia came upon a tiny, ancient woman, her face wrinkled as a dried apple, sitting on the low stone wall by the path. Despite the muggy summer heat, building already at this early hour, the woman wore heavy leggings, a long woolen skirt, a sweater, a knitted cap and ragg gloves. All were black or dark grey. Dry, white tendrils of hair curled from beneath the cap. The woman slowly looked up at Julia as she passed, stuck out her hand, and said: "Ayuda me." *Help me.*

Julia dug into her pocket and produced a few peseta coins. She placed them in the gloved hand and said: "Buen día, señora." *Good day, ma'am.*

The woman nodded, mumbled something incomprehensible, and then turned her gaze to the ocean.

Julia walked on, smelling the ocean air and feeling sun on her skin. *I could just walk forever*, she thought. But then she worried that Rico would wake and wonder where she was, so she turned and headed back, the weight of the unhappiness she never seemed able to shake off for more than a little while seeping over her again.

Rico was awake when she returned to their campsite, lying on his back under the blanket with his arms folded behind his head. "Good morning beautiful," he said and reached a hand out toward her. Julia joined him under the blanket for what had become the morning routine. She rolled onto her side, and Rico pushed up her skirt and shoved himself inside her. She was not in the mood, and it felt particularly oppressive after her glorious time in the ocean and walking alone on the beach, but she knew it never took him long. Quickly, she felt his final thrust and heard the three grunts—always three this first time in the mornings—before Rico rolled away and started looking for his clothes.

"You love me, don't you, Rico," she said without turning to look at him.

"Yeah, of course I do, Julia."

* * *

Rico left her in Guadalajara. Julia kept talking about marriage, and they started arguing frequently. When he got drunk one evening and slapped her across the face, as they stood screaming at each other on Avenida Miguel Hidalgo y Costilla, she declared that she never wanted to see him again. Rico got on his motorcycle, tossed her pillowcase full of clothes onto the sidewalk, and rode off into the night.

Julia called home, collect. Mercedes would not speak to her. She heard her daughter's voice and handed the telephone receiver to Julia's brother Luis.

"He did what?" Luis shouted angrily when she told him that Rico was gone.

Mercedes was not surprised by his tone.

"I told you that bastard was no good," Luis reminded Julia.

"I know, I know," she cried into the telephone. Julia was standing in a phone booth at a Guadalajara hotel where she could never afford to sleep. "Can you ... can you borrow a car and come get me, Luis?"

Luis was silent on the other end of the line.

"Luis? Are you still there?" she asked.

His voice was flat. "Yes, Julia. I'm here."

"You know I hate to ask you," she said. "It's such a long way. But I only have about fifteen dollars left, and there's no other way I can get home."

"Okay. Okay, Julia," Luis said. "Jorge got his old jalopy running again last week. I think it'll make it there and back. We'll scrape together some money for gas and leave tomorrow."

Her brothers knew Julia carried some invisible burden. They did not understand nor even really ponder it. They simply sensed that some inner turmoil Julia could not manage drove her behavior, and each felt he needed to protect her and defend her, no matter how outrageous her actions.

"Oh, thank you, Luis," Julia said. She was deeply and genuinely grateful. She hated having to impose on her brothers, but calamity seemed to be her constant companion. "Thank you," she said again. "I always can count on you to save me when I've gotten myself into a mess."

"You need to stop getting yourself into them, Julia," Luis replied after a pause.

"I know, Luis. I'm sorry."

"Do you have some place to sleep?" her brother asked. "If we do nothing but drive, it'll take us at least four days to get there."

Julia laughed. "Don't worry about that, Luis. I'll manage. I've been on the road alone before. Worst case, I'll find some nuns to take me in. They're all over the place here."

"Okay, Julia," Luis said. He was annoyed and concerned, but also a little impressed, by his sister's cavalier attitude. "How will we find you?"

"Just go to the Cathedral," she said. "You can't miss it. I'll hang around there like one of those Gypsy women mama always told us about and watch for you."

It did not sound like much of a plan, but there was nothing else Luis could do. "Alright, Julia. Be safe."

"I will, Luis. Thank you. Thank you. Thank you. Thank you."

"Well?" Mercedes asked when Luis returned the telephone receiver to its cradle. He and Julia had been speaking English, and their mother did not understand the half of the conversation she heard, though she suspected its content.

"She and Rico had a fight in Guadalajara, and he left her," Luis said as undramatically as possible.

Mercedes felt simultaneously faint and furious. She leaned on the back of a kitchen chair. "Oh, Mother of God, what'll she do now?"

"It's okay, mama," Luis said reassuringly as he put a big hand lightly on her back and encouraged her to sit in the chair. "Jorge and I will take his car tomorrow and get her. You know how much she's traveled on her own, so she'll be okay, like she always is. She has some money and, thanks to you, she speaks Spanish."

A small smile crept onto Mercedes lips. "Asturian, at least," she said.

Luis laughed. "Well, it'll do, mama," he said. "Now, I have to go tell Jorge about our sudden travel plans."

Chapter 15

Anmoore, West Virginia
December 1936

"Don't push until I tell you," Mercedes ordered. Julia was lying on the same bed in which Mercedes had given birth to her five children. This was Julia's first. The father was one of two young men in Anmoore, but she was not certain which. It did not matter. Neither was interested in marrying her or raising the child.

"But it hurts so much," Julia cried. "I just want it out of me!" Her long, black hair was matted to her head with sweat.

"Maybe you should've thought about that before you decided to become the town slut," Mercedes said sharply.

"Mama!" Pilar said. She was kneeling beside the bed, holding Julia's hand and blotting her forehead with a cool, damp towel. "That's a mean thing to say."

"Well, it's the truth," Mercedes snapped. "Okay, Julia. I see the top of the head. Now, push."

It was a boy. Pilar helped their mother clean and swaddle him. Mercedes held out the baby for Julia to take. "Please," Julia said, "just put it in the crib. I'm so exhausted."

"For God's sake, Julia!" Mercedes hissed. "He's your son, your first child. Don't you want to hold him?"

"No, mother, I don't," Julia said. "Not now. Please, just put it … put him in the crib."

Mercedes cuddled the baby and started out of the bedroom. Turning back, she said, "Tend to your sister, Pilar." She cast a harsh glance at Julia. "In all my life, I—" she began, but she said no more. Mercedes turned and left the room.

"He's a beautiful baby," Pilar said to Julia, in English, as she washed the sweat and blood and secretions from her sister. She rinsed the towel in a ceramic basin on the floor by the bed and wrung it out. "What'll you call him?"

"I don't know," Julia said. She looked past her sister and fixed her eyes on a blank spot on the wall opposite the bed.

"Don't worry about mama," Pilar said cheerfully. "She'll calm down. And we'll raise the baby, you and me. Oh, it'll be nice! He's a beautiful baby, and I'm sure he'll be sweet."

"Oh, please, Pilar," Julia said, sighing. She rested the back of her hand on her forehead and closed her eyes. "Stop it. I really don't feel like chatting with you about this now. Just clean me up and let me sleep."

"Yes, Julia. I'm sorry," Pilar said, getting back to her work. "I didn't mean to annoy you."

In silence, Pilar finished bathing Julia and then changed the sheet, shifting her sister from one side of the bed to the other, like a hospital orderly. For two years, Pilar had been assisting Mercedes with her midwifery. She kissed Julia on the forehead, switched off the lamp on the bedside table, and quietly joined their mother in the living room.

Julia lay on the bed in the darkness and wept.

* * *

In the American Civil War, for the large part, organized armies from the North and South slugged it out on battlefields in classic Napoleonic warfare. Generally, the territory of the opposing sides was clearly defined. The Spanish Civil War of 1936-1939 was altogether different. Nearly every city, town and village was divided almost equally between supporters of the Nationalists and the Republic. Armies did clash on battlefields, but the ugliest violence was small and close. Neighbors slaughtered each other in the places where they had lived together for centuries. *The same social strife and revolutionary fervour that fueled the Asturian labor unrest earlier in the twentieth century made it a vicious civil war battleground.*

* * *

"My dear brother and sister-in-law," Mercedes wrote. Julia still was in the bed she shared with Pilar, recuperating from the birth three days before. The baby, whom Julia finally had decided to call Richard, was alternating fitful sleep with squalling in the crib. Mercedes had wheeled the crib into the kitchen so she could keep an eye on him, and try to comfort him, as she wrote the letter at the table. "I hope you and the children are doing as well as could be expected under the circumstances. My heart is broken with yours."

Antonio and María's son Avelino had been shot to death the month before. Antonio González Conde did not take up arms in the civil war, but he did support General Francisco Franco and the Nationalists, driven by his fear of the communists who were fighting for the Republic. Like partisans on either side, Antonio justified the atrocities of the forces he backed and vilified the atrocities of those he opposed.

Avelino was betrayed by a group of young men he thought were his friends. One afternoon, riding back to Naveces from Avilés with his compatriots, the driver stopped the wagon deep in the woods and whistled three long times. A band of Republican militia emerged from the trees. The driver nodded toward Avelino. The militiamen dragged him from the wagon, threw him to the ground, and shot him in the face as he pleaded for his life.

"We are holding up relatively well," Mercedes continued in her letter. "Antonio is working for one of the new government relief agencies, building roads. He seems happier. Luis and Manuel have gotten jobs at the carbon plant which opened recently here in Anmoore. President Roosevelt's programs are making life feel a bit more normal after the terrible years of so much pain and destitution. The laundry in Clarksburg has reopened, and Julia is working there part-time."

Embarrassed and ashamed, Mercedes still had not told her brother about Julia's baby boy, her first grandchild. "I hope that awful war there will end soon, and that this letter reaches you without too much delay. Mercedes González Conde."

* * *

August 1937

"And then! ... and then! ..." Julia was laughing so hard, she was having trouble finishing the story.

Pilar, gasping with laughter as much as Julia, picked up the tale. "Just as I got ahold of the fish—oh, mercy, it was so fat and slimy—Julia slipped on the mud and fell in the river!"

"But I had a death grip on that fishing pole!" Julia struggled to add through her laughter. "Papa would've killed me if I'd lost it."

"And there was no way I was going to lose my fish!" Pilar exclaimed. "But when Julia tried to get up, the line went taut, and the fish jerked and started flopping even more, and then I slipped on the mud and piled in the river, too!"

"But, somehow, I hung onto the pole," Julia said, "and Pilar kept her fingers dug into that fish, and somehow we got to shore with both of them!"

The crowd standing around Julia and Pilar were bent over with laughter. Much of the population of Anmoore came every sunny Sunday through the spring and summer for picnicking at the clearing on the top of Pinnick Kinnick Hill, as they had for decades. The hill rose behind the town like the back of a great, surfacing whale.

These afternoons were a slice of Asturias transported across the Atlantic. Only the eucalyptus was missing, and the views of the sea. The women brought pots of fabada and cheeses and lengths of chorizo and loaves of crusty bread. The men hefted up barrels of beer and crates of Asturian-style cider, despite the despised Prohibition. Bagpipers played. The aging immigrants sang the old Asturian songs, and danced the old Asturian dances, that they had learned as children from their parents and grandparents.

Back when the smelter was still operating, the weekly picnics gave the workers and their families an afternoon of relaxation together. Now, their adopted country was in the eighth year of the Great Depression. Their native land was still convulsed by civil war, though the Republican army was disintegrating after the Battle of Ebro. And Europe appeared to be sliding quickly toward a new continental conflict, only twenty years after the end of the Great War. The weekly gatherings on "the *pico*"—as most of the inhabitants of Anmoore called Pinnick Kinnick Hill, using the Spanish word for peak—provided a few rare carefree hours each week for the immigrants and their children and grandchildren.

The Ribas sisters were sitting atop a picnic table. Julia held court in a way that would have made her uncle, Antonio González Conde, proud. She loved being the center of attention, and people loved giving it to her. Julia possessed a seemingly inexhaustible repertoire of stories and energy. Pilar, usually unwittingly, served as the perfect straight man.

"Tell us again about getting lost on that Indian reservation in South Dakota!" one young man shouted from the back of the crowd.

"Nah," Julia demurred, "people have heard that one too many times. It's wore out."

"I'm not putting that there, no matter how much better it may make me feel!" another young man shouted, quoting the punch line of the tale. That alone was enough to send a new wave of laughter rippling through the crowd.

"Where are you off to next?" a third young man asked. Julia's trips, most of which did not end as badly as Mexico with Rico, had become legendary in the town. The immigrants had been village people in Spain, and their crowded, steerage-class journeys across the Atlantic did not convert them into travelers. They generally ventured no farther than the few miles to Clarksburg. Their children, with the exception of those who moved to a different city for work, tended to be equally stationary.

"Canada!" Julia announced. "Day after tomorrow. I'll hitchhike up through Pennsylvania, New York and New England, and cross over from Maine into Québec. I've never been anywhere they speak French!"

Her neighbors would not have been more astonished had Julia said she planned to take a hot air balloon to Mars.

After the crowd dispersed, and the sisters were strolling through the picnic ground, Pilar said: "Julia, you didn't tell me you're going to Canada."

"Because I decided it just then," Julia replied. She was manic. "I'd been thinking about it for a while, but at that moment, I decided I'll go. It'll be a great adventure."

"But what about Richard?" Pilar asked. He was not yet a year old.

Julia had not taken to motherhood with any greater fondness or devotion than she showed on the night the baby was born. "Oh, he likes you and mama better than me anyway," she said. Julia waved a hand dismissively in the air. "He won't even notice I'm gone." The boy did gravitate to Pilar and Mercedes. It never occurred to Julia it was because she showed no interest in him, rather than him having little interest in her.

"Mama won't be happy about it," Pilar warned. "Not one bit."

"Mama hasn't been happy about anything I've done since I was about Richard's age," Julia said. She snatched a bottle of beer from an iced bucket beside the table of a young man she knew. "Okay?" She asked him, lifting up the bottle. She smiled and arched her eyebrows.

"Of course, Julia," he said, grinning. "I won't even charge a deposit for the bottle."

Pilar resumed their disagreement. "I'm sure that's not true, Julia, about mama never being happy with you."

"I assure you it is, Pilar. But let's not talk about that." She offered her sister a drink of the beer. Pilar waved it off, and Julia took a swig. She changed the subject. "I noticed that cute boy from your class ... what's his name? Miguel? I saw he was eyeing you when we were telling the story about the fish."

"Eyeing you probably is more like it," Pilar said. She frowned and looked down at her scuffed shoes. "The boys don't like me the way they do you. I'm too plain, and I'm too shy when you're not around."

"Oh, sweetie, you're not plain," Julia said. She stopped and took her sister by the elbow. "You're a very pretty girl, Pilar. Boys are just stupid most of the time. And it's better they don't follow you around like a pack of dogs. It'll make it easier for you to spot the right one when he comes along."

Pilar looked off toward the crowd of picnickers. "I don't know. I'd like it if they paid attention to me and brought me presents and flowers like they do you."

Julia put her arm around Pilar and pulled her close. "One will, one day, and then you'll be glad you didn't have to bother with all the jerks in the meantime."

Pilar shrugged her shoulders. "Maybe you're right."

"Of course I am!" Julia said, holding the beer bottle high. "If anybody knows those awful creatures, it's me!"

Pilar giggled and asked: "So, you're really going to Canada day after tomorrow?"

"That I am," Julia said. "And every minute that passes, the more sure I am I will. I need to get away from here for a while."

"I'll never understand that part of you, Julia," Pilar said.

Julia curled up one side of her mouth, almost their father's Gallego half-grin, and said: "Well, I'll never understand why you never want to leave this grubby little place."

They made their way back down the trail from Pinnick Kinnick Hill to Anmoore and up the street to their little house across the looming, boxy, smoke-belching Union Carbide plant which had replaced the long, brick buildings of the abandoned smelter.

* * *

As Pilar predicted, their mother was displeased when Julia announced at dinner that she would leave in two days for Canada. But Mercedes was more weary than ever. She mounted only brief, token resistance.

Julia's journey unfolded just as she had described to the adoring crowd on Pinnick Kinnick Hill. She was bored across most of western Pennsylvania—just farms and factories—but she was duly overwhelmed by Niagara Falls. She thought nothing could be so breathtaking, until she found herself in the sublime beauty of the Adirondacks. She lingered there for two weeks, meandering from village to village. As always, Julia sent postcards regularly to Pilar, and she bought a little hand-carved forest fairy for her sister near Blue Mountain Lake.

Julia did not expect to meet a man in Montreal, let alone one like Gilles. She was basking in the sun at a park near Mount Royal, marveling at the enormous six-sided dome of St. Joseph's Oratory which dramatically dominated the landscape atop the hill. Gilles came over to where she was sitting and told Julia he had been watching her for an hour.

"I am stupefied by your beauty, and I must know your name," he said and invited her to a café.

Despite her many travels, Julia was accustomed only to the rough manners of the barely educated, working class young men in northern West Virginia. This urbane French-Canadian seemed to have descended from a different branch of the human evolutionary tree.

Gilles took Julia to restaurants with white linen tablecloths and introduced her to foods and wines of which she had never heard. He showed her churches and museums and took her to jazz bars and symphony concerts. Gilles bought her three colorful Parisian dresses from a boutique in Plaza St. Hubert, and then he luxuriated in removing them at night in his spacious old apartment on Dorchester Boulevard.

"You love me, don't you, Gilles?" Julia asked as they lay panting on his bed. A chilly breeze blew in off the river through the open doors to the balcony. Julia felt like she had been transported to a different universe during this time in Montreal with Gilles, but the old uncertainty still always lurked inside her.

"I enjoy our time, very much, Julia."

"And you want marry me and love me forever?"

"Love and forever are such bourgeois conceits, my dear," Gilles said.

She had no idea what he meant. He often said things, about paintings and music and philosophy, that she did not understand. Usually, she would just nod and go on, but this question mattered intensely to her. "Well, I love you and want to marry you and live with you forever, Gilles. I've never been so happy in my life."

"I am very happy, too, that I came across you in the park," Gilles said. He looked long at her and stroked her hair. "I cannot remember passing a more intoxicating month."

"But," Julia said. She did not like the sound of what he was saying. "But what?"

"I've shared your bed for four weeks now, and I am telling you that I love you," Julia said, lifting herself up on an elbow. "Doesn't that mean anything to you?"

Gilles sat up and propped himself against the headboard of the bed. "Of course, it does, Julia. It has been a beautiful time. As pleasurable and lovely as any I have known. Our days and nights together always will be very special to me."

"I'm such a stupid cow." Julia was disgusted with herself and with him. She climbed abruptly from the bed and began to dress.

"What are you doing?" Gilles asked, truly mystified. She had seemed such a free spirit when he talked to her in the park and over the weeks since. "Come back into the bed."

"Why?" Julia said sharply. "So I can be your whore for another night? No, Gilles, I'm going."

He looked deeply offended. "Why ... why do you say such a hurtful thing, Julia? I have not treated you like a prostitute."

Julia pulled on the cheap dress she had brought with her from Anmoore. She stuffed the remainder of her belongings into the second-hand leather duffle she had purchased that spring, after a year of saving a few cents from each paycheck at the laundry. She carefully draped the three Parisian dresses from Gilles over the back of an arm-chair across from the bed.

"I'm sorry, Gilles," she said. "You're right. We've had a lovely month, and you've been very kind to me. Thank you." The duffle thrown over her shoulder, Julia returned to the side of the bed. She leaned over, kissed him on the cheek and patted his bare chest three times. "Thank you, Gilles. But I have to go. I want a man who loves me and wants to marry me."

He grabbed her hand. "Why must you be so old-fashioned, Julia? There is so much more to life than working class conventionalism."

She pulled away from his grasp. "Not for me, Gilles," she said. "You take care of yourself." She turned to leave.

"Julia, Julia, wait," he said. He started to get out of the bed. "Where will you go? It is nearly midnight."

"Don't get up, Gilles," she told him, motioning him back with her hand. "I'll let myself out. And don't worry, I'll manage on my own. I always do."

She descended the winding staircase of the Beaux Arts building and breathed in the crisp air of the Montreal autumn night. She loved that fall scent of dried leaves and wood smoke. Julia was disappointed, but not quite heartbroken. Guadalajara had been much worse. She had grown to expect little from men, and she felt foolish for having allowed herself to be so drawn into Gilles and this strange, wonder-ful, foreign world. But she also was thankful for it. Julia set off for the train station, suddenly eager to return to the familiar, comfortable confines of Anmoore.

A month after she returned from Canada, Julia miscarried Gilles' baby. She was glad.

Chapter 16

Anmoore
25 December 1939

My dear brother and sister-in-law,

I hope all of you there are well and that you have had a happy Christmas. Ours has been the nicest in years. With Luis working at the carbon plant, Antonio at the state roads department, and Julia still part-time at the laundry, we are not struggling to survive any more. The whole atmosphere of the town seems to be almost normal, for the first time since the smelter closed back in 1927. It has been a long, hard road.

We had a house full of friends and neighbors last night for Christmas dinner. Two of the men showed up with bagpipes and two others with barrels of cider. Everybody was chattering away in Spanish, and it reminded me so much of Christmas at Las Cepas. Twenty-five I have spent here now. It does not seem possible. I miss you and home even more than usual at this time of the year.

What a relief that the civil war there is finally over, though at such a cost. Pepe and Avelino both killed along with so many others. Thank God the war did not take any more of your sons. Every Spanish family in Anmoore lost family there. The Reds here, of course, think the new government is a catastrophe, but I hope it will bring peace and stability and let people get back to their lives.

At least it seems Franco will keep Spain out of this new European mess. All this killing. It never ends. I pray every night that Roosevelt keeps his promise the Americans will stay out of it too. I could not bear my boys going off to war.

But enough of that. I am glad to hear that Manuel is doing so well already at the new smelter in San Juan. I cannot believe he is eighteen already. Tell him his Aunt Mercedes loves him, even if we never have had the chance to see each other face to face. Maybe someday, after our children all are settled with families of their own, I can convince Antonio to go back so we can die at home.

Take care of yourselves. Kisses and hugs from all of us here to all of you there.

Mercedes González Conde

* * *

Anmoore, West Virginia
June 1941

"Oh, Luis, why have you done this?" Mercedes asked, white-haired and wrinkled like a prune at the age of fifty-six.

"The war's been going on in Europe for more than two years now," Luis said. "We can't stay out of it much longer. And when we get in, I want to be there." He had gone to Clarksburg that morning and enlisted in the navy.

"But what about your job at the carbon plant?" Mercedes said. "It's such good work to walk away from, and as much as I hate so say it, we'll have a hard time getting by without that income."

"I've already taken care of it, mama," Luis said. He draped a long arm over her bony shoulders. He got the job the week after he finished high school, seven years before, and Luis had a religious fervor for helping his parents and siblings. Their well-being, he believed, was his paramount responsibility. "You know I wouldn't just abandon you," he told Mercedes. "I talked to the shop foreman yesterday, and they'll hire Manuel in my place. You'll actually come out ahead, without me here to feed anymore."

"I'd rather keep feeding you," his mother said ruefully. She looked across the kitchen to Antonio. "Will you please talk some sense into your son?"

However, her husband sided with their oldest boy. "He's right," Antonio said, sitting at the table with a café con leche and cigarette. "We'll get into this thing soon, too. He might as well be ready."

"We." She nearly spat the word. "I don't see what 'we' have to do with it. My brother lost a son and a daughter in that stupid civil war in Spain. Now you're ready to sacrifice Luis for the Americans?"

"I'm American, mama," Luis said. That he was. All their children, and the children of the other immigrants in the town, had embraced the country in which they were born. Thoroughly. They spoke Spanish with their parents, but they preferred the English they spoke with their friends. Most felt no emotional connection at all to Spain. They had never been there, and no more than a handful ever would go in their lifetimes.

The new war in Europe and Asia only heightened their patriotism for the United States. "And I don't plan on sacrificing myself," Luis added. "That's why I'm enlisting now. When we get in, they'll draft everybody. I don't want to be hauled in as cannon fodder. The recruiter told me they might even make me a non-commissioned officer before too long if I enlist now."

"I don't even know what a non-commissioned officer is," Mercedes said. "But I presume it doesn't make you magically bulletproof."

Luis chuckled and hugged her. "You worry too much, mama. I'll be fine."

Julia came bounding into the kitchen. She had a tall, lanky man in tow. "Mama, papa, Luis, I want you to meet someone!"

Mercedes grimaced. Antonio slurped the last of his coffee. Luis stuck out his hand to the man.

"This is Art. Art Kelley," Julia announced, as if they should recognize the name.

"Pleased to meet you, Art," Luis said. He shook the man's hand.

"That's my brother, Luis," Julia said, "and this is my mother, Mercedes, but you can call her Martha. Everybody who speaks

English does." Mercedes flinched at the hated name and nodded, her arms crossed across her chest. "And this is my papa, Antonio." Her father shook Art's hand without getting up from his chair. "Art and I met last week," Julia said. She was nearly vibrating with delight. "I'm just crazy about him, and I couldn't wait for you to meet him."

"Where did you meet?" Mercedes asked.

"Oh, that's not important," Julia said, batting a hand dismissively and smiling wildly at Art.

"So, at the roadhouse, then," Mercedes growled. Julia had been spending most of her evenings for several months in the dark little bar at the edge of Anmoore on the road to Clarksburg.

"Why do you always have to be such a killjoy?" Julia shouted. Her mood required little stimulus to whip from one extreme to the other. "You criticize every single thing I do!"

Mercedes did not respond.

"Your brother has a bit of news himself," Antonio said in Spanish.

"Yes, um," Luis said, in English, "I enlisted in the navy this morning." He looked at Mercedes, and then back to Julia and Art, and added in Spanish: "I'll leave in a week for training."

"In a week!" Mercedes exclaimed. It had not occurred to her that he would depart so soon.

"The navy!" Julia cried gleefully. "You'll look like a movie star in that white uniform!"

"Oh, for God's sake," Mercedes said. She did not understand her daughter's comment, but her joyful tone was enough. She left the kitchen without an additional word to anyone.

"Well, Art and I are going to Florida tomorrow!" Julia announced. "He has a car and some friends who live near Miami, and we're going to the beach for a month!"

Luis and Antonio knew how this story would end. "Ah, nice, Julia," Luis said unenthusiastically. "That'll be quite a trip. Good to meet you, Art," he added, shaking the man's hand again. "I have some things to do, if you'll excuse me." Luis left the kitchen. Antonio stood, nodded at Art, and followed Luis out of the house.

"That's my family," Julia said to Art Kelley. "Part of it anyway. I have two other brothers and a little sister."

"I look forward to meeting them. I think," Art said. He had expected a warmer welcome.

"They'll loosen up," Julia assured him. "Now, speaking of loosening up" she said, "I could use a drink. How about you?"

Julia and Art drove to the roadhouse and began another beery afternoon which would stretch late into the night.

* * *

January 1942

Julia, Pilar and Mercedes were five years older, but otherwise the scene was the same. Julia was in labor on her parents' bed. Pilar held her hand. Mercedes angrily assisted the birth.

"It's a girl," Mercedes said flatly. "I'm not raising this one for you."

"I'd already decided, when Art left, that I'm giving it up for adoption," Julia snapped.

It had been Julia's longest relationship, even if it was often a blur of beer and whisky shots. Art always was non-committal about marriage, but he never ruled it out entirely. He occasionally said he loved her, unprompted. For Julia, that almost was as good as a proposal.

Then Pearl Harbor came. Art and nearly every other man under thirty in the town immediately volunteered for the fight. Julia's brothers Manuel and Antonio followed Luis into the navy. Art chose the army instead.

He would not marry Julia before he left for basic training, as she hoped and pleaded, but Art was infuriated by her decision not to keep the baby. She had told him, at the roadhouse, at the end of his three-day leave before shipping out to England.

"But it's my baby, too," he shouted as they stood at the crowded bar in the roadhouse. "You can't just give it away without my permission."

"If you won't marry me, I can do whatever I want with it," Julia shouted back.

"Hey, you two," the bartender yelled from the other end of the bar. "Pipe down or take it outside. Nobody wants to listen to your shit."

"Sorry, Bill," Art said to the bartender. He turned back to Julia. "If you do this," he said, "we're finished. I mean it, Julia."

"That's your choice, not mine," she said, her voice full of spite.

"You're not leaving me a choice," he said through clenched teeth.

"What can I do?" Julia asked. She drained off the last of her beer. "You won't marry me. You're running off to the war with the rest of the stupid men. I'm supposed to raise this kid on my own?"

"There will be lots of women on their own with their kids," Art said. "For Christ's sake, Julia, it's a world war. Why don't you try not to be so self-centered for once."

"Why don't you go fuck yourself," Julia shouted. "Don't worry, Bill," she added quickly to the bartender, who was glaring again in their direction. "I'm leaving." She took some coins from her purse and slammed them on the bar. "And give the soldier here a beer and a bump on me."

Halfway home, Julia sat down on the curb and bawled. It was so unfair. She wanted so little, just a man to love her and to want a home and family with her. She did not even care if they had a house; a little apartment in Clarksburg would suffice. He simply needed to care about her. Was that so much to ask? Was she so unlovable and difficult that no man could give her such a basic, normal thing?

After she cried out the pain to a tolerable level, Julia stood up from the curb. She wiped her face dry with her sleeve and straightened her skirt. "Well, fuck him, then," she said into the night. "Fuck them all." She fumbled around in her handbag for her pack of Camels, lit one, and marched off up the street toward her parents' house. If no man would give her what she so desired, she decided, she would just take what they were willing to give, enjoy herself as much as possible, and keep her heart to herself. Nobody wanted it anyway, it seemed.

Chapter 17

Anmoore
5 March 1943

My dear brother and sister-in-law,
    I hope you are getting by, and I am sure you are ready for spring to arrive. This was always my least favourite time of the year in Asturias, when the rain and cold seemed like they would never go away. I am saddened to hear from you that so many there are nearly starving because of the blockade. Thank God you have the farm and the bounty of the sea at hand.
    The boys write what they can, when they can. The navy censors all their letters, but the boys are crafty and always find ways to hint at where they are. I am sorry to say Luis appears to be helping inflict the current suffering on Spain. Last we heard, his ship is part of the force patrolling off Galicia and Asturias to enforce the blockade. It is a horrible irony for me, and his recent letters only make that feeling worse. He spends half of them ranting about "that fascist Franco" and saying the Americans should just invade and overthrow him. Of course, the censors are happy to let that get through.
    Manuel and Antonio Jr. are both in the Pacific, which terrifies me. One of my friends lost her only son at Guadalcanal last month, and she is, of course, inconsolable. And it is clear that this will be a long war. All I can do is pray. I go to the mass every day, and a group of us mothers pray the rosary together on Friday and Sunday evenings. Still, I am

sick from worry all the time. I know it weighs heavily on Antonio, too, though he never shows it. He fancies himself Americanized, but he is still just a tight-lipped old Gallego.

As for the girls, Pilar is excited about finishing high school in May. She already has her black robe and that strange, board-topped hat they wear for the graduation ceremony, and I see her trying it on in front of the mirror at least twice a week. I am so proud of her. My girl, a high-school graduate. The boys, of course, also went all the way through, but it makes me particularly happy that Pilar has. Julia is Julia. The least said about that the better.

Do you see anything of Ramón's daughter, Sagrario? I still cannot believe she and her husband and children got stranded there when the war broke out. Ramón says that the last he heard from her, they seem to be doing well and have opened a café in Avilés. Ramón hates Franco as much as Luis does, so he is glad they are surviving but not happy that Sagrario appears to enjoy living there. He fears she will not return, even when the war ends. I must say, though, that I envy her.

Take care.

Mercedes González Conde

* * *

Anmoore, West Virginia
April 1943

"Thank you for making time to come, Miss Ribas," the principal said. He sat across the desk from Julia in his office at the elementary school. "As I said in my note, we must address this situation with Richard."

"I don't know what you're calling a 'situation,'" Julia said testily. "Boys fight on the playground. What's the big controversy?"

"Ms. Ribas, please," the principal said. "There is no reason to be defensive. Yes, there have been fights on the playground for as long as there have been playgrounds and boys. But Richard's behavior has gone beyond that." He looked down the page in a ledger opened before him on the desk. "Your son has been involved in sixteen ... no, eighteen fights so far this school year, and three of them have been bad enough that we suspended him."

"What's he supposed to do," Julia asked, "when the boys call him a bastard and say his mother's a whore? Why don't you do something about that?"

"I know, Miss Ribas, there always are two parties in a fight." The principal's tone was even and sympathetic. "But I assure you, I have been the principal of this school for nine years, and was a teacher here for eleven before that, and I have not ever seen a boy as aggressive and spoiling for a fight as Richard."

"But—" Julia began.

The principal held up his hand and cut her off. "Please, please, hear me out. We only want what is best for Richard."

Julia crossed her arms and rolled her eyes.

"You may not accept that," the principal said, "but it is the truth. His teacher and I only want what is best for him, and, of course, for the other students. We simply cannot endure this behavior any longer."

"So, what?" Julia barked. "You're expelling him?"

"We do not want to do that, Miss Ribas. I am proposing that, with your agreement and assistance, we transfer him to the West Virginia Reform School at Pruntytown—"

Julia jumped forward in her chair. "Pruntytown?" she shouted. "You're not sending my kid to that prison!"

"Miss Ribas, please," the principal said in as soothing a voice as he could muster. "The West Virginia Reform School is not a prison. It is a place where troubled boys like Richard can receive the special attention they need to alter their behavior and grow into productive members of society."

"What a load of shit," Julia said. She stood and leaned over the principal's desk, poking her finger at him. "You're out of your mind if you think I'm agreeing to send him there."

The principal leaned back in his chair. His tone sharpened. "Miss Ribas, I invited you here in hopes that we could do this in the least disruptive way for Richard, not to debate whether we will take this action. I will not allow him to remain at this school any longer. He will be transferred to Pruntytown. It is up to you: the road can be rough, or the road can be smooth."

Julia sat back down and rested her wrists on the edge of the desk. "Please," she said quietly. "It's not his fault. I've ... I haven't always paid as much attention to him as I should. I know that. Please don't punish him for my failures."

They sat, staring at each other. The sounds of children on the playground drifted up through the open office window. After a long silence, the principal said: "You put me in a very difficult position, Miss Ribas. I understand the particular troubles you face, with Richard's father absent." He looked down and glanced over the order transferring Julia's son to the reform school. He had already endorsed it. The document required only her signature. He drew in a deep breath and sighed. "Okay, Miss Ribas. This contravenes all my experience and good judgment." He looked up at the ceiling then back to Julia. "Richard can have one more chance."

Julia leapt from her chair, ran around the desk and gave the rigid, seated principal an awkward hug. "Thank you. Thank you. I promise, he'll behave. I promise."

Gently pushing her away, the principal replied: "I hope so, Miss Ribas. I earnestly hope you and Richard will use this reprieve wisely. I cannot tolerate even one more of these incidents from him in the future. Not one more. He must exhibit model behavior from this day."

"He will. He will. I promise you." Julia shook his hand in both of hers and swiftly crossed to the office door. "He'll be an angel," she added, pausing in the doorway.

Closing the ledger and putting the transfer order into his desk— he had little doubt he would need it again soon—the principal said: "Let's just aim for not a devil."

When Julia returned to the house, seven-year-old Richard was in the backyard, catching the butterflies that fluttered around the blossoms on the plants in Mercedes' garden. Julia stomped into the yard, grabbed him by the ear, and dragged him toward the house. "Come in here, you little shit," she hissed.

Richard howled as she twisted his ear, and he stumbled along beside her.

"Oh, stop it," Julia said. "You deserve a beating. Be glad I'm not giving you that."

She hauled him into the bedroom and slammed the door. "You know where I've just been?"

Looking intently at the seam between two of the floorboards, Richard answered a barely audible: "At the school."

"Yes, at the school. And look at me when I'm talking to you." She grabbed his chin and jerked his head up. "You know what that principal wants to do? He wants to send you to Pruntytown. Pruntytown!"

"What's Pruntytown?" Richard asked sheepishly.

"It's a prison school for boys like you," she said. "You want to go to prison?"

"No!" he said loudly without hesitation. He had heard his grandfather talking once about a man he knew who was sent to prison, and it sounded like the most frightening thing he could imagine.

"Then you'd better knock this shit off!" Julia shouted. "Do you hear me?"

He nodded his head quickly.

"I'm not kidding, Richard," she said. "They're giving you one more chance. Just one. I don't care what the boys say to you."

Richard started to cry.

"I don't care what they say to you or do to you," Julia said, ignoring his tears. "One more fight, one more, and they're sending you to fucking prison."

"I don't want to go to prison," he wailed. The tears streamed down his cheeks. "Please don't send me away. I want to stay here with grandma and grandpa."

Julia looked him up and down and shook her head. She reached out and gave the boy a stiff hug. More gently than before, she said: "Just control yourself, Richard. No more fighting. None. You understand?"

He sniffed and wiped his nose on his sleeve. "I understand," he said. "Please don't let them send me away."

Julia searched around the room and found a handkerchief. She wiped his nose and dried his face. "Just do as I told you, and you can stay."

He took the threat to heart. No matter how much the boys at school taunted him, Richard turned and walked away. Not that he actually developed the ability to process his anger and frustration. He merely packed them down into himself, like stuffing garbage into a sack day after day.

Chapter 18

T he decades of smelter fumes and tobacco finally caught up with Antonio. The dry cough that began around Thanksgiving would not go away. By mid-January, Mercedes' entreaties to see the doctor were more aggravating than the cough, and Antonio went for an examination.

The lung cancer was advanced and aggressive, the doctor said. But for another month, Antonio continued to go to his job every day with the state roads department. He told only the foreman about his cancer and arranged to do the lightest work possible. Still, he took frequent breaks to lie down and rest in the back of one of the trucks.

In March, Antonio died in the bed where his five children and two grandchildren were born. His three sons were off in the war. Mercedes, Pilar and Julia were with him at the end, as they had been around the clock for his terrible final two weeks.

"I'm going to Maryland, to work in the shipyard," Julia announced without fanfare to Mercedes and Pilar at the dinner table three days after Antonio was buried in the Clarksburg cemetery.

Mercedes looked at her, shook her head, and went back to eating her stew. After they returned to Anmoore from the funeral, Mercedes had taken a long walk alone through the woods to the top of Pinnick Kinnick Hill. She stood for nearly an hour looking down at the grungy little town, the air tinted brown with the smoke from the carbon plant.

The valley was about the same size as that at home. If she were standing in San Adriano, at the top of the hill, Mercedes thought to herself, Las Cepas would be down there, a couple hundred yards below to the left, just before the valley floor. Naveces would be straight across on the opposite hillside. And off there to the right, at the valley's end, would be the sea. Oh, how Mercedes missed the sea. She had not seen it for thirty years, since she arrived at Ellis Island. From Pinnick Kinnick Hill, where the sea should be, was only Clarksburg.

In her mind, Mercedes looked down the hill to Las Cepas. She recalled that first Christmas Eve with Antonio on the steps of the granary. His face illuminated for half a second in the flame burst of the match. She gazed across the valley to Naveces, white-walled and red tile-roofed San Román Church glowing in a late-afternoon sun. She wished she could have buried her husband in the González family tomb in the cemetery behind the rectory.

Mercedes remembered reading the inscription on an adjacent tomb once, when the whole family had made one of their candle-lit All Saints Day vigils in the cemetery: *Tu nos dijiste que la muerte no es el final del camino.* You told us that death is not the end of the way. "Buen camino, Antonio," Mercedes whispered.

* * *

"You're doing what?" Pilar asked after Julia said she was moving away.

"Have you gone deaf, Pilar?" Julia said nastily. "I said I'm going to Maryland to work in the shipyard. With so many of the men gone, they're hiring women to help build the ships."

"But why?" Pilar asked. "We've just buried papa."

"Exactly. We've just buried papa. There's no good reason for me to stay around here. And, honestly, we need to replace his pay. I'll make three or four times what I do at the laundry."

"What about your son?" Mercedes asked. "Or have you not thought of him, as usual?" She was still astounded by her daughter's utter lack of maternal instinct. A casual observer of Julia's interaction with her son would have thought Richard was an orphan they took in or a boy from down the street just stopping by the house. When Richard was with Pilar, it appeared that she was his mother, but Julia did not even demonstrate the level of affection one would expect from an aunt.

"Richard's fine, mother," Julia said. "He's stayed out of trouble for a year now. And he only wants to be with you and Pilar all the time anyway."

"Maybe that's because we pay attention to him," Mercedes said. "You know, children can sense how people feel about them."

"Oh, for God's sake, let's not start this again," Julia said with a groan.

"And he's not fine," Mercedes said. "If you actually spent any time with him, you'd see that. The boy is filled from head to toe with rage. He reminds me of my father, from the little bit I knew him, and my brother José. One day, he'll explode."

"Oh, stop being dramatic, mother," Julia said. "Richard's just like any other boy his age."

Although she was always reluctant to challenge her sister about anything, most of all Richard, Pilar said: "I'm not so sure, Julia. It's not normal the way he keeps to himself all the time."

"Not you now too," Julia said. "For Christ's sake, you're both as bad as that principal at the school. Richard keeps to himself because those other asshole little boys mistreat him, and he doesn't want to get into fights and be sent off to Pruntytown."

"You always have an answer," Mercedes said.

"Well, at least I'm not sitting around here depressed out of my mind all the time like you," Julia snapped. She shoved her chair away from the table and slammed her plate into the sink. "I'm going to Maryland. I'll take the bus on Friday."

* * *

Mercedes, Pilar and Richard stood on the porch and watched Julia walk off down the street with her leather duffle bag toward the bus stop. She turned and waved before she rounded the corner. Only Pilar waved back.

"Can I go play now?" Richard asked.

"Of course you can," Mercedes said. "Just make sure you're home before dark." He ran down the steps and disappeared around the side of the house.

"Maybe you ought to go to Maryland, too," Mercedes said to Pilar after a minute.

"What?" Pilar said. "I won't go off and leave you and Richard, mama."

"We can manage," Mercedes said. "You need to get out of this town, Pilar. You've never been anywhere or seen anything. And somebody needs to try and keep Julia out of trouble."

"That's certainly true, about Julia," Pilar said, sighing. "But I'm happy being here in Anmoore and at home with you. I'm just a homebody. I always have been."

Mercedes reached over and squeezed her daughter's hand. "I know. You're as gentle and sweet as your Aunt Pilar. I wish you could have known her."

"I do, too, mama." When they were young, Mercedes told the children many stories about her life during those thirteen years at Las Cepas with her brother and his family. Pilar's favourites were the tales about her mother's visit to Avilés to see the processions of the penitents during the Semana Santa.

"And all of them over there," Mercedes said. "My brother Antonio and María, and all our family. There are so many of them, and they're such good people."

"Like Uncle Ramón," Pilar said.

"Yes, like your Uncle Ramón, and all his kids. It's good we at least have him over here, even if he is all the way over in St. Louis. But it's a shame you don't know the rest of them. Maybe someday, after this war is over, you can go visit them in Asturias."

"Oh, mama," Pilar said, giggling. "I'd love to meet them, you know that. But I can't go all the way to Spain. I don't even want to leave Anmoore!"

Mercedes knew that was the truth. If Pilar married the richest man in town and had all the time in the world, she still would never venture so far as Asturias. "Well, as I said, you ought to at least go to Maryland and get yourself a job like Julia, and keep an eye on her."

"If you think so, then I will," Pilar said. "But don't run me off just yet!" She hugged her mother. "You need to eat more, mama. You're as skinny as a bean pole."

"I'm fine," Mercedes said. "Just fine." She looked up at the sooty, brown sky. "But I'd be better if I could breathe the fresh air blowing in off the Cantabrian Sea, and smell the eucalyptus trees, just one more time."

Pilar patted her on the back and went inside the house to begin preparing their dinner.

Chapter 19

Baltimore, Maryland
June 1944

Julia was jumping up and down like a little girl as her sister climbed off the bus. "Pilar!" she cried. "I still can't believe you pried yourself out of that shitty town!"

"There's nothing wrong with our town," Pilar said. She hugged her sister tightly and then looked her all over, as if she had not seen her for years, rather than four months. "It's so good to see you, Julia. We've missed you something terrible."

"I've missed you too," Julia said. "But not that shitty town."

"Oh, Julia, you'll never change," Pilar said.

"Not if I can help it!" She took Pilar's suitcase in one hand and her sister's hand with the other. "Come on, now. We'll drop your bag at the apartment—can you believe I have my own apartment! Then I'll show you Baltimore. And there's somebody I want you to meet."

"A man?" Pilar asked warily.

"Of course, a man, silly," Julia said, laughing. "You'll like him. He's a hoot!"

"I'm sure he is," Pilar said. "They always are."

"Oh, for Christ's sake. It's good you came here," Julia said. "You're turning more into mama every day."

Julia hauled Pilar off to the apartment and gave her a perfunctory tour of the major Baltimore sights before they met John Goad in a bar at Fells Point on the shore of Baltimore Harbor.

"Well! Julia's little sister!" John called out loudly as they entered the bar. "She tells tales about your adventures in the West Virginia hills eighteen hours a day!"

"We didn't have that many adventures," Pilar said primly. She shared neither her sister's enjoyment of boisterous men nor her fondness for whiling away the hours in bars, though this one was more pleasant than the few Julia had dragged her to in Anmoore and Clarksburg. With its brick walls, polished wood bar with brass railings, and view out the window of the harbour, it was not a disagreeable place.

"Didn't I tell you she's a card!" Julia said. "Hank," she shouted at the bartender. "Bring a beer and a bump for me, and a Coca-Cola for my little sister." She turned to Pilar. "I assume you haven't started drinking since I escaped Anmoore."

Pilar grinned a bit. "No, that I haven't."

"It's just as well," Julia said. "Makes you a cheap date!"

Julia told Pilar about the new friends she had made and about the work at the shipyard. "I never imagined life could feel this good," Julia said. "I have my own place, and I come and go without having to answer to anyone. I feel as free as a bird. And even with what I send back to mama, I make enough money to shop a little and go to the movies with the other girls."

Pilar had seen Julia in her manic moods before. She worried that this was another of them, destined to deflate as soon as she struck some impediment. But Julia did seem genuinely happy, and this life was completely different from her existence in Anmoore. Pilar felt guardedly hopeful that Julia had actually reached a place of true satisfaction after so many years on a stony and troubled path.

As the afternoon faded into evening, John told story after story about his adventures on the road and rails, tramping during the Depression. He seemed to have traversed from coast to coast and stopped at every place in between. To her surprise, Pilar even found herself liking Julia's latest companion. Eventually, Pilar asked John: "So, why aren't you off in the war with the rest of the men?"

"Four-F, on account of a lung condition from when I was a kid, thank God," John told her. "Don't get me wrong. I've got nothing but respect for all those boys over there whipping up on the Krauts and Japs. But I never was much of one for fighting. I'm content to be one of the few left behind to tend to the maidens." He squeezed Julia high on the thigh.

"John Goad!" Julia howled in mock protest. "You're a devil! Save that for the bedroom. Hank!" Julia shouted to the bartender. "Another round."

"Not for me, Julia," Pilar said. "I'm dead on my feet."

Julia dug a key out of her handbag. "You go on back to the apartment, then. You remember the way don't you?"

"I do," Pilar said.

"Good," Julia said. "Make yourself at home. There should be some food in the refrigerator."

Pilar hugged Julia goodbye and shook John's hand. "It was very nice meeting you."

"I'm glad you're here, Pilar." John said with a toothy smile. "We'll show you some good times in this old town!"

As Pilar started out the door into the cool night, Julia called to her from across the bar: "Don't wait up! We'll be late."

Later that week, Pilar bought stationery and wrote to Mercedes while Julia was at work.

Dear Mama,

I am glad you had me come here. Baltimore is so different and so much more interesting than Anmoore and Clarksburg. I can't believe it's me saying that! Julia has shown me all over, and I have gone out exploring on my own in the afternoons when she is at work, and I always discover some new place or thing. I am still a homebody at heart, but I feel for the first time that I'd like to see more of the country some day.

Julia is doing good, really good. She is happier and more content than I've ever seen her. She loves the work at the shipyard—she is just like that Rosie the Riveter poster!—and has a lot of girlfriends from her shift. They've taken me to buy a new dress and some shoes that are so nice I never want to wear them, and we went to see the movie Going My Way *last night, and I could see it a dozen times. I would marry Bing Crosby tomorrow!*

Julia has also gotten me on at the shipyard, and I'll start next week. With the big invasion last month in France, they can't build fast enough, and the yard is working around the clock. I'll start just helping push things around in carts and cleaning up, but I hope I'll get to do more before too long. You just wouldn't believe the sight of all these women in overalls doing men's work and building these huge ships! It's a new world.

So, don't worry about us, though I worry about you alone there with Richard all the time. I hope he's not being difficult and is helping you with the housework. I love you and miss you!

Pilar

* * *

April 1945

John Goad was gone. Pilar and Julia had cooked dinner for the three of them, as they often did; then he and Julia went to her room, as they always did. There was no indication that anything had changed. But in the morning, Julia came into the kitchen for her coffee alone. John always woke first and had the coffee percolating in the electric pot by the time Julia rose.

"John sleeping late this morning?" Pilar asked.

"No," Julia said without elaborating.

Julia took only two sips of her coffee and did not touch the eggs, bacon and toast Pilar had prepared. Julia stood and stared out the kitchen window, and smoked a cigarette, and left the kitchen without saying anything else. Pilar heard the bathroom door latch and then the sound of Julia vomiting. Pilar knew it was not a hangover.

After a few minutes of silence in the bathroom, Pilar went across the hall and knocked tentatively.

"Everything okay in there, Julia?" she asked.

"Goddamnit, Pilar," she shouted from behind the closed door. "Can't you just leave me be? Go outside and do something. Or are you incapable of leaving the apartment alone?"

Pilar did not take the rude outburst personally. Julia always stung blindly, like an angry hornet, when she fell into her black moods. After the frustration loosened its grip, she would apologize and vow never to speak harshly to Pilar again. It had happened ten thousand times. Julia would lash out again, of course, but she was always sincere when she made the promise.

Pilar effortlessly deduced what had transpired. Julia clearly was pregnant again, and when she told John after dinner in the bedroom, he left. *Mama is going to be so disappointed in me*, Pilar thought. *And furious with Julia.*

Julia had gotten pregnant again a year after she delivered Art Kelley's daughter, whom she gave away for adoption, back in 1942. She miscarried that fourth pregnancy. Standing in the hallway of the apartment in Baltimore, Pilar felt guilty about hoping Julia would lose this one as well.

"I'll go out, then," Pilar said through the door. She put on a cheerful tone, as if they were sitting placidly together on the sofa. Pilar always felt responsible for helping Julia pull herself back together. "I found this park with a view of Fort McHenry that I like very much, and it's a beautiful day. I'll get myself a newspaper and go there and read it."

"You do that," Julia said through the door.

Pilar stayed away all day. When she returned to the apartment, Julia still was in her nightgown and bathrobe, but her mood had improved.

"Hey, kiddo," Julia said when Pilar came into the kitchen. "I'm sorry about being so nasty this morning. I promise not to take it out on you like that again."

"It's okay, Julia," Pilar said.

"I guess you figured out what's going on," Julia said. "It's pretty obvious, especially to you. We've been through this, what, four times already?"

"Yes, I know, Julia," Pilar said. "I'm sorry. Is John not ever coming back?"

Lighting a cigarette, Julia forced a grin. "I think we can count on that."

"I'll fix us something to eat," Pilar said. "Do you need anything? A blanket? It's getting a little chilly in here."

"No, I'm good, thanks," Julia said. "But some hot food would be very nice. I haven't eaten anything today, and I feel my appetite coming back."

Pilar made *tortilla con patata*—the thick egg and potato omelet ubiquitous in Spain—and they ate mostly in silence.

Pilar cleared away the dishes and returned to the kitchen table with coffee and some pastries she had bought that afternoon at the bakery around the corner. Julia said: "I guess we should quit our jobs at the shipyard and go back to Anmoore."

"Yes," Pilar said, though it made her sad to think of leaving the city so soon. "We've saved enough money to last us a year anyway."

* * *

Once again, in November 1945, Julia was on Mercedes' bed. Her mother had barely spoken to her over the six months since they returned from Maryland.

"I'll deliver this baby," Mercedes said coldly. "But I don't want to hear a sound out of you. Not a sound."

Julia obeyed, and silently gave birth to another daughter.

"What'll you do with this one?" Mercedes asked.

"Adoption," Julia said and closed her eyes.

Chapter 20

Anmoore
December 1945

My dear brother and sister-in-law,

All three boys arrived home to stay this week, just in time for Christmas! It feels like a miracle they all made it through the war, and without a scratch. Of course, I should not call them boys. The years in the navy have turned them into big, strapping men, but they will always be my boys, no matter how old they—or I—get.

The carbon plant across the street is busier than ever, and because the foremen remembered how well Luis and Manuel worked before the war, the company is hiring the three of them immediately. How I wish Antonio had lived to see this day, the boys home and set to make good lives for themselves.

Now, I feel I must tell you something that I have hidden from you over the years. I have wrestled mightily with how and when and whether to write you about it, and never have because I find it such a horrible thing. But I suppose my advancing age and the many hours I have spent looking back at my life over this year and a half since I lost Antonio make me want to settle all the things I have left undone. And this certainly is one of the biggest.

As you know, Julia never has married. What you do not know is that she has not lived a virtuous life. She has three children, and would have two more but miscarried them. All of them have different fathers. Her son was born in 1936, and he lives with us. Pilar and I have done our best to raise him because Julia has never had much to do with him. The second, a girl, Julia gave up for adoption in 1942, and next month we will take the newest, another girl, to the woman who arranges the adoptions.

It pains me greatly to see my daughter debasing herself and damaging her soul, and I detest that she is throwing away her own children as our father threw me away. I have been so angry and frustrated with her that I have barely been able to be in the same room with her, which, of course, puts me, in a way, down on the same vile level as our father. I know I should just love her and forgive her and pray for her, but I have been unable to find that in myself. And I feel like a complete failure as a mother that she grew into such a wanton creature in the first place.

I hid this from you for a selfish reason, because you always have lived such moral and responsible lives, and I feel that I have brought shame to our family even from so far away. And now I tell you for a selfish reason, because I do not want to reach the end of my life knowing that I have kept something so significant from the two people I have loved more than anyone other than my own children. I hope you will forgive me for all of it.

Mercedes González Conde

* * *

Steubenville, Ohio
January 1946

Mercedes, Pilar and Pilar's husband, Jim, climbed out of his car with the baby girl wrapped warmly in a wool blanket on the winter day.

"They're here, Ginny," Elsie shouted back through the rambling house toward the kitchen. She let the curtain fall back across the front window and went out to the porch. "Hello again," Elsie said cheerfully as Mercedes, Pilar and Jim approached. Virginia quietly emerged from the house and stood behind Elsie. Mercedes lingered at the foot of the stairs. She still spoke no English, and she wanted this shameful business concluded as quickly as possible. Pilar introduced Jim to Elsie.

"Just married? Well, that's wonderful," Elsie said. "Congratulations! What happy news."

"Yes," Pilar said. She beamed at Jim. "It's been a whirlwind, and it still seems like a dream. Jim was just back from the war, and he came into this coffee shop with some buddies where I was with some of my friends. One of the girls pointed him out and said he'd been looking constantly in my direction. I was embarrassed, but I nodded at him when we made eye contact. And then he got up, came over to our table, introduced himself and sat down."

"She was so pretty," Jim cut in, letting loose a booming laugh that matched his burly frame, "that I had to talk to her."

"And two weeks later, we got married," Pilar said with a big smile.

"Two weeks!" Elsie exclaimed. "That must be Fate."

"It sure feels like it," Pilar said.

Mercedes, standing away from the rest of them, had no idea what they were talking about. But it annoyed her that they all were so jovial. Pilar looked down toward her. "And you remember my mother—"

"Martha, right?" Elsie said. She descended the stairs.

Mercedes winced at the sound of her Anglicized name and limply shook Elsie's hand.

"Th-that's right," Pilar stammered. She knew her mother hated the name, but it was what the Americans all called her. Looking up to Virginia, who had remained on the porch standing silently near the door, Pilar said: "I'm sorry. Hello there. I don't think we've met."

"Oh," Elsie said. She turned from Mercedes. "That's Ginny. She helps me around the house with my kids, and with the babies while they're waiting to go to their new families."

"Nice to meet you, Ginny," Pilar said with a friendly wave. Virginia mumbled something Pilar took to be a greeting.

"Don't let her shyness fool you," Elsie said. "I've never seen anybody with a bigger heart and a better way with children. They'll be screaming their heads off, and I can't do a thing with them. Then

Ginny comes in, and in five minutes, all is happy and peaceful. I don't know how she does it."

Pilar looked down at the swaddled little girl in her arms. "I'm glad she'll be in good hands." She kissed her niece on the forehead and handed her to Elsie. "I'm sorry we've had to call on you again."

"Aw, there's nothing to be sorry for," Elsie said. "These things happen all the time. The preachers and politicians like to act like they don't, but they're too wrapped up in their own business to really give a hoot and holler about what happens with real folks."

"Thank you," Pilar said.

"And how's your sister, the baby's mother?" Elsie asked.

"She's fine, thanks," Pilar said, though Julia was far from fine. She was depressed and swilling at the roadhouse until all hours of the night again as soon as she had recovered from the delivery. Julia was taking the birth, John Goad's unceremonious departure, and the return to Anmoore hard.

"And did she give this little girl a name?" Elsie asked.

"We've been calling her Mary," Pilar said. She extended a finger for the baby to grasp with her tiny hand.

"Mary. That's a nice name. Hello there, Mary," Elsie said to the baby, but Mary's black eyes were fixed on Virginia, who had come down from the porch without anyone but the infant noticing, and stood at Elsie's side. "We're going to take good care of you."

An uncomfortable silence fell. There was nothing else for them to say or do. Jim cleared his throat and spoke up. "Well, I suppose we'd better be going."

"That is a fair bit of a drive for one day," Elsie said. She handed Mary to Virginia. "You folks have a safe trip home," Elsie told Pilar and Jim as they started down the stairs. "And don't you worry about little Mary. I already have a nice couple lined up who can't wait to get her."

Pilar turned back and asked: "Can you tell me where she'll be living?"

"No harm in that," Elsie said. "She's going to be a west-coast girl. The couple is from California."

Pilar frowned. "California. That's a long way."

"Yes," Elsie said, "but I promise, you have nothing to worry about. I insist on spending some time with all the prospective parents, and these are kind, loving people."

"That's good. Thank you," Pilar said. She knew she should feel assured, but it made her miserable to think of Mary growing up in such a distant place. Elsie had placed Julia's first daughter with a couple only a few towns over from where Pilar and Jim lived, and she was able to keep surreptitious tabs on the girl. With Mary across the country, she never would know anything of her again.

Pilar nodded and the three of them trudged toward the street. Mercedes was sad and disgusted with Julia. Jim was shocked that a perfectly healthy woman would give away her children like a litter of barn cats.

"It was good to see you again, Martha!" Elsie shouted across the yard. Mercedes looked back at her, and got into the car without a word.

* * *

The California couple took a baby closer to home. Two months had passed since the adoption fell through, and Elsie was beginning to feel desperate. She could not find another adoptive family. With three young children of her own, she could not afford to keep Mary much longer. Then her brother came rolling back into town.

"Good lord, Sammy," Elsie said as he climbed out of the big Buick. The car's spotless navy blue body and generous adornment of chrome glistened in the late-March sunshine. "Where'd you get that?"

"I won it!" Sam exclaimed, "playing cards over in Columbus." Sam was living wherever the cards were hot. The army had discharged him four months before, under circumstances that were still not entirely clear to Elsie.

"So you'll probably have it until the next card game," she said. "Come on in the house. We were expecting you two hours ago. Supper's on the table."

Sam eagerly tucked into his heaping plate of food. "Ginny, you make the best fried chicken I ever ate," he said. He grinned at her from the other end of the dining room table. His new gold-capped incisor gleamed like the Buick. "Better than my mom's even."

A very slight smile came to Virginia's thin lips, and she looked down at her plate. She never knew how to take a compliment.

Sam turned to Elsie. "So, how's the baby business, sis?"

"Not so good," she said. "A Spanish family from over in Anmoore brought me a little girl two months ago, and the new family fell through. I don't know what I'm going to do."

"What the hell's the matter with them spics, anyway?" Sam said. "Giving their kids away. We ought to send them all back to where they came from. We didn't just fight a war for that kind of trash." He helped himself to another piece of chicken and more mashed potatoes from the platter and bowl on the table.

"Sammy, for God's sake, don't say things like that," Elsie chastened. "A girl just got herself in trouble. Like any girl from anywhere can. Like plenty of white girls do."

Sam sucked a lodged strand of poultry from between his teeth. "Well, if their parents took a belt to them more often when they were growing up, they wouldn't get themselves in trouble. Spics and white girls."

Rather than descend into yet another shouting match with her brother, who would never change anyway, Elsie got up and went to the kitchen to get the fresh pot of coffee that had been brewing as they ate.

"So, how are you doing, Ginny?" Sam asked after his sister left the dining room. "You look as pretty as a picture. I couldn't hardly wait to get back here and see you again."

"I'm okay, Sammy," Virginia said. She pushed the last of the food around her plate with her fork to avoid meeting his gaze. "We've been busy with the kids."

"I'm ready to be busy with some kids of my own," Sam said. He grinned wider and winked at her. Sam craned forward, his elbows on the table. "I haven't told Elsie yet, but I got me a job with the city, down in Huntington."

"I been to Huntington a couple times. I growed up down in Logan," Virginia said.

"Huntington's growing like crazy," Sam said. His voice brimmed with excitement. "The steel mills and glass factories are booming. I'll have a good, easy job for life, working for the city."

"What kind of job is it?" Virginia asked.

"Sanitation engineer," Sam said. He reared back in his chair and pulled a cigarette from a pack of Winstons, lighting it with a battered Zippo. He was going to be a garbage man. "And that's just to start. My brother went to work for the city six months ago, and he's already been promoted twice."

Elsie returned from the kitchen with the pot of coffee. "What are you two conspiring about in here?" she asked.

"I was just telling Ginny about my new job," Sam said.

"You got a job?" Elsie was astounded.

"Yep. Down in Huntington, working for the city," Sam said proudly.

"Well, that's great, Sammy." Elsie tapped a Pall Mall from her pack on the table. "I was starting to think you'd make a career of gambling."

Sam laughed heartily. "No, that's just for fun. If I'm going to get married and have kids, I need a steady job."

"Get married and have kids?" Elsie asked, astounded again. "I didn't even know you had a girl."

"Ginny's my girl," Sam declared. "Ain't you, Ginny?"

Virginia dropped her fork, and it clattered to the floor. For a few seconds, Virginia was unable to form any kind of response. "Oh, Sammy, you're so full of shit," she finally said.

"You're not the first person to say that," Sam said, chuckling.

"Amen!" Elsie said.

"But I'm serious," Sam said to both of them. "I ain't married. Ginny ain't married. And now you've got that little baby with no home. What do you say, Ginny? Let's you and me get married and take that baby to Huntington."

"You're crazy, Sammy," Virginia scoffed. But she did not say no.

"What're you going to do?" Sam asked. "Hang around here at my sister's house, taking care of her kids and these cast-offs all your life?"

One other factor spurred Sam's enthusiasm for the idea. He was sterile. Only he and an army doctor knew it. From the time he was old enough to throw a punch, Sam had been an enthusiastic brawler, especially after he got some booze in him. He was a private in the army during the war, serving in the Canal Zone in Panama. The dearth of combat provided many opportunities to swill beer, throw dice and fight. His constant boasting did little to endear Sam to his fellow soldiers.

One night as he was sleeping in the barracks, a group of other privates bound him in a blanket and proceeded to beat him relentlessly. One took particular pleasure in pummeling Sam's scrotum with the belt from his uniform. The soldier made sure to land as many blows as possible with the heavy brass buckle.

For a month, Sam recovered in the post hospital. His testicles had swollen to the size of navel oranges. "There is no way to be certain at the moment," the army doctor told him, "but my guess is that the damage has been too extensive. It is highly unlikely you ever will father children."

"So, what do you say, Ginny?" Sam prodded. "Will you marry me?" He removed the garish gold and diamond-fleck ring from his pinky finger. It also came from a poker pot. Sam pushed his chair back from the table, got up and walked over to where Virginia was sitting. He took her chafed hand and slipped the ring onto her finger. "What do you say?"

Virginia looked at the ring, at Sam, at Elsie, and back to the ring. "You're crazy, Sammy," she said again. She looked at him, and then Elsie again. During his visits over the past months, she had suspected he fancied her, though she could not imagine why. No man ever had taken an interest in her, and the way he talked about the big times he had in one city or another, she presumed he had a string of women.

However, Sam had surmised correctly. Elsie always was kind and fair to her, but Virginia wanted a life of her own. She never dwelt on it, because she had no other prospects. Until that moment. She looked once more at the ring and then at Sam's eager face. "Okay," she said. "Okay, Sammy. Let's get married."

Three days later, a Justice of the Peace administered the minimal vows and signed the paperwork. Elsie and her husband served as the witnesses. Sam, Virginia and Brenda—"We're naming her ourselves," Sam had announced to his wife and sister, and then told them the name he had chosen—loaded up in the big Buick an hour after the marriage ceremony and drove the four hours south to Huntington.

Chapter 21

Steubenville, Ohio
February 1947

"You tell them that we don't want to, but we're bringing her back to them," Sam said loudly to Elsie. She was on the telephone with Pilar.

When Mercedes, Pilar and Jim brought Brenda to Elsie, they completed no adoption paperwork. Elsie was waiting for final word from the couple in California. They had no birth certificate because Brenda was born at home, and Julia had not bothered to file for one later.

Sam and Virginia took the girl without a thought about any of that, and now the murky legal situation had become problematic. The city would not include her on Sam's health insurance without proof she was legally his daughter, and they had learned that they could not register her for school when the time came.

Elsie put her hand over the mouthpiece of the phone. "Stop yelling at me, Sammy. That's not helping anything." She returned to the conversation with Pilar. "I understand that your sister is being difficult and your mother is worried about signing any document she can't read, but you have to do this. They can't even take her to the doctor, because she's not legally theirs."

Elsie paused, listening to Pilar on the other end of the line. Sam paced back and forth in the living room. "Sit down, Sammy. You're

driving me crazy," Elsie said. Then to Pilar, she added: "As you probably heard, my brother is saying he'll drive over there and leave her
with you, today, if you can't get one of them to agree to sign some
papers. And it's not just talk, I assure you … Okay … Okay. I'll wait
for your call."

"Well, what are they doing?" Sam asked, still on his feet.

"She's going to try again to talk some sense into her sister and
mother and call me back."

"This is ridiculous," Sam said. "I don't know how you deal with
these people all the time."

"It's just a hard situation, Sammy," Elsie said. She was tired of his
carping and condescension. "The mother—"

"Don't call her that," Sam snapped. "Ginny's her mother."

"The woman who had her," Elsie began again, "is a bit unbalanced,
and her mother is a Spanish widow who doesn't speak any English."

"I don't give a rat's ass about their problems," Sam barked.

"Just calm down, Sammy," Elsie said wearily. "They'll sign the papers. Pilar heard you ranting. They won't want you to bring her back."

Thirty minutes later, Elsie's telephone rang. "Yes, I have the papers
here," she said. "It's just one document for a witness to her birth to
sign and another saying you agree to Sam and Virginia adopting her.
I know a notary who'll stamp them for us later. All you need to do is
have one of them sign the papers … Okay … Very good. They'll be
there in a couple hours … Yes, I have the address. Thank you, Pilar."
As she returned the phone receiver to its cradle, Elsie said to Sam: "I
told you there was nothing to worry about."

"There's always something to worry about, especially with those
people," he grumbled.

Elsie ignored his comment. "Here are the papers, and here's the
address." Sam and Virginia had already signed the documents. "It
would be best if the mo … if the woman who had her signs them, but
her mother will do."

Sam, Virginia and Brenda drove the winding, narrow roads
through the bleak winter landscape to Anmoore. Virginia and Brenda

waited in the car. Sam walked up to the house and knocked on the door. Pilar answered.

"I'm Sam Blevins, and somebody needs to sign these papers," he said brusquely. The soldiers in Panama had not beaten the anger out of him, nor had marriage and fatherhood reduced his volatility. He was like an old box of dynamite. Not much jostling was required for him to explode.

"Hello, Mr. Blevins. I'm Pilar, Julia's sister." Sam merely glared at her. "Julia. Mary's mother."

"Her name is Brenda, and my wife is her mother," Sam said.

Pilar nodded. "Julia and my mother will sign the papers. Please come inside."

"I'd rather wait out here," Sam said.

"As you wish, Mr. Blevins." Pilar took the documents and disappeared into the house. When she returned, Mercedes came out with her. She extended her hand to Sam, and he shook it. He could not be angry with this woman whose weariness was so palpable that it made him tired to look at her. She spoke something to him in Spanish.

"My mother asks how Mary... uh ... Brenda is," Pilar said.

"Tell her she's happy and healthy," Sam said. "We've given her a good home."

Pilar translated his reply. Mercedes' lips remained clenched, but she nodded her head in grateful acknowledgment.

"Would your mom like to see her?" Sam asked. "She's out there in the car." He motioned toward the big Buick with his thumb.

Mercedes understood the question and shook her head no.

"Muchas gracias, señor," she said to Sam, grasping his hand again. Mercedes looked over his shoulder toward the car parked at the curb. Then she turned and went back inside the house.

Pilar handed the signed documents to Sam. "I hope this takes care of it, Mr. Blevins. I'm sorry if we caused you any trouble. My sister can be difficult sometimes."

"I understand that," Sam said. "Mine can be, too."

"Elsie?" Pilar asked. "I can't believe that. She always was very sweet with us."

"Oh, no not Elsie," Sam laughed, lighting a cigarette. "My other sister. That one's a handful." Sam looked over the papers with a judicial air, though he could barely read. "This should be fine. Thank you."

"Take good care of her," Pilar shouted across the yard as Sam opened the door to get into the car. He smiled and waved. Pilar stood on the porch in the cold wind until the Buick was out of sight.

Chapter 22

Pilar's husband Jim could have taken a job at the Union Carbide plant in Anmoore along with his brothers-in-law. Pilar had pressed him to, so they could live near her mother, but he loathed the idea of being confined in the factory. He gleefully applied for and accepted a job as a truck driver with a new long-haul company in central Ohio when a friend told him about an open position.

Pilar missed her family. Jim was glad to live six hours away from them. He got on well with Pilar's brothers, but Julia and her son Richard daily tested the limits of his patience and his generally cheerful demeanor.

Advancing to junior high had liberated Richard from the close oversight of the elementary school principal and his threat of banishment to the reform school at Pruntytown. Physically, Richard took after his uncles Luis and Manuel. Over the summer after elementary school and during first months of junior high, he grew a head taller than the other boys. He became more muscular and broad-shouldered with each passing month.

For Richard, his new found freedom and physical domination finally provided an outlet for his years of suppressed anger and frustration. He became one of the worst bullies in the junior high school.

He joined the football team and quickly gained a reputation for leaving opponents writhing on the ground in pain. Richard balked fiercely at every remonstration from Julia and Jim, who had unwillingly been drafted into the role of surrogate father.

The atmosphere frequently was tense at the little house in Anmoore after Pilar and Jim moved away. Mercedes, Julia and Richard survived mostly on the charity of Mercedes' sons. Julia still worked only part-time at the laundry. She spent most evenings at the roadhouse, leaving sixty-two-year-old Mercedes to deal with Richard.

"Beer and a bump, Dave," Julia said as she climbed onto her usual stool at the end of the bar.

"Hard day?" the bartender asked as he set the frosted mug of beer and the shot of bourbon on the bar. "You look beat."

"Hard day. Hard week. Hard month. Hard year. Hard life." Julia threw back the shot and took a long swallow of the beer. "My kid's driving me nuts."

"Boys his age can be tough," Dave said. "Especially without a man around to knock some sense into them every now and then."

"Tell me about it," Julia said. "You know he ran off again last week? He was gone for two days, and when I asked him where he'd been, he told me it was none of my goddamned business."

"He said that?"

"Yep. 'None of your goddamned business.'"

"My old man would have beat the shit out of me for that," Dave said. "My old lady, too."

"Well, he's too big for me to thump, or I would have, trust me," Julia said. She took another long swallow of the beer.

From a booth table along the wall across the dimly-lit roadhouse a man said: "Like Dave suggested, you need a man around."

Julia thought she recognized the voice, but it could not be. She turned on the barstool and looked into the shadow. "Art?" she asked.

He slid out of the booth and walked across the room. "That it is. How are you, babe?"

Julia nearly fainted. "Wha ... How ... Whe ... ," she sputtered.

Art Kelley laughed and slung his arm around her shoulder. It was less lanky than she remembered. "I just got to town this afternoon, and I figured you'd show up here sooner or later."

Julia looked at him, and then at the bartender. "Dave, you knew he was here?"

"He did," Art said. "But I swore him to secrecy. I wanted to surprise you myself."

Julia finished her beer in one more gulp. "Well, you certainly did that. Jesus, Art. What the hell are you doing here. It's been … it's been—"

"Five years and four months."

"A lot of water under the bridge," Julia said, though suddenly it felt as if he had never left. She was at once comforted and confounded by his reappearance.

"A whole world war," Art said.

"And a lot of other shit," Julia added. She thought of Art's baby, John Goad's baby, Richard, her father's death. "It's been a tough five years."

Art nodded and ordered a beer for himself and another for her.

Julia looked him over. Had she not been on her first beer, she would have sworn he was a hallucination. "You still haven't told me why you're in Anmoore, Art. I assume you haven't come for a job at the carbon plant."

"Christ, no," Art said chuckling. "Actually, I've come for you."

"You've done what?" Julia said. Surely she misheard him.

"I still think about you all the time, Julia," Art told her in the most sincere and tender tone she ever recalled hearing from him. He put a hand over hers that was resting on the bar. "I've regretted more times than I can count how things ended with us."

Julia did not think about Art all the time, though he did pop into her mind occasionally. It always made her sad. She had loved him, and he was the only man she had known who actually made her feel loved.

"But what do you want, after all these years?" she asked, indignant. "You think you can just waltz in here and back into my life, into my heart, because you want to? You don't get to do that."

"I was hoping we could try again," he said as calmly and sweetly as he could. "You know, if you're not with somebody else, which you don't seem to be."

"Oh, Artie, I don't know." Separating from him had been one of the most painful episodes in her life. Julia was not eager to risk that agony again. "How am I supposed to trust you now, after what happened before?"

"I'll make it right this time, Julia," he said. "I promise. I was a mechanic in the army, and I have a regular job at a garage in Cleveland. I've even rented a little apartment of my own. I'm as domesticated as a Labrador retriever. We'll get married and do it right."

Julia was exasperated. "You have no idea how many times I've wished for that, dreamed of it, that you would come back and want to marry me. But now, I just don't know, Art. It's too much somehow. It doesn't even seem real that you're here. Honestly, I don't know how I feel about you, or about us. I can't make such a decision on the spur of the moment."

"I understand," Art said. "I had this image in my mind of coming in here and sweeping you off your feet—"

"Well, life's not some fucking movie, Art," Julia said, interjecting.

"I know, I know," Art said. "It was naive. How about this? Just come with me now for a bit. We'll take a drive and talk, or not talk. We'll get some supper in Clarksburg and see what happens and how we feel."

Julia considered it for a minute as Art stood in front of her, his eyes pleading. "Alright, Artie," she finally said. "I have to admit, it's good to see you. Fucking crazy, but good to see you."

Though Julia had absolutely ruled it out in her mind as they were leaving the roadhouse, they ended up at Art's room in the motor lodge outside Clarksburg after dinner. They lay in each other's arms in the lumpy bed, and she began to cry. "Oh, Art," she said, "all these men I've been with the past five years, I never really wanted them. I just wanted you."

He lightly stroked her naked back, tracing down her spine and around her shoulder blades with his fingertips. He was unsure how to respond and desperate not to misstep.

"But I still don't know, Artie," Julia said. "You have to understand that this, tonight, it doesn't mean we're back together. It doesn't mean I'll marry you. It doesn't even mean I want to see you again." A tornado of competing and conflicting emotions swirled up inside her. "I need time to figure out what I think and feel and want now. Do you understand?"

He did, and he did not. But of one thing Art was certain: pushing too hard would drive Julia away. "I do," he said. He pulled her body tighter against his own and kissed her on the forehead. "In the morning, I'll take you home and go back to Cleveland. Then we'll take it a day at a time."

"Thank you, Artie." Julia snuggled her head against his chest and drifted off to sleep.

* * *

Art was persistent. He drove down from Cleveland whenever Julia would agree to meet him. Some days were pleasant and easy: walking on Pinnick Kinnick Hill, going to eat and to a movie, drinking beer at the roadhouse. Some visits were wildly passionate and they spent the entire weekend in his shabby motel room.

Other times, Julia would be hostile from the moment Art arrived or whip from hot to cold without warning. They would be whiling away an afternoon when some seemingly innocuous strain of conversation caused her to erupt, her body rigid as she ranted and the look in her eye distant and detached. "You can't just step back into my life like this!" she would shout and storm away, leaving him sitting alone in his car. Art would drive back to Cleveland and call her a day or two later, and she would be calm and want to see him again.

After five months, Julia—who was pregnant but not showing and had yet to tell Art—accepted his proposal. They were married at the city hall in Clarksburg. She put everything she owned into her leather duffle bag and the suitcase Mercedes had brought from Asturias but never used again, and Julia and Art drove off to Cleveland that afternoon.

Richard refused to go with them. Despite his litany of psychological and emotional troubles, or perhaps because of them, Mercedes agreed to let Richard stay with her in Anmoore.

Chapter 23

Anmoore
September 1947

My dear brother and sister-in-law,

It is a miracle. Julia married today. Despite the many kind and accepting things you wrote to me after I told you about her behavior, it has continued to torment me until this day. I know that God is merciful and will forgive her, and I feel that I can forgive her now—and maybe myself, as well. Her husband has a good job as an auto mechanic in a big city in Ohio about five hours from here, so I believe they will have a decent life. It is as if a double bow ox yoke has been lifted from my shoulders.

What wonderful news from you also. I cannot believe your "baby boy" Manuel and África have now had their third child. And a girl this time! I remember when Luis, Julia and my Manuel were the same ages, and it is one of life's sweetest times. Please tell Manuel that his Aunt Mercedes loves him every bit as much as the others, even though we have still only seen each other in photographs. Nothing against his brothers, but I believe he is the most handsome and dashing of them all!

I hope you are both healthy and well. I am only sixty-two, but I feel so old and worn out. I think back to the spinster aunts helping us with the harvests at Las Cepas, and I do not know how they did such work so far into their eighties. It must be something in the Asturian air.

Take care.
Mercedes González Conde

* * *

Anmoore, West Virginia
March 1948

At last, Mercedes was elated to be assisting Julia in childbirth. She still did not hold Art Kelley in particularly high esteem, but her oldest daughter was having a baby in wedlock, planned to raise it herself, and appeared to be genuinely happy with the entire situation.

Julia came down from Cleveland and stayed with Mercedes for the last month of her pregnancy. Many nights they sat up late, sitting in the kitchen and drinking coffee. Mercedes talked incessantly about Asturias. She told Julia stories her daughter had never heard, about her childhood exile from the farm, about her brother Antonio's adventures in Cuba, and about life at Las Cepas after her return.

"That Christmas night when I met your papa seems like it was yesterday," Mercedes told Julia one evening. "I can remember every detail."

"What was he like then, mama?" Julia asked.

"I first thought, 'What an odd little man,'" Mercedes said, laughing. "He didn't talk much, and he was overwhelmed by the crowd of people. The house was full, and your Uncle Antonio was dragging him around by the elbow introducing him to everybody. But then, when we met, and he looked into my eyes and said, 'Encantado,' my heart just melted. Calmness and warmth and generosity radiated from him like heat from a fire. Everybody in my family always said he was the kindest, gentlest man they ever knew. And he could be so funny and charming."

Julia was nine years old when the smelter closed, and eleven when the stock market crashed. "You know how much I loved papa," she said, "and I remember some of the good times we had before the Depression, but I mostly remember him being quiet and sad for so long. I wish I could've known him then, back when you were in Spain."

"I do, too," Mercedes said. "I wish he could have stayed like that. Life didn't treat him very fairly." She reached across the kitchen table and took Julia's hand. "There's so much I wish you could know about Asturias, so many people there I wish you could meet." Julia started to speak, but Mercedes pressed on. "You know how your sister is. She hates to be away from home overnight. And your brothers, well, after four years in the war, they'll never set foot outside this country again. But you're different."

Julia laughed. "That, I certainly am."

Mercedes had grown too serious to acknowledge the joke. "I know I was always angry about it, but you love to travel and explore."

"I did, mama, but I have a husband now, and a baby on the way. Those days are over."

"But it's in your nature, Julia," Mercedes said. "Of course, you're in no position to do it now. But promise me, promise me, that one day you'll go there, that you'll go to Asturias and know our family, that you'll walk along the high bluffs looking out over the sea, and through the eucalyptus groves at Las Cepas. Please, Julia, promise me you'll go."

Julia squeezed her mother's hand. "If it means that much to you, mama, of course I will, if I ever can afford it. To be honest, sometimes I still miss my wanderings, most of them anyway. And even though it ended disastrously, I really liked Mexico."

"You would love Asturias," Mercedes said. "I know you would. I can't tell you how much I've missed it, how much I miss it still."

Not long after that night, Julia was back on her parents' bed. Mercedes supportively talked her through the labor. Julia finally understood why her mother was the most popular midwife in every town for miles around for so many years. Pilar was in Ohio, so a young woman Mercedes was apprenticing knelt by Julia's side. But Julia barely noticed the girl's presence, she felt so connected to her mother.

Art paced and chain-smoked in the kitchen. Even had he been inclined to be in there with Julia, Mercedes firmly believed that men had no place in the birthing room.

"Okay, Julia," Mercedes said gently. "Now, push. Push as hard as you can."

The baby slid into Mercedes' hands. "It's a boy!" she announced with relish and lifted him up for her daughter to see.

"Can I hold him?" Julia asked.

"Of course, you can," Mercedes said. She was amazed and relieved that Julia had asked. "Let us clean him up a bit for you, and then you can hold him for as long as you wish."

"Thank you, mama," Julia said.

"You're welcome, sweet girl. It's good to see you so happy."

* * *

November 1948

Antonio González Conde sat in his favorite armchair in the parlour at Las Cepas and wept. The letter from his brother Ramón in St. Louis lay in his lap.

"What is it, Antonio?" María asked when she came into the room with his evening tea.

"My dear sister is gone," he croaked.

There was not much of Mercedes to waste away when the cancer came, just after Julia and Art's son Harry was born. She had taken great pleasure in the baby boy and in Julia getting some direction to her life. But a leaden feeling remained at her core to the end, the emanation of unaddressed traumas stretching all the way back to Casilda's death and Bernardo's abandonment.

Pilar returned from Ohio to help care for her mother. Mercedes died four days before Halloween 1948, in the bed where she gave birth to her children and where Antonio passed away. She had not seen her brother or Las Cepas in thirty-four years, but her two daughters and three sons were there with her in the little bedroom when she slowly exhaled a last, rattling breath.

They buried her in the Clarksburg cemetery, next to Antonio. Luis insisted on putting "Martha" on her gravestone.

Chapter 24

Cleveland, Ohio
August 1953

Harry knew he was not in his room when he woke, but it took a few seconds for him to remember they were at the neighbor's apartment. His three-year-old sister slept soundly beside him in the twin bed. The bluish glow of the television faintly illuminated the hallway. He got out of the bed and followed the light to the living room.

The rotund, elderly woman dozed in her big, threadbare armchair. Her knitting had fallen to the floor. Harry tugged at her skirt, and she stirred. "Mrs. Miller, where's my mom? When are we going home?"

She pulled the five-year-old boy onto her lap. "I don't know, dear. They said they'd be back hours ago. I hope they come before too long. I gave the baby the last of the formula, and she'll be hungry again soon."

"I want to go to my own bed," Harry said. "It's dark in there. The streetlight shines through our bedroom window."

"I'm sorry, Harry. I didn't know you were afraid of the dark," the old woman said.

"I'm not afraid!" he said, bristling. "I just don't like it."

"I understand," Mrs. Miller said, smiling. "When my boy was your age—that was his room you're in—he was afr ... he didn't like the dark either."

"Where is your boy, Mrs. Miller?" Harry asked.

She paused and looked away. "He didn't come back from the war, dear."

Harry did not know what that meant, but he had heard his father say it about friends of his. A lot of men must have stayed somewhere after the war.

"But we should get you back into bed, Harry. It's late." He slid off her lap. Mrs. Miller slowly hefted herself from the armchair. "And I'll put the bathroom light on for you. It makes the hall nice and bright."

As she tucked him in, Harry asked: "Where do my mom and dad go when they leave us here? They're always loud and their breath smells when they come back."

Mrs. Miller sighed. "They just go out and meet their friends, dear. You know, the way you see your friends at the playground, except they go to … to restaurants."

"I wish they'd stay home and play with me more," Harry said as he nestled under the wool blanket.

"I know, Harry," the woman said. She patted him lightly on the shoulder. "But I'm always glad when you and Laura and Elizabeth come to visit."

"I like it too, Mrs. Miller. You always make us good food. Mom doesn't like to cook so much." He rolled over and then sat halfway up. "And cookies! Can I have another cookie?"

"You really shouldn't, Harry," Mrs. Miller said, though her tone indicated she was not firm on the decision.

"Please?" he begged. "I won't tell."

She hated to deny any request from Julia and Art's children because she knew they frequently went without so many things children should have in their lives. "Well, I suppose half a cookie won't hurt," she said.

When Mrs. Miller returned from the kitchen, Harry already was asleep again. She switched on the bathroom light for him and returned to her armchair in the living room.

* * *

November 1954

"For Christ's sake, Julia, can't you do something with those kids?" Art shouted. "They're tearing the place apart." Six-year-old Harry and four-year-old Laura were playing a raucous round of tag in the cramped apartment.

Julia, with two-year-old Elizabeth on her hip, came into the living room. "Are your legs broken?" she snapped.

"I'm trying to watch TV here," he moaned. Art motioned toward the flickering black and white screen in its big, wooden casing.

"Well, I'm trying to wrestle some food into her, and I'm fucking exhausted," Julia said.

"You're always fucking exhausted," Art grumbled. "Maybe you ought to go to the doctor. I'm tired of listening to you complain about it."

"I am, Art," she said bitterly. "On Tuesday."

He had not actually meant it. Art knew she was constantly occupied with the children, and it weighed on her. Mothering did not come easily to Julia. Still, whenever Art tried to express his frustration, it came out as an attack. "You are?" he asked, his tone shifting from anger to concern.

"Yes, Art, I am." Julia was still angry. "Something's just not right. My stomach is killing me all the time, I ache all over, and every little thing tires me out."

"Well, with this gang of kids, I'm not surprised," Art said. "I'm sorry, Julia, for sniping at you like that." He got up and extended his arms. "Give me Lizzy. I'll finish feeding her. You sit down here and have a rest."

Julia's tone softened as well. "Thank you, Artie." She shivered as she sat down. "And I'm always cold. Or burning up."

Art awkwardly clutched Elizabeth in one arm and handed Julia the flannel throw from the sofa with the other.

"I hope the doctor can figure it out," she said. "Surely, I'm not going though the change of life already. I've been having a lot of female problems, too."

"Oh, hell, Julia, of course you're not," Art scoffed. "Your mother was only halfway through having babies when she was your age. You're just worn out by this pack of wild animals. Harry! Laura!" he yelled back through the apartment. "Knock it off! Your mom doesn't feel good."

* * *

"I'm sorry, Mrs. Kelley," the doctor said. Julia had returned to his office three days after her initial appointment to learn the results of the battery of tests. "I ... this is always so difficult, especially with a woman of your age."

"What? Spit it out, doc. You're scaring the shit out of me," Julia said.

"Mrs. Kelley, I wish more than you can know that there could be some mistake, but the tests are clear." He paused. "Where is your husband, by the way? Are you here alone?"

"Yes, doc, I'm here alone," Julia said impatiently. "He's at work. For Christ's sake, you act like I'm dying."

The doctor took a deep breath and looked at his hands resting on the desk, his fingers interlaced. He looked back up at Julia. "I am afraid you are, Mrs. Kelley."

As Julia had lain awake in bed the past three nights, that possibility kept worming its way into her mind, but she immediately pushed it away. "No, no," she said slowly to the doctor. "There must be some mistake. I ... I'm only thirty-five. I'm just tired from the kids. You know I have three under the age of six."

"Yes, I know, Mrs. Kelley," the doctor said. "I am very, very sorry. But the tests are definitive."

Julia felt as if she were sitting in a vacuum chamber with all the air sucked out. "But how? What? What is it?"

"We really should get your husband here," the doctor told her. "Nurse!" he called out from his office then looked back to Julia. "What is the telephone number for your husband's workplace, Mrs. Kelley? Nurse Davis here will call him for us."

"Uh, it's, uh." Julia could not call it to mind. "Oh, that's not necessary, doctor," she said.

"Please, Mrs. Kelley," the doctor insisted.

She thought about it hard and came up with the number at the garage. The nurse wrote it down and returned to the reception desk.

Regaining some of her composure, Julia asked: "So, what is it?"

"Wouldn't you prefer to wait for Mr. Kelley?" the doctor asked.

"No," Julia replied. "I want to know now."

"I really believe it would be best—" the doctor began.

"Damn it, doctor, just tell me," she ordered

"Okay, Mrs. Kelley," the doctor relented. "It is cervical cancer. This is the source of your extreme abdominal pain. And I am sorry to say it has metastasized."

"What does that mean?"

"It has spread, to other organs, and to the bones, which is why you have been aching generally."

Julia began to cry. "I don't understand, doctor. Why's this happened to me?"

The doctor reached into his pocket and handed her his handkerchief. "There is no explanation, Mrs. Kelley. I know it is little comfort, but it seems to strike randomly, and often among women around your age. There is nothing you could have done to prevent it."

The doctor was correct. His explanation provided no comfort. "So, what do I do now?" Julia asked.

The doctor's calm faltered. "In a less advanced case, I would recommend surgery and chemotherapy." He paused.

"But?" Julia said.

"But in your case, with it so advanced, I think this route of treatment would merely deprive you of any quality time you have left, with your husband and your children, without offering any real hope of extending your life."

The nurse stuck her head through the doorway. "I reached Mr. Kelley, and he is on his way."

"Thank you," the doctor said. He rose from his tufted leather chair, came around the desk and sat in the seat next to Julia. He always tried to maintain a certain distance and detachment from his patients, but her distress was overwhelming. He took her hand and looked into her eyes. "I promise you, we will keep you as comfortable as we can and give you as many good days as possible."

* * *

Pilar came to Cleveland to care for her sister. Julia's son Richard had joined the Air Force the day he turned eighteen, and he made no effort to get leave to come see his mother. Julia died on a bitterly cold January day in 1955 at a hospital in Cleveland. She had just turned thirty-six.

For half a year, Art struggled to care for their three children by himself. He and Julia had generally been poor parents when they were trying to do it together. Alone, he was a disaster. By June, he could not go on.

Jim and Pilar were out in their back yard, working on the fish pond they had dug the summer before. Pilar dashed into the house when she heard the telephone ringing.

"Hi, Pilar. It's Art."

"Hello Art," Pilar said, out of breath from her sprint to the kitchen. "It's good to hear from you. How are you? How are the kids?"

"Well, that's why I called, actually," he said in a dejected voice. "I … well … it's … ah. Oh, hell, Pilar, I just can't do this on my own."

She and Jim had been braced for this call since Julia died. "I know it's hard, Art. I thought your sister was going to help you."

"She did, for a while, but she couldn't stay here forever, and I'm at the end of my rope." He went silent on the other end of the line, waiting for Pilar to make the suggestion.

"What exactly do you want us to do about it, Art?" She anticipated what he had in mind. But if he was going to make this decision, and so dramatically alter the course of her and Jim's life, he would certainly have to ask.

He hemmed and hawed, never getting to the point.

"What, Art?" Pilar finally interrupted him. "What do you want?"

"Well, I know it's more, a lot more, than anybody could reasonably expect. But, could you … will you … will you and Jim take them?"

"Oh, Art. Mercy," Pilar said. Expecting the question did not make it any easier to swallow when it came. "Richard's barely been gone two years, and that was so difficult for us. And then Julia was sick. We're just beginning to feel that we have a life of our own."

"I know, Pilar. And I swear to God, I wouldn't ask this if I thought there was any other way." Art sounded so exasperated, she could not help feeling sorry for him. "But there's not. I'm not asking for myself. I'm asking for them. I can't give them the attention and life they deserve."

Pilar did not doubt the accuracy of that observation. "Let me talk to Jim," she said, "and I'll call you back."

Jim was up to his thighs in the fish pond when Pilar wandered back out into the sunny afternoon. When he saw the strained look on her face, he quickly sloshed out over to her. "Who was it?" he asked. "What's the matter?"

"It was Art."

Jim's thick jaw clenched. He slowly shook his head as he looked at the ground without speaking. When his eyes returned to Pilar, his jaw relaxed, and Jim reached out and gave her a bear hug. "You don't have to explain, or ask," he said. "We knew this day would come, and it's fine."

Pilar craned her neck up to look at his face. "Honestly, Jim? You don't mind?"

"Hell, no, I don't mind," Jim boomed, grinning. "Those little ones aren't Richard, and we've both wanted a family since the day we married. Well, now we'll have one." They had been trying to have children without success for a decade. Jim knew adoption had become their only option, and what better than to take in Pilar's nieces and nephew? Jim also thought Art was about as shiftless and useless a man as he had ever met. It would be the right thing to rescue those children.

Pilar loved him more at that moment than she thought it possible to adore another human being. She rubbed Jim on his thickly-muscled back. "I knew I was smart to let you buy me that cup of coffee back in Clarksburg."

Jim laughed and said as he waded back out into the pond: "Best decision you ever made."

184

Chapter 25

Huntingon, West Virginia
September 1957

Collecting garbage did not make for much of a living, even in Huntington. Until Brenda was five years old, she, Sam and Virginia lived in a two-room apartment above a hardware store across the street from the farmer's market sheds. Virginia and her daughter shared the one bed. Sam slept on the sofa. With only two windows at front and a small one in the kitchen to the rear, the apartment was perpetually gloomy. In the summer, it was stifling. What little breeze managed to find its way in the windows seemed only to bring the stench of the refuse from the market.

So Brenda was exhilarated when they moved to the four-room, wood frame house in Guyandotte on the outskirts of the city. The neighborhood had declined precipitously since its heyday as a town in the nineteenth century, before Huntington was founded. But a child does not notice such details. The house had a yard, and Brenda had a bed of her own. She was so content that the lack of indoor plumbing and trek to the reeking outhouse seemed only minor inconveniences.

It did not last. After six months, they moved to a different house two streets away. Brenda and Virginia were back to sharing the bed. Sam again bunked on the sofa, which was fine with his wife. Nine months later, they packed up their few belongings and moved to another house in the neighborhood.

They changed homes so frequently because Sam had played cards one night with the owner of these and several other similar properties. The man preferred not to have them sitting empty when they were not rented, and Sam preferred not having to pay rent. Over a beer and a shot of whiskey, they agreed that Sam, Virginia and Brenda could live in the houses in exchange for maintaining them, provided they were willing to depart on short notice if the man found long term tenants.

Eventually, even Sam tired of the nomadic lifestyle. He bought a little two-bedroom house in a tidy, leafy working-class neighborhood. In the kitchen of this house, one Sunday afternoon, he sat Brenda down at the table and told her she was adopted.

"That woman who had you," Sam said, "didn't want you, and we did. They were just no-account people. She didn't even know who got her pregnant."

It was too stark and sudden a pronouncement for Brenda to comprehend. When Sam called her to the kitchen, she thought he was going to punish her for knocking the drying laundry from the clothesline that morning while she was playing in the yard.

"I ... I don't understand," Brenda said. "What do you mean? You're not my dad and mom?" She had sensed for as long as she could remember that something was off with their family. It was an inchoate feeling, and she always suppressed it when it crept in. She never imagined that Sam and Virginia were not actually her parents

"Of course, we're your mom and dad," Sam said angrily. "I just told you, she didn't want you, so we took you."

"But ... but how did you find me?" she asked.

Sam was tremendously irritated by having to reveal even this much information to her. "Your Aunt Elsie knew the people, and she got you for us."

"But wh ... why didn't my mom want me?" Brenda asked. She began to cry.

"Ginny's your mother!" Sam thundered. "That woman's nothing to you. And don't you go telling anybody now that you're adopted. And don't ever talk to me or Ginny about it again."

"But why?"

Sam leaned across the table. His face was so close to hers that Brenda could smell the coffee and cigarettes on his breath. "Because it means you don't really love us if you do. And stop that crying. You're twelve years old, not some little baby."

But Brenda desperately wanted to know more. "Who was my mo … who is she? Where does she live?" she asked.

"I told you," Sam shouted, "I don't want you to talk about it. It doesn't matter who she is or where she lives. I'm only telling you now because we had to let them know at your school, and I didn't want you to hear it somehow from somebody there."

"But—" she began again.

"That is enough, Brenda!" Sam yelled even more loudly and smacked his hand on the table. "No more questions. And I'm telling you, don't you breathe a word of it to anybody, anybody, if you love us."

Virginia sat silently in the bedroom she shared with her daughter, listening to the conversation in the kitchen.

* * *

Dear Diary,

Today I turned thirteen. Aunt Elsie gave me some money for my birthday, and I bought you with it. I've got to find a good place to hide you because Dad can't ever be able to find you.

I wonder where my real mom is today and if she is thinking about me. I hope she remembers that it's my birthday. I wish I knew why she didn't want me. I guess she thought I wasn't worth keeping. Sometimes I think she was right. I'm always doing something that makes Dad mad.

I hate junior high. Some of the girls are so mean to me. They make fun of my shoes and my coat. I can't help it that they came from the Salvation Army. When I'm grown up I'm going to get a good job and buy myself nice clothes all the time. And if I ever have a little girl I'd never give her away and I'll always buy her pretty things. Everything she wants.

We're going to visit Aunt Elsie on Saturday and I'm soooo excited. Dad never yells at Mom and me when we're there and Aunt Elsie always is so nice to me and she always has a bowl of the best cookies. I can't eat enough of them fast enough. I wish we would stay for a month with her.

Brenda

* * *

Dear Diary,

I love these kinds of days. Dad and Mom and I went fishing at the river for the whole day. I caught two fish and Dad caught three but we threw them all back because he said it's not safe to eat them because of the stuff in the water from the factories. But I didn't care. It was so much fun just to catch them. Mom made fried egg and bacon sandwiches and Dad bought two bottles of pop for each of us and we had such a good time. Then when we got home we all sat on the porch and Dad played his guitar and sang us songs. He never yelled once all day and Mom laughed a lot. I wish it was like this all the time.

Brenda

* * *

Dear Diary,

Today was the last day of school. I'm so glad. I like learning stuff, but there are too many mean girls and boys. My friend Caroline and I are going to bicycle together every day. Dad brought a bicycle home for me two weeks ago from the dump where he works and fixed it up and painted it red. It is beautiful! He is always bringing things home and fixing them up for us to use. I can't believe what all people throw away.

We're going to visit Dad's other sister Aunt Louvina in Kentucky next weekend and I wish I could stay home or that we were going to Aunt Elsie's instead. Aunt Louvina always treats me like I don't belong there and she and Dad always end up drinking a lot of beer and fighting with each other. Mom doesn't like it either and we always try to go to bed early before they start yelling about something.

Brenda

* * *

Dear Diary,

I'm sorry I haven't written in so long. I stopped a couple years ago because it seemed like a little girl thing to do, writing in a diary. But I found you hidden in the bottom of the chest of drawers, and reread all my entries, and I feel like you are an old friend.

I'm in the spring of ninth grade now, my last in junior high. I met the sweetest boy, Tom, this year, and he has asked me to the prom! He's shorter than I am, but most of the boys are, and a little skinny, but he treats me like a princess, and he is the star shortstop on the baseball team. I go to all of his games (when they're at home or at other Huntington schools—Dad won't let me go on the bus to the games in other towns), and the other girls envy me, which is nice.

Mom and I went last weekend to buy my prom dress. It is the most beautiful thing I've ever had. White with lots of lace on the top and a flared satin skirt with a petticoat. Three more weeks till the dance. I can't wait!

I promise I'll keep writing, now that I've started again.

Brenda

* * *

Huntington, West Virginia
May 1961

"Wait for me at the fence at the back of the schoolyard," Virginia whispered to Brenda as she started out the door, so Sam could not hear her from the kitchen. "I'll bring the money to you there."

"Thanks, Mom," Brenda whispered back and kissed Virginia on the cheek.

After classes ended on sunny Fridays, many of Brenda's friends went to the nearby dairy shop for a hotdog, Coca-Cola and ice cream.

Sam always refused to give her the dollar and a quarter it cost, even when he had the money. Embarrassed by standing around and watching the others enjoy their treat, Brenda usually made some excuse to beg off.

It was one of the thousand things that made Virginia furious with Sam, though she never confronted him about it. He shouted at her enough without provocation. She did what she could to scrape together a little spending money for Brenda, gathering the loose change which slipped from Sam's pocket and into the crevices of the sofa and selling the crafts she made in her free time.

In the evenings, Virginia liked to crochet, mostly doilies and little teacups which she would starch so they would stand upright. She sold them, for a quarter or fifty cents, to the middle-class women for whom she cleaned house. Sometimes she went door to door with them in the nicer neighborhoods of the town. A lady who lived near Brenda's school had ordered eight of the teacups, and on this Friday, Virginia was delivering them and collecting her payment.

"Here you go," Virginia said, slipping the folded dollar bills through the chain-link fence to Brenda. "Have a good time, and don't stay too long so he doesn't know you were there." She never used Sam's name in conversation, just an acidic "him" or "he."

Brenda unrolled the little clutch of cash. "Oh, Mom, this is too much," she said. "I only need a dollar and a quarter. Here." She pushed two of the bills back through the fence. "And I'll bring you the change tonight."

"No," Virginia said. She refused to take the money. "Save it somewhere he won't find it, and go again next week." She turned and walked away down the alley.

Chapter 26

Many of the Scots-Irish Protestants who made their way to the United States in the mid-eighteenth century were a ragtag, unrooted lot. Their great-great-grandparents had supported the English king in the conquest of Scotland. Their grandparents had gone to Ireland to help the English subjugate the Catholic natives there. They were tired of being a despised minority always fighting for an English aristocracy which treated them like the mercenaries their forebears had been, and as many as could set sail for the American colonies and settled on the Appalachian frontier. They hoped that in the isolation of the mountains they could tend their bit of land and make a life far removed from the political intrigues in which their families had been embroiled for centuries.

* * *

Waynesville, Ohio
June 1983

Robert was captivated by the image in the black and white photo, though he thought his great-grandparents inscrutable with their emotionless staring into the camera. "What were their names? Where did they come from in Spain?" he asked Pilar.

"Mom's name was Mercedes"—Mer-THEY-des, she still pronounced it—"but everybody called her Martha. Dad was named Antonio. She came from Barcelona, but he was Gallego. He came from Galicia. He was an orphan."

Robert's gaze lingered on the creased photo. He wanted to know everything about these people. He was familiar enough with Spanish geography to know those two places were far apart. "How did they meet?" he asked.

"Mom's family had a farm, and Dad worked there," Pilar said. "He never talked about it much, but I know things were hard then, and he had a lot of trouble finding work. That's why he came to America, back in 1912, and went to work at the zinc smelter in Anmoore. Mom came two years later."

For as long as he could remember, Robert had felt an intense attraction to all things European, a craving for a sense of historical identity which seemed to be located somewhere across the Atlantic. Logically, it made little sense. He knew nothing about his father's Scots-Irish ancestors. They were faceless, nameless people who arrived in the English colonies thirty years before the American Revolution.

Still, the countries of his paternal ancestors' origins were enough for fourteen-year-old Robert to latch onto Britain. He had shown no interest at all in his mother's Spanish heritage, partly because he knew only his biological grandmother's name, partly because his vibrant Anglophilia fostered disdain for the Castilian kingdom. Spain was the dark-hearted country that launched the Inquisition in 1478 and the Armada against England eighty years later. More generally, Robert was a child of Anglo-America, which ignored its Spanish history for the most part, and of Protestant Appalachia, which distrusted any-thing Catholic.

But now, with a story and a photograph of real European great-grandparents, Robert's curiosity swelled. "How did he get to Barcelona? What was her family like? Did they like him? Are our rela-tives still there, in Barcelona? Have you met them?" he asked Pilar, in rapid fire succession.

She laughed lightly and said: "I'm sorry, honey, but I don't know any more than what I told you. Nobody here talked to Mom's people in Spain after she left. One of my brother Lou's daughters went over there a few years ago, but I don't know much about it. I remember she said the ones she met were rich, had some kind of store and properties, but that's all I know."

Robert was disappointed his great-aunt could not tell him more, but his questions about Mercedes and Antonio faded to the back of his mind as they spent the next two hours examining the photographs and listening to Pilar talk about her siblings and their years growing up in Anmoore.

"Who is that boy?" Brenda asked. He appeared to be about ten and was wearing a short-pant suit and saddle oxfords. In the photo, he and Mercedes stood in the grass on a little knoll with a row of humble clapboard dwellings in the background.

"That's Richard," Pilar said. Pain and reluctance edged her voice. "He was Julia's oldest boy."

Brenda peered at the picture. Her older brother. "Where is he?" she asked. "You've never mentioned him."

It was clear Pilar would rather keep it that way, but she said: "Richard had a lot of problems his whole life." She looked at the photo again. "He gave us all fits. He came and lived with Ed and me for a couple years after Julia moved to Cleveland. That was real hard."

"Where is he now?" Brenda asked.

"Nobody really knows," Pilar said. "I don't even know if he's still alive. After Richard got out of the air force—that must have been about 1958—he got married and had two kids and moved to Florida. It seemed that he had finally gotten his life on track." She looked long again at the photo. "But then, a few years later, he just up and left one day. Got in the car without saying anything to anybody and disappeared."

Brenda and Robert were stunned.

"I think it was 1966 or '67, when the phone rang one day, and it was the police in California. They said Richard was in some kind of asylum out there and had given them our name and number. Well, Jim told them that we'd had all the trouble we could take with Richard and hung up the phone. That was the last we ever heard about him."

Pilar returned the photograph to the box. She pulled out another, of her, Julia and their brother Manuel's wife. "Oh, I love this one."

The buoyancy returned to Pilar's voice, but Richard's ghost seemed to hang in the air. "It's from, let's see, 1949. We had gone to get our hair done together and bought new dresses, and we were on our way to a big dance at the VFW hall. Oh, we used to have such fun together."

Pilar's descriptions of Julia were always limited to the platitudes one would expect from a devoted sister speaking to her long-lost niece about the woman's long dead mother: "She was the sweetest girl I ever knew." "I loved her so much." "We always had the best times." Robert already had two grandmothers he adored: Virginia, and Tom's mother, Shirley. He was interested in information about Julia, but he felt no connection to her.

Brenda's emotional reaction, as they looked at the photos and listened to Pilar's stories, was more complicated. "I've always felt like a chicken hatched from an egg," she had told Pilar during their first meeting. Now, she had a brother and sisters, aunts, uncles and cousins. Her mother was no longer just a name on a piece of paper.

Yet finding her family and learning about Julia did not answer the question which had tormented Brenda from the day Sam told her she was adopted: why didn't my mother want me? The revelations about Julia's struggles, and that she had put another daughter up for adoption, helped Brenda understand it cognitively. But knowing some new facts did not relieve the pain nor repair the psychic damage of Julia's abandonment.

Brenda had always felt hurt when she thought about her unknown birth mother, but Julia's transformation into an actual person spurred a new, intense anger. Although it was a legitimate reaction, Brenda felt guilty about it. She suppressed her fury whenever it rose. "I just should be happy I found them," she would tell herself, "and forget about Julia. She was a mess and is nothing to me."

When she met her family for first time, on a crisp November afternoon in 1982, it seemed as if they had been standing watch every day for her return. Brenda and Tom were surprised to see such a crowd of people when they entered Pilar and Jim's house. Mercedes and Antonio's three sons were there with their wives, as well as Harry, Laura and Elizabeth, whom Pilar and Jim had adopted after Julia's death.

At first, everyone stood there in the packed living room smiling anxiously. None of them had experienced such an emotion laden moment in their lives. Pilar's brother Antonio, thick tears filling his big eyes, stepped forward and said: "You look so much like Julia, it's like she just walked into the room after all these years." Brenda's apprehension and fear evaporated as they introduced themselves and each person hugged her tightly.

Then everyone started talking at the same time. Brenda whipped from one ongoing conversation to another, responding to a barrage of questions and comments and trying fretfully to keep all their names straight. The feelings racing through her were so intense that Brenda could hardly breathe. The entire scene unfolded like a fantastic dream, though its joy and beauty exceeded anything Brenda had envisioned over the years when she imagined such a reunion.

For decades, imagining it was as close as Brenda had come to finding them. She and Tom married when she was twenty years old. She felt that getting from under Sam's roof finally gave her the license to look for her family. But Brenda was terrified by the prospect of finding them. Her mother had not wanted her, so why would any of her relatives, whoever they were? Her search never went beyond looking up the name Ribas in the telephone directory of every city she visited on vacations. She would read the names and touch them on the thin page, as if one would touch her back.

Brenda was thirty-four when her best friend Cathy decided to act, after another angst ridden conversation with Brenda about her constant sense of displacement and abandonment. Brenda knew only her mother's name and that some of Julia's siblings had lived in Clarksburg. Cathy got a copy of the city's phone book at the library. Four Ribases were listed. She wrote down the names and numbers and started calling when she returned home. The first three had never heard of Julia. The last was Julia's brother Luis.

Luis gave her Pilar's name and telephone number in Ohio, and Cathy drove directly to Brenda's house to tell her. The discovery was too important, it felt too powerful, to report over the telephone. As she left, Cathy said, pointing to the piece of paper Brenda still clutched in her hand: "I don't know what you'll do with that, but if I were you, I'd call."

Brenda carried the paper around with her for four months. She could not muster the courage to call. She would take it out, unfold it and look at the name and number, nearly faint from anxiety, and stuff it back into the bottom of her purse. But the harder she tried to ignore it, the stronger the anxiety grew. Emotions are not like plants; they do not require the light of consciousness to grow.

Eventually, the stress became more than she could bear. Brenda was lying awake every night, thinking about the piece of paper in her purse. Her digestive system, always irritated, was a complete wreck.

One Saturday morning, Brenda closed and locked her bedroom door and picked up the telephone receiver. She put it down and sat for a minute looking at the name and number on the paper. She picked the phone up again and dialed. A woman answered. Brenda's throat was clenched and dry, but she managed to ask, "Can I speak to Pilar Miller?"

"This is Pilar Miller," the woman said.

"I'm Brenda Stevens." She tried to swallow. "Julia's daughter."

"Oh, my," Pilar said.

"I don't want anything from you," Brenda added quickly. "I just want to know any important family medical history, for me and my kids."

"Oh, honey," Pilar said, sniffing and wiping her eyes, "I thought you'd never call. I've been waiting ever since Lou told me your friend called him. It's been months."

Brenda had so steeled herself that Pilar's response only made her more confused. "I ... I ... wasn't sure about it ... about calling. I still ... I ...."

"It's okay, it's okay," Pilar said. "Hold, hold on a second." Brenda heard her call away from the phone, "Jim! Jim! It's Brenda! Yes, Julia's girl!" Pilar returned to their conversation. "I'm sorry, honey, I had to tell my husband. We were afraid you'd lost the number or didn't want to talk to us."

Didn't want to talk to them? Brenda almost laughed at the irony. "I've wanted nothing more than to talk to you, well, to my mother or somebody, for most of my life. I always thought you wanted nothing to do with me. "

"Of course we've wanted you, to have you back in our lives. You're part of our family, and family is the most important thing in the world."

Brenda began to sob so hard that she had to put down the telephone and lie back on the bed. Pilar sat down in a kitchen chair and wept. She held the receiver to her ear and painfully listened to thirty-six years of agony pouring out of her niece.

Chapter 27

August 1984

As a child, Brenda longed for something—material or emotional—nearly every day. The deprivation coloured most of her adult attitudes, desires and actions. Shopping became her favorite form of recreation. She was determined that her children, Robert and Marilyn, would receive a surfeit of the parental love that Virginia had shown her when she could summon the energy amid Sam's relentless tyranny. Brenda showered her children with presents, whether she could afford them or not. Every August, their closets swelled with new clothing for the school year. Her heart was large. Her love was deep. Her inner woe was vast.

From the week after she turned eighteen, Brenda had worked full-time for the telephone company. In those days, there only was one: AT&T. Additionally, every November and December, their house turned into a ceramics cottage industry. Each day after work, until late into the night, Brenda painted angels, crèches, trees and Santas by the carload to sell for the cash to buy dozens of Christmas gifts for Robert, Marilyn and Tom. There were so many that the children grew weary of unwrapping on Christmas morning, and Brenda had to prod them to remain focused on their task.

Other than Christmas, Brenda's great passion was the summer vacation, and Robert adored these far-flung excursions. Brenda, Sam and Virginia never had taken one. Accordingly, she, Tom and their children took one every year without fail, for the full two weeks she had off from the telephone company and Tom from the bank where he worked making loans.

Brenda could have made a career in logistics. The scope of these summer trips often stretched the bounds of physical ability. She crafted them to the smallest detail, mapping driving routes, reserving hotels at every stop, purchasing as many entry tickets as possible in advance by mail.

She funded these grand excursions with another round of spring-time ceramics: summer planters shaped like frogs and baskets, and eggs and bunnies of all sizes and configurations for Easter. Tom, more or less, enjoyed the trips once they were underway. But he made it clear from the start that they were Brenda's project. He would have been equally content to spend the two weeks off work at home, golfing and tossing a baseball in their yard with Robert.

Brenda's vacation expeditions reached their apogee in the summer of Robert's fifteenth year. To her regular income and the seasonal ceramics sales, she had added selling cosmetics at home shows. Brenda worked as tirelessly and obsessively at the makeup business as she did in every other venture she undertook. Not only was she flush with cash by the start of summer, but she would be honored for her voluminous sales totals at the company's annual convention in Philadelphia in July. Sam never acknowledged anything she did as she was growing up, and Julia's abandonment had hobbled her self-confidence. Brenda craved public recognition. The anticipation of the convention filled her with ecstasy.

The trip contained enough activity for three vacations. They would drive from their home in western West Virginia to Niagara Falls, then on to Toronto, Montreal, New Hampshire, Boston, Cape Cod, Cape May and Philadelphia. In two weeks.

It was nearly midnight as they approached Montreal in their enormous, light blue Pontiac station wagon. Marilyn was stretched out on the back seat asleep, but Robert was too excited to rest. He perched as far forward as he could, hanging halfway over the back of the front seat, and peered intently at the city lights in the distance.

A dense string of multicolored incandescence hugged the ground along the horizon. In the center rose a dark hill topped by a huge pointed dome. It gleamed in white light against the black sky. Robert could not take his eyes off it. "What is that?" he asked his parents, pointing toward the dome.

"Have no idea, Buddy," Tom replied, exhausted already from the endless driving. "We'll find out tomorrow."

They learned from the hotel desk clerk the next morning that they had seen the Oratory of St. Joseph, a nineteenth-century Catholic basilica and the largest church in Canada. Robert insisted they visit. Brenda added it to their itinerary.

Robert had never set foot in a Catholic church. When he did on that day, he experienced a sense of peace and holiness he had not known in his life. And he had never seen anything so beautiful. He walked through the Neo-Gothic nave with his mouth gaping open and gazed up into the soaring dome. The Baptist church they attended was typical: low-ceilinged and devoid of grandeur. This place transported him to a different world.

Robert read in the guidebook that the thousands of crutches they saw hanging along the walls and stuffed into every recess were left by the pilgrims who had arrived physically impaired and walked away on their own power. They had prayed for intercession from a priest called Brother André, who had preached and healed at a small chapel on the hilltop in the nineteenth and early part of the twentieth century.

The church and the story were a revelation for Robert, but they also felt like a dangerous flirtation with the Devil. In their doctrinally strident Baptist church, most other Christian denominations were condemned as false, and the Holy See most of all. They believed that a Pope would one day be the Antichrist. Just that spring, his church had withdrawn from an interfaith boys' basketball tournament on dogmatic grounds. "What if the Episcopal priest wanted to say the prayer before the game?" the youth minister had asked the disappointed team. Well-indoctrinated, the boys required no further explanation.

Now, however, Robert was thrown unexpectedly into a crisis of faith, though he did not really recognize it as such. He just felt tremendously confused.

Doubts had begun to squirm in the back of his mind for the first time when they met his mother's family. They were the first Catholics he knew. He questioned, though only to himself, how such good, loving people could be headed for eternal damnation. Now this kindly looking Canadian priest in the little black-and-white photo in the brochure, who had apparently helped heal all these people. How could he be in Hell, burning forever? And what about this strange inner comfort he felt in the Oratory of St. Joseph? It gnawed at him for the remainder of the day.

Robert did not mention any of this to his parents as they toured Montreal. They never discussed religious matters, or much else of any significance. They were an openly affectionate family, and they spent most evenings and weekends together, but Brenda and Tom were not ones for talking about personal things. The lack of reflection and communication did not consciously trouble Robert. They never had those sorts of discussions, so it didn't occur to him that things could be otherwise. It would have been like an aboriginal child in the jungle suddenly wondering why they had no electricity. Robert accepted without a second thought that this new religious quandary was his to sort out alone.

But for the moment, the wonders and pace of the vacation distracted him. The experience at the basilica in Montreal slipped into the recess of his mind as they followed the tourist trail through Boston. The Revolution was the only part of US history which interested Robert, and he was astonished by the age of the buildings they saw.

They had taken a summer vacation for as long as he could remember, but they usually went to the beach, professional baseball games and amusement parks. This was their first visit to New England and the first to include so many historical sites. Huntington, where they lived, was founded in 1871. To Robert, a hundred-year-old farmhouse seemed ancient. Here he saw buildings from the seventeenth century. Robert could not drink in enough to slake his thirst.

Chapter 28

Dear Aunt Pilar,

Thank you very much for the money and the card. It always makes me happy that you think of me, and I am so glad we found you.

I got lots of great things for my birthday, the biggest being a car! I sure am glad I passed that driving test last month. I opened this little package from Dad, and it was a Volkswagen key. I didn't know what to think, and he told me to look out the window, and there it sat on the street in front of the house. It is a silver Scirocco. Dad bought it from one of his friends and had it painted and it looks like new. I love it. Maybe one day Mom and Dad will let me drive to visit you.

I am enclosing two calligraphies I did for you. They are prayers I got from a Catholic devotional book I found at the library. I joined a calligraphy club at the museum a few months ago, and I like it very much. I can sit in my room for hours at night, with just candles for light, and work on it. I feel like a monk at some monastery in the middle ages. Mom gave me a really nice set of pens for my birthday, and I bought the parchment with the money you sent me.

I hope you're well, and I'm looking forward to us visiting you at Thanksgiving. Your turkey is the best, and I can't wait to have some of Aunt Elizabeth's chocolate chip cookies. I have to get the recipe from her this year.

Love,
Robert

* * *

Huntington, West Virginia
September 1985

Robert looked around nervously as he ascended the steps to the open doors of St. Joseph's, Huntington's primary Catholic church. His parents would have been no more horrified had someone told them they saw him entering a strip club. He slipped inside quickly and sat in the back pew.

The Gothic Revival nave was illuminated only by the early evening sunlight coming through the stained glass windows and by the two spotlights shining on the large crucifix in the apse. It was aesthetically more pleasing than the Baptist church he attended every Wednesday night and twice on Sundays with his parents, but St. Joe—as everyone in the town called it—had none of the grandeur of St. Joseph's Oratory. A year had passed since that day in Montreal, but the same sense of peace and stillness rose again within him as soon as Robert entered the silent nave.

After half an hour in the stillness, a tall, burly, slightly hunch-shouldered priest plodded from the vestry. He stopped, bowed at the waist and crossed himself before the spotlighted crucifix and then finished tidying around the altar from the Saturday evening mass. As he came up the center aisle, the priest noticed Robert. "Say one for me," he called over as he passed.

A bit startled, Robert said: "Excuse me?"

The priest stopped and looked back. "A prayer. Say one for me." Then he continued with his work, stacking and straightening the missalettes, brochures and offering envelopes on the table in the vestibule. As he passed again, this time down the side aisle next to Robert, the young man asked: "Is it okay if I come back in the morning, for the mass?"

The priest crunched his brow and looked at him curiously. "Well, of course. Why wouldn't it be okay?"

"I'm not Catholic," Robert said tentatively.

"You don't have to be Catholic to pray!" the priest declared and let loose a robust laugh that echoed through the empty church. He tromped off toward the side door midway down the nave. As he started out, the priest said without looking back to Robert: "I'll leave those lights on if you'll be in here longer. I'm going next door to eat my dinner."

"Thank you," Robert said. "I would like to stay for a bit more."

"No rush, sit as long as you want," the priest said. "Hope to see you tomorrow."

Brenda and Tom were out of town for the weekend. They had left seventeen-year-old Robert at home alone overnight for the first time in his life. Marilyn was staying with a friend. Robert relished the freedom and having the house to himself.

He had wanted to come to St. Joe for months, but he could never find the courage, or come up with a good explanation for his parents about where he was going. Robert had grown increasingly frustrated and angry with them over the past year. The more his doubts about their church and its rigid, exclusionary doctrines grew, and the more he tried to avoid the host of Baptist youth group activities, the harder they pressed him to participate.

That spring, Robert had declined an offer from the youth minister to narrate a religious puppet show because it conflicted with his high school elections. He was running for student council president. His parents were greatly displeased when the youth minister informed them—Robert was too afraid of their disapproval to tell them himself—and Tom told him gravely one night in his bedroom: "You need to get your mind right with God."

Further complicating the turmoil swirling inside him, Robert was in love with his debate team partner. Isabel was Catholic, and she worshipped at St. Joe. Isabel did not share his affection—which he never even came close to revealing—but she was happy to talk about her faith and answer his endless questions about it. Robert was glad to learn about Catholicism, and focusing on the topic allowed him to surmount the social anxiety which usually rendered him mute around girls.

Despite the concern someone would see him and tell his parents, Robert attended his first mass that Sunday morning. Over the following year, he went regularly on his bicycle to St. Joe on weekday evenings. He told his parents he was going to the park or just out for a ride. He sat alone in the church, thinking and feeling. When he was there, it seemed as if he had recovered a piece of his identity that he did not even know existed. With increasing frequency over the months, he also spent time in the living room of the rectory next door, chatting with the two parish priests.

Father Moore was an irascible, voluble old West Virginian. He was the priest Robert encountered on that first evening. Father Callahan hailed from Massachusetts and was his compatriots' opposite: diminutive, avuncular, almost bashful. "The sweetest, truest man of God I've ever known," Father Moore once told Robert. The priests had met in seminary and served together ever since, almost fifty years. Father Moore's simple declaration, "You don't have to be Catholic to pray," endeared him to Robert, though the priest's imposing physical size and forceful personality also scared him a little.

Sprightly little Father Callahan, however, Robert loved unequivocally, and the priest reciprocated his sentiments. Father Callahan was the supportive and gentle grandfather that life had denied Robert. Robert was the beloved grandson celibacy had denied Father Callahan. One summer evening as they strolled over to the church to turn out the lights and lock the doors, Father Callahan told him: "When I'm Pope, I'll appoint you Secretary of State!"

When Robert was nineteen, Father Callahan suffered an aortal aneurism. He lay placidly unconscious in his upstairs bedroom at the rectory, breathing softly when Robert came in to see him. The housekeeper left when Robert came in, and Robert talked to the old man about the things they always discussed: history, theology, architecture, vegetable gardening. Father Callahan looked so small and childlike under the sheet on the twin bed. A single lamp on the bedside table cast a faint glow across the oak paneled room.

Robert had brought a little gold-painted plaster frame with a picture of Christ pasted on it. He had made it in Vacation Bible School when he was a child and had placed it beside the bed of Tom's father as he lay dying of cancer when Robert was five years old. Sitting in the rectory, he put it on Father Callahan's bedside table beneath the lamp. For more than an hour, Robert sat on a wooden chair beside the bed and recalled the many pleasant, easy evenings he had passed with his friend.

Eventually, the housekeeper returned and clambered around the room, making it clear that she was ready for Robert to go. He stood and leaned over the old man and kissed him on his bald head. "Sleep well, Father," he said. He lightly squeezed Father Callahan's boney shoulder beneath the sheet. As Robert walked toward the door, the catatonic priest stirred. He grunted fiercely, as if he knew Robert was going for the last time.

Two days later, Father Callahan died. Father Moore asked Robert to serve as an honorary pallbearer at the funeral. Robert accepted. Although he no longer lived with his parents, Robert worried what they would say if they found out. At the same time, another part of him did not care.

Chapter 29

S ix days after his eighteenth birthday, Robert packed all his belongings and crammed them into his Volkswagen. He began, working furiously, as soon as his parents departed for work. He left a long letter for them on the desk in his bare bedroom, pouring out his feelings and frustrations and asking them not to look for him. Paralyzed by his need to be the good boy and unable to face any kind of interpersonal conflict directly, Robert could do it no other way.

He had started college earlier that month. Two better, out of state schools had accepted him, but he decided to attend the mediocre local university instead. He could go there without paying tuition. His desire to sever all reliance on his parents trumped getting a good education.

As long as they were paying his bills, Robert reasoned, he would not be free. Late in the summer, he got a job hauling ice and kegs and cleaning up at a bar near the college. On the eve of his birthday, he rented the shabby little apartment to which he transported his things on this late-September morning.

Robert was spent, physically and emotionally, after unloading the car and stacking everything at one end of the apartment's living room. He had no furniture. He rolled his sleeping bag out on the wooden floor and crawled in. As he drifted off to sleep, Robert considered it a good sign that his stomach did not hurt. He had been devouring antacids all day every day for a year.

The next morning, when Robert emerged from his French class at the university, Tom was standing in the hall. He looked distraught, his eyes puffy and red.

"You need to come home, Buddy," Tom squeezed out of his dry throat. "Your mom is just sick about this."

"I ... I can't," Robert said. He swallowed the powerful urge to cry. "Didn't you read my letter?"

Tom reached into the inner pocket of his blazer and withdrew the folded letter. "Of course I read it, about ten times." He unfolded it and began to read from Robert's missive.

"Don't," Robert said. "I don't want to debate it with you. I ... I said what I had to say, and ... and—"

"Just come home with me," Tom pleaded.

Robert was not prepared for this face to face confrontation. He had believed naïvely that his parents would read the letter, understand his position and leave him alone. Now, standing in the narrow hallway as students bustled past to their classes, he did not know what to do.

"At least show me where you're living," Tom said. "Let me drive you back."

Robert could resist no more. "Okay," he said, and they walked together in silence to Tom's car in the university parking lot. They drove in silence to Robert's apartment.

"Oh, Buddy, you can't stay here," Tom said as they entered the apartment. He pointed to the old, unventilated natural gas heater in the fireplace, its row of blue flames whooshing. "That thing'll kill you in your sleep." Motioning to the sleeping bag on the wooden floor, Tom added: "And you don't even have a bed."

"It's not that bad," Robert said. "And I can't come back. I just can't."

Tom stood in the middle of the gloomy living room, looking around with his hands in his pockets. Robert's overflowing suitcase was open in one corner. A row of books sat on the floor beneath the drafty windows looking out on the wet, grey day. "Just think about it then," Tom said. "You don't have to live like this, and we want you to come home." He could not contain his agony any longer. With "home," Tom gasped and wept. He grabbed Robert and hugged him tight. "Come home," he choked out through his tears.

Robert's head was swimming. Too many emotions were competing for dominance within him, which left him feeling numb to all of them. He hugged Tom back. "I'll be okay," he told Tom as they released each other. "Don't worry."

Tom wiped the tears from his face with his hand and opened the apartment door. A cold draft swept in, and the blue flames of the space heater flickered in the rush of air. "Turn that thing off when you go to sleep tonight," he said. "I'll buy you a safe one tomorrow and have it installed."

* * *

Robert quickly settled into the routine of taking classes at Marshall during the day and working in the Hunter's Run bar at night. He had always been outgoing and precocious with adults, but agonizingly shy and awkward with his peers, so the lack of the traditional college freshman life agreed with him. Robert got on well with the bartenders and cocktail waitresses, who treated him like a younger brother. Most of them were already bar-work veterans in their mid- to late-twenties. Several took an occasional course at university and maintained at least the public fiction that their saloon jobs were temporary, but for most this path was permanent.

Robert's social life consisted primarily of regular visits after work to an illegal after hours club in the basement of an old warehouse by the railroad tracks with the other denizens of the bar community. On this Saturday night a week before Christmas, already three hours into Sunday morning, he and one of the Hunter's Run bartenders who had befriended him tromped through slushy, new snow to their regular stools at the end of the bar in the dingy after hours club.

"Oh, Robby, that's fabulous news," Bobby said as he fired up another Parliament cigarette. "Just fabulous." He reached over and squeezed Robert's forearm with his thin, pale hand. "You should be very proud of yourself."

He was. Robert had received his grades in the Saturday mail for his first semester of college: A's in all four classes. Bobby was the first person he told. Robert's relationship with his parents remained strained and complicated to the degree that he would not pick up the telephone and call them about anything, let alone something that seemed like a major personal milestone. And Robert felt a strange kinship with Bobby.

The skinny, haggard, pasty-skinned, chain-smoking bartender was the first openly gay person Robert had known. It was the mid-1980s, but in socially conservative West Virginia, most people still considered gays and lesbians to be fringe deviants. Robert empathized with Bobby's sense of marginalization and estrangement from mainstream society, and he appreciated the compassion and concern Bobby always showed him.

"My mom wanted me to go to college when I was growing up, but I never really took to school," Bobby lamented. He looked around at the motley crowd packed into the after hours club. "Since I was younger than you, I've always felt more at home in this world anyway."

Robert was glad he had become friends with Bobby, and he was intrigued by the nocturnal subculture he had discovered over the past months. As he always did in whatever circumstances, Robert fit in somehow—or at least did not clash—without making any particular effort. He coped with an agonizing social anxiety by adapting to those around him and remaining unfailingly amiable. Still, Robert did not feel any more at home among the bartenders and waitresses than he had in any other community or situation in his life.

It had been the same in high school. Robert maintained friendly relations with nearly everyone in all the different cliques—so much that he was elected school president, a victory that had caused his first open conflict with his parents—but he had no friends with whom he truly shared himself. And he always felt like some observer from another planet, completely self-contained, navigating without a compass through an alien world.

"What was your favorite class?" Bobby asked.

"Oh, introduction to ancient philosophy, without a doubt," Robert said.

"Ancient philosophy," Bobby said. "Wow. That sounds interesting—and hard."

"It was wonderful," Robert said. "I never knew such a world of thought and ideas existed. The Bhagavad Gita, the Iliad, the Odyssey, Plato, Aristotle, Cicero, the Bible as literature. We read and read and discussed and discussed. I still feel drunk on it all, and like I am beginning to see the world for the first time." Robert gesticulated so animatedly that he knocked his drink over on the bar.

"Jesus, Robbie," Bobby said, laughing as he helped mop up the amaretto sour with a handful of bar napkins, "I don't think I've ever been that excited about anything in my life."

"It's incredibly exciting, and a bit frightening," Robert said. "The professor, Dr. Vanderfelde, told us in the first class that if he did his job well, by the end of the course we'd be questioning everything we believed, and I certainly am."

"That does seem to be the point of getting an education," Bobby said.

"It is!" Robert agreed. "Although I didn't understand that until now. I always just saw it as the road to a good job. I feel so strongly the opposite that I'm going to change my major to ancient philosophy."

"What is it now?" Bobby asked.

"International Relations."

Bobby laughed so heartily he nearly choked on his amaretto sour. "That's quite a change."

"I mainly declared IR because I won a scholarship to go to Egypt on a study program this past summer, after I graduated, and I didn't know what else I should major in," Robert explained.

"You won a scholarship to study in Egypt?" Bobby was astounded. Such experiences were not in the background of the typical Huntington bartender. "What the hell are you doing slinging booze at the Hunter's Run and going to Marshall? You should be at Harvard or someplace."

"Well, no," Robert said. "Harvard is way out of my league, but that is a long, different story. Egypt was a bit of a fluke—the guidance counselor recommended me and nobody else from here applied—but it was fascinating, and it gave me a taste of being abroad. It is a big world out there, and for as long as I can remember, I've been more interested in international things than domestic ones. Plus, I really like the International Relations professor at Marshall I met through the Egypt scholarship, so I thought I would study with him. But philosophy is … is inspiring and beautiful and true unlike anything I've ever experienced. I can't imagine staying with IR now."

"I don't know a damned thing about either of them," Bobby declared, "but if you're that passionate about philosophy, you should do it. Life goes by too quickly to get stuck in one you're not crazy about. When I was your age, I used to think about getting out of Huntington and finding something I loved to do. I even considered joining the navy—see the world on a ship full of cute boys!—but I never did."

"Why not?" Robert asked.

Bobby drained off the last of his amaretto sour, bit off the maraschino cherry and tossed the stem into the empty glass. "Oh, first my mom needed help taking care of my grandma, then she needed help taking care of herself. And my friends are here and my life isn't anything to make a movie out of, but it's okay. And now I'm too damned old and set in my ways." He waved to the bartender. "Kim, give us two shots of peach schnapps." Turning back to Robert, Bobby added: "But enough of my sob story. It sounds like you've made a big, life changing decision, and that deserves a toast!"

Chapter 30

Robert did not change his university major, only his focus from international relations to American politics. In the spring of his freshman year, the non-profit organization which took him to Egypt offered him an internship in Washington, D.C. Robert accepted it immediately, elated by the chance to get out of Huntington for a few months and live in a real city. He returned to Huntington and Marshall inebriated by the whorl of life in the capital and captivated by dreams of a career in politics. The quiet contemplation of the ancients could not compete with such excitement at hand.

Robert volunteered with the college Democrats in the next election, and his unflagging enthusiasm laboring in the colossal failure that was the Dukakis presidential campaign won him a job working for the local congressman. He unenthusiastically continued to attended his classes at Marshall, wedging them into his work schedule. The job felt like real life. It gave him the identity he craved. The congressional work was all he actually cared about.

Six months into his job with the congressman, Robert made the first true friend in his life. Jack was hired as a part-time constituent-services worker in the office. He had interned with the Congressman in high school and was occupying himself for a few months after finishing his degree at the Virginia Military Institute before starting the four years of army service his college scholarship required. Robert and Jack went for happy hour at a bar near the office on Jack's first day of work in early June, drank and talked until the bar closed at 2 a.m., and were inseparable until Jack departed for officer basic training in November.

* * *

The Great Plains
April 1992

The black furrows of freshly turned soil undulated off into the distance in the grey, dawn light of the Iowa morning. Jack was at the wheel of his midnight blue Saab. Robert gazed drowsily out the window at the slumbering farmland.

"Oh, man, I need some coffee," Jack groaned. "I knew it was a bad idea to open that second bottle of sake at eleven. Three came way too early."

"But it seemed like such an excellent proposal at the time," Robert said, chuckling. "Plenty of time to sleep when we're dead."

"That may come sooner than either of us wants if I don't get some caffeine in me soon," Jack said. "I suddenly snapped to about half an hour ago and had no idea how long I'd been sleep-driving."

"Thank God," Robert said. He motioned toward a point of bright yellow light on the horizon.

They tumbled out of the car, stretching their legs and backs, and meandered slowly toward the doors of the blazingly lit Shell station. "I am so fucking fatigued already," Jack said as they entered. "And we still have at least 700 miles to go."

Jack had been posted to an army recruiting company in Des Moines. Robert flew out to spend an extended Easter weekend visiting him, and they decided to drive across the Great Plains to see the Little Bighorn Battlefield, where George Armstrong Custer met his end. They each had dreamed of such a trip since they were boys but never imagined they would get around to making it. The Greasy Grass, as the Lakota called the Little Bighorn River, always seemed impossibly remote from West Virginia.

"Fuel," Robert said, dragging the Pyrex pot full of sludge-black coffee from the warmer. He sniffed it and added: "This would make a corpse stand up and dance."

"Pour me the biggest cup they have," Jack ordered.

Sipping from thirty-two ounce Styrofoam cups of the bitter, scorched coffee, they raced through the rolling swells of the western Iowa landscape—seemingly as endless as the sea—and into Nebraska. Mile after mile of tilled, fertile earth awaiting another annual round of germination, growth, ripening, harvest, and winter sleep. Bruce Springsteen's *Greatest Hits* blared from the Saab's CD player, then U2's *The Joshua Tree*. Robert and Jack sang along enthusiastically, delighted to be on their little adventure.

"So, how's the wedding planning coming along?" Robert asked somewhere in eastern South Dakota, as a tumbleweed—the first he had ever seen—bounded across the highway ahead of them.

Jack would marry in June. "Oh, hell, mostly as much aggravation as you can imagine. But Beth did agree to let me pick out the china and crystal. I love her, but I wouldn't trust anybody—except you, of course—with that decision. Speaking of which, on the crystal: if you could only have three, would you get? A water glass, multi-purpose wine glass, and champagne flute? Or a white wine glass, red wine hock, and champagne flute?"

The question consumed the next forty miles of South Dakota countryside. They debated the relative merits of each combination with an earnestness that most people would find absurd, including Jack's fiancée, which is why she had gladly agreed to leave the decision to him. Robert and Jack could, and often did, go on like this for hours about obtuse topics, wheeling tangentially from one to another. Beth's maid of honor had said just the weekend before—when Jack and Robert launched into a comparison of china patterns over dinner—that they should be the ones getting married. They had laughed it off and continued their conversation.

The highway stretched westward, the sun crept higher in the vast expanse of blue sky, and Robert and Jack talked and talked and talked about things great and small. Robert had never in his life enjoyed someone's company as much as he did Jack's. He also fed off his friend's strong self-confidence and buoyant personality, and Robert appreciated deeply that they engaged in so much frivolity. When

Robert passed his time alone—as he was generally between his periodic disastrous romantic relationships, he tended to over-seriousness and dark thoughts.

At the Kimball Motel and Liquor—a gas station and weather-beaten line of welded-together mobile homes in a particularly desolate expanse of South Dakota—they sat in the car laughing until their sides ached. A dog that looked like a rabid wolf had chased them, snarling and barking, back across the parking lot when they had strolled over for photos with the establishment's crudely hand-painted sign.

They heeded 150 miles of roadside signs urging travelers to "See Wall Drug" and spent half an hour wandering around the rambling tourist trap, which sat alone in an equally desolate patch of South Dakota. Buying stamps for their postcards at the Wall Drug post office, Jack offended at least half the other patrons when he shouted to Robert at the other end of the counter: "Which do you prefer: the young, skinny Elvis, or the bloated, drugged-out Elvis? I tend to think the latter is more true to life."

Time felt suspended as the day wound on and they covered more territory in one drive than either of them had before. "Everybody should do this at least once," Robert said as they left the interstate and turned onto a winding, two-lane road which cut across the northeast corner of Wyoming. "There's no way to appreciate the enormity of the plains unless you drive across them."

A fierce storm rolled in from the west as they gained elevation and entered the Cheyenne Indian Reservation. The slate-grey skies and gusting sheets of sleet-laced rain deepened the grimness of the scenes they passed: household garbage strewn along the roadside; the rusting carcasses of thirty-year-old cars in one barren field; battered refrigerators and washing machines piled like blocks in another; rickety houses without windows and doors.

"They strip the copper from the houses and anything else they can get their hands on, to sell for cash," Jack said. "Mostly to buy booze. It's ungodly what we've done to these people. I never fully realized it until I got posted out here. We recruit heavily on the reservations. What an irony: the best hope for most Indian kids, thanks to the shitty lives we condemned them to when we stuck them on the rez, is to get into the US Army."

When they descended from the mountains, the storm broke apart as if on cue, and a rosy, golden light bathed the low hills of eastern Montana. In the distance, Robert glimpsed the dark outline of a squat obelisk perched atop a bulbous, grassy swell in the terrain. "Look! Look!" He nearly shouted. "That must be Last Stand Hill."

Robert had long before discarded any illusions he once harbored about the nineteenth-century Indian Wars, and the drive across the Cheyenne Reservation only enhanced the reality of the injustice meted out to the Native Americans. Still, for a time in his boyhood, he had been enthralled by the stories of westward expansion and the Civil War—and the romanticized exploits and demise of General George Armstrong Custer in particular—and Robert could not help but feel giddy about seeing this iconic bit of American history first-hand.

Ten minutes later they pulled up to the entrance of the Little Bighorn National Monument. The gate was closed. They climbed stiffly from the car and stared in disbelief at the chain and padlock.

"For fuck's sake," Jack howled. "We drive a thousand miles, and it's closed?"

Robert looked at his watch. "It's only a little after six. And it's a hill. How can it be closed?"

They had planned to stop and see the battlefield and then drive on to the Black Hills, two hours to the south. They paced around like tigers in a cage, looking at the gate and up the lane going into the park and back to the gate.

"Look down there," Jack said suddenly. He pointed into a gulley off to to the left of the road. About thirty yards away, the six-foot wire fence which ran in both directions from the gate was crunched down to the ground. "I don't think Custer would've let closing time and a fence stand in his way, do you?"

"Hell, no," Robert said and sprinted down the steep hillside through the scrub brush to the breach.

Feeling like conquerors, they strolled up the lane past the little museum and to the top of a rise. The ridge and its footpath ran away from them, gently downhill and up again for a couple hundred yards to the knoll with the granite obelisk. The Little Bighorn River, not much more than a wide creek, wended sluggishly along below in the valley to the right, its banks lined with budding cottonwood trees.

Robert silently recounted the details of the battle as they walked up the path past the white marble stones which marked where Custer's troopers had fallen. Robert had enjoyed visiting historic sites for as long as he could remember, but this was the first time he actually felt the spirit of the place and the events which had unfolded there. He could sense the U.S. soldiers' fear and the Lakota warriors' triumph. He could hear the pounding of a thousand hooves, war cries, shouting cavalrymen, cracks of gunfire, fusillades of arrows slashing the air. The slaughter. The pyrrhic victory. And then, when he reached the top of Last Stand Hill, silence. The ghosts of the battle faded away, and Robert returned to April 1992.

They felt no need to speak. Robert and Jack stood looking at the granite monument and the sweep of western landscape, the wind buffeting the burgeoning prairie grass. After a few minutes they sauntered toward the car, looking back every few yards to fix the image of the historic ridge in their minds.

"What a gift," Robert said as they drove away. "To see it like that, all alone."

"We couldn't have asked for more," Jack replied.

Anticipation had energized them for eighteen hours and a thousand miles. Now the weariness and fatigue of the journey took their turn. "I say we postpone the drive to Deadwood until tomorrow," Jack suggested, "and crash at the first place we see."

"That is an excellent plan, Lieutenant," Robert said.

The American Inn—thirty minutes from the battlefield in the scruffy Montana town of Hardin—was a relic from the 1960s. The worn out, two-storey motor lodge catered primarily to big-game hunters, and the reception desk was dominated by a moth-eaten mounted moose head with a rack the size of a loveseat. Robert and Jack checked in, plodded into their overly bright and tackily decorated room and collapsed on the hard beds.

Jack sat up and unzipped his duffle bag. "I'm whipped, but this day deserves a final celebration." He pulled a fifth of Jim Beam from the duffle. "Normally, neither of us would drink this shit on a bet. But I couldn't think of anything that better shouts The Old West."

"That it does indeed," Robert said. He dragged himself from the bed and fetched two plastic cups from the bathroom sink.

Jack poured two inches of whiskey into each cup and raised his. "To George Armstrong Custer, Sitting Bull, and a fine, fine day."

"Hear, hear," Robert said.

They emptied their cups, and Jack refilled them. Animatedly recalling the day, they drained the bottle of Beam before they realized it. Robert and Jack crawled into their beds bleary-eyed from exhaustion and bourbon.

Chapter 31

Virginia would not have been more thrilled if Robert had taken her to Washington and introduced her to the president. Probably less so. *The Waltons*, the 1970s television program chronicling the life of a family in bucolic 1930s rural Virginia, was her all time favorite. She never missed a weekly episode during its original broadcast, and she still watched it nearly every day in reruns. Now she and Robert stood looking at the set of the program's farmhouse kitchen, in which many of the title family's joys and struggles had unfolded.

"It looks just like it does on the show!" she said.

"Well, yes," Robert replied. He was delighted to see her enjoying the day so much. "It's the set. They brought it here from California and reassembled it." They were in Sharkey, a village strung along a forested ridge south of Charlottesville, Virginia. The family on which the program was based had lived there, and the old elementary school converted into a museum of the show.

Surrounded by the gold, orange and red autumn foliage, Robert and Virginia strolled down the blacktop road to see the actual farmhouse. Virginia was a little disappointed that it did not look like the one on television, but she was excited to hear that descendants of the real family still lived there.

At the general store / souvenir shop, Robert bought her a light blue "Walton's Mountain" T-shirt. Virginia insisted on wearing it out of the store, and she was beaming as they got back into the car. "Thank you, Robby," she said and squeezed his hand. Hers was plump, with crinkly skin like a lizard's. Robert generally loathed when people called him the diminutive of his name, but he liked it when Virginia did.

He was in graduate school at the University of Virginia in Charlottesville, five years after that late afternoon in April on Last Stand Hill with Jack. Brenda and Tom had brought his grandmother to visit for three days. Over the years since his abrupt departure from their house, Robert and his parents had managed to establish a more or less manageable framework for a relationship. As long as they steered clear of any substantive issue, and did not spend too much time together, it worked. They avoided confrontation. No psychologist would call it particularly healthy, but it was the best they could cobble together on their own.

"Why do you like *The Waltons* so much, Granny?" Robert asked her as they drove back to Charlottesville. He and his sister always called her "Mommaw" when they were children, a particularly Appalachian appellation. But Robert started calling her "Granny" as a joke a couple years before, and it had become their term of endearment.

"I reckon because it reminds me a little of what it was like at home, before my mom died," his grandmother said. "And what I wish it could've always been."

Her mother was killed in a car accident when Virginia was six. On one side of a black line in Virginia's memory lived those idyllic times of her early childhood on the southern West Virginia farm when she chased butterflies and waded in the brook beside the rambling clapboard house and felt her mother's love. On the other side stretched the wretched years after her father remarried to a woman who despised her stepdaughter's presence.

The clouds which accumulated over Virginia after her mother's death rarely, and only briefly, dissipated over the decades that followed. Her life with Sam was so burdened that the moments of joy with Brenda and her grandchildren were like January sunlight in

Lapland: merely a slight brightening on the horizon before the quick return to darkness.

But Sam died the summer before this visit with Robert, and Virginia felt as if the hard lifetime between her mother's death and Sam's had been a long, bad dream. Every new day seemed a marvel to her, and the few people whom she knew well—Sam never permitted her much of a social life when he was alive—were astounded by how she blossomed.

While Sam was alive, she rarely spoke unless spoken to. Now, Virginia volunteered opinions and observations about nearly everything. Her frequently dour and pained demeanor became expansive and cheerful. All her life, Virginia was gaunt. With each passing month now, she grew more jollily rotund. She felt guilty about feeling so well, but not overly so. Sam had reaped what he had sowed.

"Why didn't your dad do more to make your stepmother less difficult?" Robert asked. His grandmother never talked about her childhood, unless pressed, and even then she offered only crumbs. The older he got, the more he wanted to know her better. Robert felt closer to Virginia than any other person, but he knew little other than the surface details of her story and virtually nothing of her inner life.

"Oh, I don't know, Robby," she said. Virginia looked distantly out the side window of the car. It was easier to pry open a live oyster than to loosen her tongue. "It's just how he was," she said without turning away from the window, "and how she was." Virginia continued to gaze absently at the colorful passing trees. "I loved my dad, though. I still miss him."

Several years before, Robert had driven her down to the West Virginia coalfields where she grew up, to put flowers on her parents' graves. Virginia had not been there for twenty years. After an hour of traversing gravel tracks barely wider than the car—out one to its dead end, back to the two-lane blacktopped road, up the next, and back down again—they found the little cemetery on a bare hillside at the edge of the woods. It sat behind a cluster of the decaying former coal company houses that were scattered along the narrow, serpentine valley.

The cemetery was typical of the extended-family graveyards in that part of the country, overgrown and abandoned. Several of the tombstones had tumbled prone. Decades of weather-erosion had rendered at least half unreadable. Still, the sunny patch of ground in the peace and quiet of the countryside was not a bad spot for one's eternal rest.

Virginia walked straight to her parents' graves. Once they located the cemetery, she seemed to know every plot. Robert helped her jab the green metal legs of the plastic flower arrangements into the mossy ground, and then they stood in silence looking at the graves. As usual, his grandmother did not volunteer any of her thoughts. Robert did not inquire. "Okay, Robby. Let's go," she had said abruptly after two or three minutes, and they had returned to the car and driven the two hours north to Huntington.

After Walton's Mountain, Robert and Virginia visited Monticello— Thomas Jefferson's neoclassical mountaintop manse overlooking Charlottesville—and then they ate dinner at his favorite restaurant in the town. She insisted on paying despite his protestations. They returned to his apartment, and Robert prepared the fold-out sofa bed for her. He had tried to talk Virginia into taking his bed, but she absolutely refused.

"Do you need anything else, Granny?" Robert asked as she settled under the blanket.

"Just a kiss goodnight," Virginia said.

He leaned over and kissed her dry cheek. It was slack with age. "I had a very nice day with you, Granny."

"Oh, me too, Robby. Thank you," she said and patted his forearm.

It is strange, Robert thought as he lay in bed recalling their day, that they were related only by law and love. He never longed for his biological grandmother, Julia Ribas, nor wondered how she might have been in Virginia's place, had she kept Brenda and lived to old age. But he did often wish to know more about her and about their lost relatives in Spain.

Not long after he moved to Charlottesville for graduate school, Robert had gotten the address of his great-uncle Luis' daughter who had visited Spain thirty years before and met some of the cousins there. He wrote to her, telling her he wanted to try to contact them, but she did not reply. When he asked his great-aunt Pilar about it, she said: "Oh, she's a strange one, Robert. She never visits or calls, and I don't really have any contact with her." A frustrating dead end, he thought again as he drifted off to sleep.

Chapter 32

Robert's cell phone rang as he climbed into his forest green Jeep Wrangler at the Safeway supermarket. He was living in Arlington, Virginia, outside Washington, DC. He worked at night as an editor for a company that produced news briefings every morning for lobbyists and politicians. He did his grocery shopping at 8 a.m., after finishing work and before dragging home to try to sleep for the day. No one ever rang him in the morning.

"Mom?" he said, recognizing the number but not expecting her call. "What's up?"

Panic fringed Brenda's voice, and she talked in a rapid stream. "It's Mom. The distress alarm sounded in her apartment half an hour ago and they can't get in because she has the safety lock on. They're waiting for the fire department to come and break in, and they keep calling to her through the door, but she's not answering them back. They just hear the cat meowing constantly."

For the first decade after Sam died, Virginia lived in a condominium Brenda and Tom rented for her. She loved decorating it as she wished and sitting on the terrace watching the robins, cardinals and blue jays splash in her cast-concrete birdbath and eat seeds and suet from her feeders. But a series of mini-strokes had made her left leg stiff and unreliable, forcing her to move into an apartment in a semi-assisted living facility. The physical impairment took a toll on her psychic health. The joyful time of freedom had passed so quickly.

When Robert visited her on his rare trips to Huntington—his nocturnal work schedule and the difficulty of getting any time off from the small startup company made normal life nearly impossible, Virginia was usually sitting in her apartment with her cat, watching television.

"Why don't you go down to the lounge with the other people, Granny?" he would ask.

"Oh, I don't want to sit down there with those old women," she would scoff, though Virginia was older than most of them. The one thing she did like about the place was that it had bingo night on alternate Mondays. They played for a quarter a board, and she proudly returned to the apartment most times with a handful of coins.

"I'm afraid she's had a major stroke," Brenda said. "I've called her phone a dozen times, but she doesn't answer, and she always has it with her. I'm on my way down there now."

With minor incidents and irritations, Robert managed only with great difficulty not to erupt in a fit of frustration. But in moments of true crisis, a single-minded focus overcame him. "Okay," he said to his mother. "Try not to overreact. It could be anything, not necessarily the worst thing. I'll go home and pack a bag and drive straight there. Let me know when you hear something definitive."

Brenda called back a few minutes later. "She's alive," she said without a greeting. "She went to the bathroom, without her walker, and she fell. Probably that bad leg gave out."

"How is she?" Robert asked.

"They think she broke her hip," Brenda said. "She's in a lot of pain and is on her way to the hospital."

A broken hip at eighty-four was a bad thing. "Will they replace it?" he asked.

"Probably … maybe … I don't know." Brenda sounded terrible. "They'll have to see how bad it is and then decide. Are you on your way?"

"Just about," Robert said, zipping his suitcase. "I just have to corral the cat and get her into her box and in the car, and then I'll leave." He checked the time. "I should be there by five. Call me as soon as you know anything more."

While Robert was driving, his mother called and said that it was indeed a bad break. The doctors wanted to fuse the hip. The procedure was much less difficult, and they doubted she could recover from replacement surgery well enough to have any mobility. Virginia overruled them. She insisted on the full hip replacement. She would rather die now than be confined to a bed or wheelchair for the remainder of her life.

His grandmother was resting when Robert arrived. He hated everything about hospitals: the smells, the sterile corridors, the machines, the lighting, the angst radiating from every room and person. He could not believe he had dreamed of being a surgeon when he was a boy.

Virginia was sedated, but she stirred when he came in. She took his hand weakly and spoke to him softly. "Hi, Robby. I'm so glad you're here." Her lips, creased by wrinkles from decades of cigarettes, were sunken without her false teeth in, but her hazel eyes smiled.

"Of course, I'm here, Granny," he said. He stroked her thin, white hair. "How are you?"

"Not so good." She sighed and closed her eyes.

"I know, Granny," he said. "But it'll be okay. Tomorrow, you'll get a bionic hip. You'll be like the Six-Million Dollar Man."

Virginia opened her eyes and managed a weak smile. "I don't know about that, Robby. We'll see." Her heavy lids slipped closed again.

Robert kissed her on the temple. "You sleep now, Granny, and I'll see you in the morning before the surgery." She had already sunk again into slumber.

* * *

Virginia dreamed she was a young woman again. Standing on an empty beach, she curled her toes down into the wet sand and relished the squishing, grainy coolness. The stiff, warm breeze felt as if it was blowing through her and carrying with it every pain and worry of her life. It seemed as if she could float off the sand and fly out over the blue sea on the wind like the gleaming white gulls.

She turned from the surf and saw a cheerful-looking man walking slowly but purposefully up the beach. He wore a long, white tunic and flowing cloak. The coverts of pale grey wings rose above his shoulders. She thought, but did not say aloud, "Who are you?" when he stopped before her.

"I am Gabriel," he replied with a wry smile, though he also did not speak.

She stared at him, unable to form a specific thought.

"It will be difficult," he said, again without speaking aloud. "But I will be with you. Robert will be with you." He spread his powerful wings, a magnificent sight, and leapt out over the rolling waves, without another word or glance.

The gulls cried. The surf crashed. The breeze blew. Virginia stood alone on the beach and watched a white sailboat move silently across the horizon.

* * *

The surgery was a success. The recovery was not. Medicare paid for thirty days of intensive physical therapy in an excellent private rehabilitation facility. Despite her weakened condition and the intense pain, Virginia progressed little by little over the month. At the end, she could take several halting steps on her own, supporting herself on the waist-high parallel bars. Her determination had endeared her to the therapists and nurses. To continue paying hundreds of dollars a day for the treatment, however, Medicare demanded more rapid progress than Virginia could achieve.

Robert had returned to Arlington and work the week after Virginia's surgery. Brenda and Tom met with the rehab hospital's administrator. The woman was supportive and sympathetic during the brief encounter in her well-appointed office, but she made it clear that Virginia would have to be moved out of the facility by the end of the week unless they could begin covering the costs personally. Four days.

Brenda and Tom trudged slowly and silently down the pastel-colored corridor toward Virginia's room. Brenda was sad, because she knew this place was her mother's only hope of walking again. She was frustrated, because the Medicare bureaucracy was so inflexible. She was angry, because they could not afford to pay the bill themselves for Virginia to continue the treatment.

"Hi, Mom," Brenda said as they entered Virginia's room. She struggled to keep as much emotion from her voice as she could. The room looked more like a hotel than a hospital.

Virginia turned her attention from the local television news and smiled. "I took nine steps today," she said.

Brenda leaned over the bed's barely noticeable rail and gave her a quick hug. Tom sniffed and blinked hard and looked to the distraction of the television.

"That's great, Mom," Brenda said. "You're doing so good. And they all like you so much."

"I like them, too," Virginia said. "I don't hardly even feel like I'm in the hospital."

Brenda felt nauseated. "I know, but you know it's not the only nice place in town. And you're getting so much stronger, you could keep improving even if you weren't here."

Virginia did not like Brenda's tone, at once hollow and edgy, or that she was clearly beating around something. "What is it?" she asked curtly.

Brenda looked at Tom. He glanced at her, then back up at the television.

"It's Medicare, Mom," Brenda said, indignation creeping into her voice. "They will only pay for one month, and this place charges way too much for us to pay for it. They just told us that you have to go at the end of this week."

Tears began to pool in Virginia's eyes, but she continued to stare directly into Brenda's.

"I'm sorry, Mom, but we're going to have to move you to a … uh … a retirement home."

Virginia looked away, turning her face as far away from Brenda as possible.

Brenda reached out and touched her on the arm. Virginia shook it off. "Oh, Mom, please. Don't make this worse than it already is."

Virginia refused to look in her daughter's direction.

"It's not like they used to be. It won't be some awful old nursing home," Brenda insisted.

Virginia exhaled sharply at the words nursing home.

"They're retirement communities, with lots of activities and people there to help you," Brenda said. She knew it would never happen, but she added: "To give you more physical therapy so you can walk again."

Virginia acknowledged nothing. Her anguished gaze remained fixed on the wall to the side of the bed.

Brenda grew quickly frustrated. *After all I've done for her*, she thought, *she shouldn't treat me like this*. "I'm sorry, Mom," she said. "There's nothing else I can do. Look, I know the woman in charge of a nice place just over in South Point. I'll call her first thing in the morning and see if we can get you in there. It would be perfect."

It was as if Virginia had turned to stone.

Brenda lay a hand on her mother's rigid shoulder. "Love you. We'll see you in the morning, Mom," she said. "Come on Tom, let's go."

Chapter 33

The Thanksgiving after Virginia fell, Robert started working remotely for the news briefing company. He moved to New Orleans. The city had enthralled him since the first time he visited it when he was living for a time in Lafayette, Louisiana. He disliked the trashiness of Bourbon Street, but he adored the rest of the French Quarter. "Of course you love it," Jack had wisecracked. "It's the least American place in the country."

There was some truth to the joke. In the Quarter, off the drunken-tourist vortex of Bourbon Street, the city's colonial soul still lurked among the French Creole cottages and Spanish townhouses. The pace and spirit of the city bore no resemblance to any American place he knew. Robert found an apartment in a two-hundred-year-old triplex on Orleans Avenue, four blocks back from the Cathedral.

He roamed the streets for hours, day after day. He sat reading in cafés and in his walled courtyard, the cat lolling under the banana tree. He explored the bars, restaurants and jazz halls with his teacher friends from Lafayette. In his attic bedroom, he could hear the steam whistle music of the sternwheelers on the Mississippi. Other than still having to work at night, Robert was in heaven.

Like many other lovers of New Orleans, Hurricane Katrina drove him from the city where he had quickly begun to hope he would live for the rest of his life. His apartment on the high ground of the French Quarter survived with little damage, but the city's wrecked infrastructure made it impossible for him to work from there.

Robert landed in Naples, Florida, after two months of wandering from one friend's house to another and staying with his parents and sister. Naples could not have been more different than New Orleans, all posh and manicured, but he found the prospect of living ten minutes from the Gulf of Mexico inviting. The Florida beach town atmosphere almost was as satisfyingly different as the Mississippi Delta had been.

And there was a woman in Naples, a teacher with whom Robert was intensely involved when he taught U.S. history at a private high school in Lafayette between graduate school and the job in Arlington. Shortly before the hurricane, they rekindled their relationship. She had come to New Orleans to visit her family. They met for a drink at Napoleon House, and they each felt the tug of their old affection.

The tempestuous relationship foundered a second time less than a year after Robert moved to Florida. But he enjoyed the quiet life he found there. He spent every morning after work sitting in the sun on his little patio. He read voraciously, drank too much, and watched the ducks, cranes, cormorants and pelicans living out their routines in the artificial lake. On the weekends, Robert drove over to a pristine beach in protected parkland and luxuriated in the solitude by the gently lapping Gulf.

For his second year in Naples, Robert's cat and a retired man from Indiana who lived two condominiums down were his only companions. The man would walk past Robert's patio every morning with his black Scottish terrier, and they would chat about politics and the news of the day while Robert petted the feisty little dog. At Thanksgiving, Robert prepared the full traditional fare and invited the man and the Scottie for dinner.

* * *

Huntington, West Virginia
August 2007

Robert drove the twenty hours up to West Virginia to visit his parents and his grandmother. A month remained on his second, one-year lease for the condominium in Naples. He had decided to move to St. Augustine, on the Atlantic coast in north Florida. The artificiality of Naples had begun to grate on him, and he had taken an instant liking to the old Spanish colonial capital on a recent weekend trip there.

He stayed in Huntington for two weeks, as had become his custom over the years. It was long enough to feel like a substantial visit, yet short enough that he and his parents could accept each other just as they were at that moment, without activating all their old conflicts and patterns.

Robert went nearly every day to the nursing home to sit with Virginia after he woke in the afternoon. The nurses and aides, friendly despite their long hours of difficult labor, always greeted him when he arrived and reported on how Virginia was doing that day. Still, it was a nursing home, no matter what it said on the sign at the entrance.

The low corridors were depressing, with their dull white walls, linoleum tile floors and fluorescent lights. Whether the building was overheated in the winter or over-cooled in the summer, the air seemed to recirculate, hermetically-sealed from the outside. The halls and rooms always smelled faintly of food, bowel movements and cleaning solution. Depending on the time of day, one of the scents overwhelmed the others.

All residents had to share a room. Virginia lived in a double with a frail woman who was approaching a hundred years old. The woman had a brother who visited three or four times a year and a nephew who came less frequently. She passed her days and evenings sitting in a chair in her half of the room, looking at the floor. She was nearly deaf, which suited Virginia. She never felt like talking anyway.

Except for the one morning a week when the aides would haul her up and take her down the hall to be bathed, Virginia had rarely been out of her bed for a year. The physical therapy at the nursing home was occasional and brief. She was not there long before she took the last tentative steps of her life.

For the first year, Virginia would let them hoist her out of bed and into a wheelchair to join the other mobile residents for bingo and other games in the commons room. But as the realization set in that she would never return home, Virginia grew increasingly withdrawn and uninterested in the activities. The lack of physical movement exacerbated her emphysema, and she became dependent on bottled oxygen to breathe.

Virginia did get to attend the wedding of her granddaughter Marilyn, the summer after she entered the nursing home. Marilyn hired an ambulance to take her to the church and the country club reception. For those few hours, Virginia's lively post-Sam personality returned. She was surrounded by people she had known for decades and out in the fresh air. She loved having her hair done and wearing the bright purple dress she chose from a catalogue for the occasion. Her strength waned late in the evening, and the sadness returned as the ambulance came to take her back to the nursing home, but Virginia was thankful for that day.

She was also freed from the home the first two Christmases she lived there. Tom and Robert took her to his parents' house in a borrowed van to visit for a few hours on Christmas day. The process of getting her there and back severely tried everyone. Virginia was dead weight. Tom and Robert had to wrestle her into and out of the van, from and to the wheelchair. They were terrified they would drop her. So was she, and the fear constricted her breathing, which made her more anxious. The second Christmas, she had put her head on Robert's chest and wept as he held her sprawled on the floor in the back of the van.

When Virginia was safely in Brenda and Tom's house, however, amid her little family and the familiar Christmas decorations, the light came back on within her. She had laughed and talked and eaten like a lumberjack. She had so wished she could stay.

At the end of this two-week, late-summer visit from Florida, Robert sat on the metal folding chair beside Virginia's bed. She had eaten the entire plate of buttermilk biscuits and sausage gravy he brought her. Virginia despised the bland nursing home food. Bob Evans Restaurant's biscuits and gravy was her favorite, and Robert always brought her an order when he was in town.

"You go back tomorrow?" she asked suddenly as they watched the local news on the television at the foot of the bed.

"I do, Granny. First thing in the morning." The time had passed quickly. Too quickly. Robert was ready to be home and back to his solitary routine, but he already missed his grandmother.

Virginia said nothing, as if she had not heard him. She returned her absent, melancholy gaze to the television. The oxygen tube snaked from her nostrils to a tap in the wall behind the mechanical hospital bed.

An hour later, Robert stood and leaned over the high bedrail to tell her goodbye. He put his hand on hers, which was resting on her stomach atop the cotton blanket. "I need to go now, Granny. I work tonight, and I have to eat and nap a little before eleven."

"I know, Son," she said. Her voice had gotten gravelly from the years of oxygen.

Robert did not know why she had started calling him son recently, rather than Robby. But she had, and he liked it.

Virginia began to cry. Robert was startled. He could not recall seeing her weep before. It made his heart ache.

"I'm sorry, Son," she said. "I know you have to go. I just miss you when you're not here. That's all."

Without thinking about the idea, which popped into his head unbidden, Robert said: "What if I move back here for a while, so we can see more of each other? Would you like that?"

The tears still rolled from the corners of her eyes, but a smile spread slowly across Virginia's face. "I'd like that very much."

Robert's decision surprised him. Usually he agonized for weeks or months over such major changes in direction. He was terrified of making a wrong choice. And he had hated living in Huntington with a passion. The day he left for Charlottesville was one of the happiest in his life. Not once in the twelve years since had he thought for a second about moving back. He would rather have cut off an arm. But Virginia needed him, and he could not recall anything ever feeling so right.

Robert kissed his grandmother on her damp cheek. "So, I'll see you in about a month, okay? I love you, Granny."

"I love you too, Son." .

She still was smiling, cherubic in the ugly little room, when he looked back at her from the hallway.

* * *

Every detail fell into place for Robert's return. A week after he drove back to Florida, Tom called and said that a high school classmate of Robert's, whom he had insured, was just completing renovations on an apartment building. He would rent Robert an apartment for as long as he needed. The owners of the condominium were sorry to see Robert go, but they waived the requirement of two-months' notice, given the circumstances, and refunded his deposit early.

Robert had left most of his possessions in a self-storage space in Arlington, Virginia when he moved to New Orleans, taking only as much as would fit in his Jeep. On his way to Huntington, he added the majority of what he had with him to his storage bin. He bought a comfortable chair which folded out into a bed, a wheeled table for his laptop, and a television. Otherwise, the apartment was empty. Sometimes he wished that a fire would consume all the things he had packed away in storage.

As usual, sleep was not his friend. Working at night and struggling for rest during the day was too unnatural, and switching back to diurnal life at the weekends made it worse. After four or five fitful hours, he could make himself lie there no longer. Robert would drag himself from the fold-out bed, feed his old cat, and drive across the river to visit Virginia.

They quickly established as pleasant a routine as possible. Robert brought her a café latte from Starbucks every time he visited. She loathed the nursing home's watery, burnt coffee more than she hated the tasteless meals. And at least once a week, Robert brought biscuits and gravy from Bob Evans. Virginia always slurped the entire twelve-ounce coffee enthusiastically and ate every scrap of the food.

They did not talk much. Robert was back, but Virginia was still depressed about her confinement. They spent most of his visits watching television and enjoying each other's presence.

As autumn faded into winter, Virginia drank less and less of the coffee and came to barely touch the food. In January, Robert stopped going to Bob Evans altogether. Often, he poured her coffee down the drain before he went home. But he could not bring himself to stop purchasing the coffee. It would acknowledge her decline too painfully.

By the end of February, Virginia was absent more than she was present. If Robert was not working or fighting for some sleep, he sat at her bedside. Then he took off work and began rotating shifts with Brenda and Tom so she never was alone.

Virginia's breathing became labored. Three ragged, shallow breaths, then nothing for five seconds that felt like two minutes. Three ragged, shallow breaths, then the five seconds of silence, as if her body was undecided whether to battle on or surrender. Over and over. Occasionally, she opened her eyes, clearly afraid and confused, and tried to speak, but only grunts emerged from her clenched mouth.

"It's okay, it's okay," Robert would say, squeezing her hand. "You can go now, Granny. It's okay. We'll miss you, but we'll be fine. You've taken such good care of us."

"You should go home and get some sleep," Brenda said just before twelve one night. "We'll call you if anything changes."

Robert relented and hauled himself home. He slept poorly, despite the exhaustion, and woke at five. He showered, fed and pet the cat, and was dressing when his cell phone rang.

Brenda's voice was thick and choked. "She's gone, Robert."

"When?" was all he could ask. It could not be. He had been away for only six hours.

"Just a few minutes ago," Brenda said. "Her breathing became smooth and even, and she didn't wake up scared anymore." She paused and sobbed. "Then she was gone."

His vision blurred by the tears, Robert raced through the empty streets at dawn. He did not know why he was hurrying. His grandmother was gone, but he needed to be there.

Virginia's forehead was still warm when he kissed her lightly, but her body was an empty shell. "Goodbye, Granny," he said. He stroked her wispy white hair for the last time.

They sat with her for half an hour, until the two aides came quietly into the room. The bearish young man with the thinning flattop and braided necklace towered over everyone else. He wiped away his tears and put one of his meaty hands on Brenda's shoulder. "We need to prepare her now," he said in a near whisper.

"Yes, yes. Thank you," Brenda said. She stood and took one more long look at the body of her mother lying on the hospital bed. "Oh, Tom," she said and started to weep again. He held her close and walked her from the room.

Robert left the nursing home through the service entrance. He had always parked on that side of the building when he came to visit. Virginia's window faced that way, and he could peck on the glass and wave to her when he arrived and departed. When the automatic door opened, he saw the undertakers in their black suits pulling a stretcher bearing a purple velveteen body bag from the back of the hearse.

* * *

A week after they buried his grandmother, Robert had to put his beloved old cat to sleep. He had never felt so utterly alone.

The year before, visiting a friend in Prague, Robert saw one of his graduate school professors, who was there for a conference. "Let me get this straight," the jovially acerbic professor said after Robert told him about his job. "You can work anywhere you have an Internet connection, and in the U.S. you have to work all night. Why the hell have you not moved here?"

Sitting on the one chair in his lifeless Huntington apartment, Robert recalled that conversation and decided to go.

Chapter 34

Prague

December 2008

Robert turned forty less than a month after he moved to Prague, but he felt ten years younger and as if his life, in some amorphous, signficant way, had just begun. He spent most weekday afternoons at a cafe called Meduza, reading and drinking hoppy Czech beer among the hodgepodge of antique furnishings and walls covered with early-twentieth-century photos and lithographs in dark wooden frames. On the weekends, he spent countless hours revelling in the magical city, meandering the grey and white cobblestone sidewalks and feasting on the endless baroque architecture. It was like living in a dream.

Robert and Marlene had arrived in Prague a day apart, though they did not meet for another six weeks. Robert noticed her on the first evening of the Czech class at Charles University. That wild mane of blonde curls and her ice-blue eyes. It was a course for expatriates of myriad professions and interests seeking some understanding of the ridiculously complicated language. Nothing about Czech resembled anything of their native tongues: Finnish, Dutch, French, Spanish, German, English. English was the lingua franca. It did not make learning Czech any easier, but it at least allowed them all to communicate.

Clearly, Marlene was younger than he. All of them were. Robert turned forty the day before the course began and was pained to say it

240

when—as part of the second-night exercise in the names of the numbers—the teacher went around the room asking the students their ages. The closest was a diplomat from Finland—thirty-two—and the youngest the fifteen-year-old son of an American businessman. Marlene was twenty-nine.

They were paired for a conversation exercise for the first time a month into the class.

"What time do you get up in the morning?" Marlene asked in Czech.

"Four forty-five," David replied. None of the numbers even sounded like numbers, and he recalled them and expelled them from his mouth with difficulty.

"Four forty-five!" Marlene exclaimed, in English.

Robert laughed and answered in English. "Yes, I know. It's awful. I start work at five. But it's much better than before I moved here. In the U.S., I had to start at eleven and work through the night." He was amused by the mixture of horror and disbelief on Marlene's face.

"Only in America would that be possible," she said.

"Yes," Robert agreed in a resigned sigh. "And what time do you get up in the morning?" he added in Czech.

"Nine!" Marlene replied gleefully in Czech. She continued in English: "I could never force myself from the bed as early as you do. It is hard enough at nine."

Robert had been disappointed when the brief exercise ended but delighted by the several chances they had to chat during breaks and after the class over the next two months. On the Saturday night before the course ended, the students had gathered for dinner at Hlučna Samotá, a traditional Czech restaurant in the expat saturated Vinohrady neighborhood. Only the Dutch landscape architect with a Czech girlfriend had learned much of the language, but the class had bound them into a happy little social band.

"Snow!" Marlene howled like a child when they emerged from the toasty restaurant into the freezing night. At least six inches had fallen during their long, loud repast, and fat, wet flakes still were streaming down.

"Perfect!" the Finnish diplomat declared. "We certainly can't call it a night already on such an evening. Who's up for moving this party to the next location?"

Most demurred. It already was past midnight, and they had consumed half-litre glass after half-litre glass of Czech pilsner over dinner and two rounds of shots of the gullet-burning plum liquor called *slivovice* to cap the meal.

"I'm in," Robert said. He had never felt so securely part of a sympathetic group as he did with this eclectic gang of expatriates. He had not passed on a single outing with them over the three months they had known each other.

"Ahhh, we can always count on the New World," said the bulky, redfaced Finn. "Who else will rise to the challenge? France?"

"Non, non, non," the French software engineer muttered as he rolled his usual post-dinner joint. "I was supposed to be home an hour ago."

"I'll go, but just for a little time," said the twenty-four-year-old Spanish embassy intern. "I'm meeting friends for brunch tomorrow, but not until eleven."

The others all gave their excuses and bade their farewells. Marlene lingered at the edge of the remaining few, looking undecided.

"Come on, Marlene," the Finn encouraged her. "It's too early to go home, and it's our last night before we all march off to our homelands for Christmas."

"Okay," she said with a slight hesitation, and then: "Okay! Yes! Where should we go?"

"Oh! Oh! I know," the Finnish wife of the Finnish diplomat shouted. "I just read the other day about this new, authentic Japanese karaoke bar not far from here, and I'm dying to try it!"

Her husband groaned. "God, no, not karaoke. Anything but karaoke. You're with me on that, aren't you?" he pleaded to Robert.

Robert was unsure which position to declare. He felt more self-confident among this group than he had with any other, but he still reflexively tried to adapt to the prevailing sentiment on the rare occasion a difference of opinion arose. It was a deep, hard old psychic condition to break. He adored both the Finns, and he did not want to alienate either of them. Before he chose a side, the Spanish intern and Marlene leapt in.

"Some friends at the embassy went there last weekend said it's great!"

"I love karaoke!" Marlene said.

"Well," the Finnish diplomat said, looking in Robert's direction. "We must keep the ladies happy. And I'm sure it'll have slivovice. Karaoke it is."

They tromped giddily through the slushy snow, found the karaoke bar, and bounded down to their room. Round after round of slivovice. Round after round of bellowing along—microphones clutched in hand—to the lyrics scrolling down the fifty-inch flatscreen TV. At four o'clock, the Japanese waiter poked his head through the door and announced apologetically that they had fifteen minutes until closing time.

Standing again in the cutting wind on the snowy sidewalk, the Finns and the Spanish intern called for taxis. Emboldened by the hours of Czech plum brandy, Robert turned to Marlene, offered his arm and said: "I don't live too far from here. Do you want to come back?"

"Okay, yes," Marlene said after a moment's consideration. They waved goodbye to the others and began slipping and sliding away, the Finnish diplomat grinning at them as they went.

After the always fumbling and uncertain first-time sex, Robert and Marlene spent the next sixteen hours talking in his bed. At around four in the afternoon, as the winter night descended again over the gloomy, grey December Prague day, Marlene fetched paper and two pens from Robert's desk. "Let's play Stadt, Land, Fluss!"

"What?" he asked, chuckling.

"Stadt, Land, Fluss!" she reiterated.

"Never heard of it," Robert said as he pushed upright and gathered the down comforter around him.

"How can that be?" Marlene squealed. "It's the best game ever." She explained the details: each player makes columns on his page and labels them city, country, river, and then whatever other topics they want such as books, movies, writers and actors; then they take turns calling out a letter of the alphabet and making an entry to each column as quickly as possible with a word starting with that letter.

Robert generally disliked these sorts of games, but at this moment with Marlene—naked and radiant with her magnificent mane curling and cascading over her shoulders and half-way down her back—he would have gladly agreed to anything. They laughed and played until their pages were full, and Robert won by five when they calculated the points at the end. "Beginner's luck," he assured her.

After a second, slightly less awkward go at sex, Robert had said as he held Marlene in the warm cocoon of the comforter and looked out the window at the black sky: "I haven't spent the whole day in bed in ten years, and that was when I had the flu."

"The Americans," Marlene had said, shaking her head. "We won't wait that long to do it again."

Now they stood, a week later, amid the festive bustle of the Christmas market at Naměsti Miru. The frigid air was laced with the scent of baking Christmas pastries and mulled wine from the little wooden huts erected for the month around the square. Marlene slipped her hand into his jacket front and placed it flat on his chest over his heart. "I can feel the pain in you," she said. Her voice carried a profound stillness.

Robert had the sensation of a powerful current flowing between them: from his heart through her hand to her heart and back again.

The red and beige tram rang its flat toned bell as it approached the Naměsi Miru stop. Marlene glanced away to the tram and then back to Robert. "I don't want to go, but I have to."

"And I have to pack," Robert said. He reached into his jacket front and took her hand. "I'll only be gone three and a half weeks. I can't wait to see you."

They kissed as the tram doors clanked open, and then Marlene dashed for the steps as the bell growled again. Robert stood in the cold wind, but did not feel it, as he watched the tram crawl away past the festive market huts, the garish Christmas tree, and the towering Gothic church at the back of the square.

Chapter 35

Berlin

April 2012

"What the fuck is wrong with you?" Marlene yelled at the top of her voice.

Robert worried what the neighbors would think.

They had moved from Prague to Berlin a year before, after Marlene finished her clinical internship, and they had lurched from one angst ridden, agonizing argument to the next. Robert had begun to think it would be better to die than keep living like this.

"What kind of man doesn't want to have a child and build something up with the woman he says he loves?" Somehow, she had managed to increase her volume ten decibels.

These conflagrations always unfolded the same way. Marlene, her irritation boiling to the point where she could not contain it any longer, would launch into Robert, usually about the children topic. Robert would immediately shut down emotionally. He felt like a radio in an electromagnetic storm. He could not put together a coherent thought. His brain and emotions scrambled, and his whole body felt chilled to his core.

"Well?" Marlene screamed. She was perched at the opposite end of the black, velvet sofa, her body rigid with anger. "Do you again have no fucking thing to say?"

He did not. He could not. Robert was frozen, and he and looked at her blank-faced, which intensified her fury.

Marlene jumped to her feet. "I will walk out that door and go to my brother's and this is over—over!—if you don't have some response."

Robert just looked at her.

"Fine," Marlene spat. "Fuck you." She stormed into the bedroom and crammed some clothes into her backpack.

When she emerged, Robert was standing in the hallway, his hands in his trouser pockets. "Oh, for fuck's sake," he barked. "What are you doing?"

Marlene stopped in the vestibule, clutching her knapsack in one hand. "I'm going, Robert. I've had enough of this shit." She turned and flung open the apartment door.

"You live to make my life a fucking nightmare!" he shouted. Robert's relationship with Marlene had opened a well of love and connection like he had never known with any other woman, but it had also tapped a reservoir of frustration worse than any he had felt and unleashed a fury he had never indulged.

Marlene looked back at him, let loose an exasperated hiss, and stormed out.

Robert instantly felt relieved, though he knew the respite would be brief. He wished Marlene would not return, but she would. Marlene was never gone for long. This was not the first time one of their eruptions had ended this way, though they usually burned out before reaching the dramatic exit.

Twenty minutes later, reading on the bed, Robert heard the key turn in the apartment door.

Marlene plunked the backpack on the floor and sat on the edge of the bed beside him. Robert's body stiffened. She said, in a soft, pleading tone: "Come with me to the therapist. That's all I ask."

Robert drew a deep breath and exhaled sharply. "Fine. I'll go to the fucking therapist." He knew his response was unnecessarily harsh, and it had exploded out of him despite the fact he had resolved to be less confrontational when she returned. He saw the anger flash anew in Marlene's face, and then her swallow it down.

"Thank you," she said. Marlene took the book from his hands and put it on the bedside table. She took one of his hands and placed it on her breast and slipped his other up her skirt between her legs. She leaned over and kissed him deeply. The volcanic arguments always ended this way.

It was not merely make-up sex. They always returned to this subterranean space undisturbed by the rampaging sandstorms on the surface. Every time. Robert had not experienced anything like it. His previous relationships had all followed the same trajectory: initial flirtation, overwhelming attraction, unquenchable carnal desire, quick professions of eternal love, suffocation and a passive aggressive campaign against his partner, the death of all physical desire, bitter separation. But with Marlene, the tensions rose, she lashed out, he sat stonily until he exploded—and when the maelstrom passed, they collapsed wantonly into each other and tried again.

"You and me," Marlene said as they lay entwined on the bed. "We're something else."

* * *

Robert was as prickly as a porcupine all the way across Berlin on the U-Bahn, to the appointment with the therapist. Marlene let his barbed comments dissipate into the crisp November air. Seated in Frau Frei's therapy room—a sunny parlour in the pre-war apartment where she also lived—Marlene poured out a vociferous stream of emotion, aggravation and pain at the therapist's initial prompting.

Robert was harder work. Frau Frei labored patiently to pull every terse sentence from him at first. But then he opened up, bit by bit. Eventually, he talked more about his feelings and his family than he had before to anybody. To his astonishment, Robert actually felt a little less burdened by the end of the two and a half hours.

"Well," Frau Frei said, looking down at the pile of notes she had taken during the session. "To look at you, a first child and a second child, one of you," she said toward Robert, "more cognitive and structured, the other," she said toward Marlene, "more emotional and spontaneous, I would say you are a perfect couple who should have a beautiful, mutually-supportive relationship." The matronly therapist shuffled through her notes. "But, sadly—and I mean that, it makes me truly sad—there are these other things that pose enormous barriers."

Robert looked over at Marlene in the wicker chair beside him and felt an engulfing sadness himself.

"Ms. Schröder," the therapist continued, "you are the daughter of an overprotective, older father and an angry, emotionally distant mother. It compels you to try to manage every relationship and makes you unable to establish your independence. Of course, you've developed this overly-intense desire for an unquestionably secure relationship, and a child which locks it into place."

Marlene nodded and wiped the tears from her face. She had been crying for an hour.

"Mr. Stevens, you are the son of an adolescent minded father and an emotionally devastated mother. What more could we expect? You had the responsibility for your mother's emotional well-being thrust upon you nearly from birth, which forced you into this role of adult-child, made you unable to set boundaries or express your needs in a relationship, and imbued you with an unusual desire for independence."

An unexpected sense of relief and calm filled Robert. It was the first time his emotional reactions made any sense to him.

"I ... I must admit," Frau Frei said, "that I am unpleasantly surprised by what we have uncovered here today. When Ms. Schröder and I spoke briefly on the telephone, I expected that yours would be a fairly typical case which primarily required some strategies for better communication. But this ... this is difficult, complicated. I believe you both suffer from a severe attachment disorder, but it expresses itself in the exact opposite ways. You are matter and anti-matter. You clearly love and care very much for each other. However, your parents have saddled you with terribly heavy burdens. It was inadvertent, of course—they also are emotionally and psychologically damaged— but that makes it no less destructive for you."

* * *

Robert and Marlene returned to Frau Frei a month later. They delved deeper into the same issues of their family histories and the cycle of their emotionally unhinged clashes, but the two-hour session was their last together. Despite his initial skepticism and hostility toward the idea of therapy, Robert had embraced it by the close of their second visit; still, it had become clear to them and Frau Frei that at this point, more couple's therapy likely would yield few results. A month later, Robert came back alone.

"You told me again today," the therapist said, "that the thought of having a child makes you feel physically ill. Nauseated, you put it. Would you say that's an extreme reaction?"

"I suppose it is, yes," Robert said. He took a sip of the hot tea Frau Frei always offered at the start of each session. Robert was glad he had come again, but talking openly about his feelings caused him severe stress and stoked his anxiety. His throat was tight and unquenchably dry. "I just feel like I'll have to give up everything in my life that makes it worth living and spend the next twenty years slaving away to do nothing but raise a child."

"What would you have to give up that makes your life worth living, if you and Marlene had a child?" Frau Frei asked.

Robert took a sip of his tea. "Travel. Reading. Solitude. Independence."

Frau Frei smiled at him. "Yes, children certainly can wreak a bit of havoc on solitude, at least for the first few years. And, of course, activities such as reading and travel become more complicated, although I know parents who managed those needs with the child-rearing well, after they worked through the changes. It isn't easy, of course. Your concerns are understandable."

"And independence?" Robert asked. "How can you really maintain any freedom when you're responsible for a child? It dictates every decision, large and small. And I'm not saying that's wrong. It's what's right. Raising a child is the most consequential duty you can take on, and it has to become the center of your life."

"A grim prospect, isn't it?" the therapist replied. "It's difficult to imagine anyone surviving it and remaining sane."

"I do understand, though, why it's okay for most people," Robert insisted.

"For most people, but not for you."

"Yes. I … I just can't imagine it not eating at me every day, consuming my life and all my energy, and making me bitter and angry, and a terrible parent."

"Are your parents bitter and angry, or your friends who have children?" Frau Frei asked.

"No, of course not," Robert said. "But they're different. They're delighted by it, more or less, despite what it does to their lives."

"They don't appear to require the same level of independence you do."

"They don't," Robert said. "But I know that's a problem with me. It's not normal."

"What's normal?" Frau Frei scoffed. "If you feel it, it's normal for you."

Robert was not convinced, but he liked that someone seemed to understand him.

"But this question of independence is a big one for you," the therapist said. "Has it always been an issue in your other relationships, before Marlene?"

Robert thought about it, looking out the parlour's big windows at the cold, pouring rain. "I never thought of it being so," he eventually said. "In each one, we had other, specific issues we couldn't resolve. But when I think about it, my need for independence was always there, at least in the background, and it seems connected somehow to the other things, now that I think about it."

Frau Frei nodded and scribbled on the tablet in her lap. "In what way, do you think?"

Robert sipped the last of his tea and refilled his cup from the vacuum pot on the small table beside his chair. "I always felt … smothered. Suffocated by what they needed, regardless of the particular issue. And like all I wanted to do was to get away from them and get my life back."

She scribbled again on her tablet. "So, your life with your partner, in the relationship, felt as if it were something being imposed on you and separate from your real life, the life you wished you could lead."

"Yes," Robert said. He had ruminated on these ideas and questions more times than he could count, but saying them aloud was entirely new. The mere act of speaking them made him feel lighter. "In every relationship," his mind was jumping from one former love to another as he talked, "I felt … I came to feel … responsible. Responsible for doing the things they wanted and they needed, regardless of what I wanted."

"And needed," Frau Frei added.

"And what I needed," he said, realizing it for the first time. "And now with Marlene, too. I adapt to the other person and lose myself. At first, it's fine, because the relationship is new and exciting, but then those feelings of loss and suffocation creep in and grow. In the end, all I feel is frustration and depression."

"Have you ever discussed these feelings with your partners?"

"Jesus, no," Robert said.

"Why? That seems the logical thing to do, don't you think?"

"I have often wanted to, but I just can't. I've even had conversations in my head about what I could say and how I could explain what I feel. But then, when the moment arrives to say it, I can't open my mouth. I'm paralyzed."

"Well, that certainly is miserable," Frau Frei said. "Why do you think that, instead of just confronting the issue and talking about it, you adapt and abandon yourself and spiral down into frustration and depression?"

"Fear, I suppose," he said after a minute. "I'm afraid that if I start some argument and push too hard, it'll destroy the relationship."

"And what has this approach achieved in your past relationships?"

Robert grinned and felt both silly and suddenly aware. "Destroying them."

Frau Frei smiled. "Well, at least you've conducted sufficient field tests to establish with great certainly that this method is ineffective. Unless, of course, the goal is to blow up a relationship."

"Which it is not," Robert said.

"No, it is not. Why do you think you do this?" she asked. "Why do you think you react and feel this way in a relationship?"

Robert pondered the question until the silence made him uncomfortable. "I really don't know," he said, sighing. He felt sad and deflated. "What do you think?"

"Well," Frau Frei said, chuckling and fumbling with her pen. "We're here for you to talk about what you think and you feel. But it's a fair question, especially after I've been holding your feet to the fire for nearly two hours."

She took a sip of her own tea and appeared to collect her thoughts. "I have two observations. First, there is a relationship dynamic I like to call parental partnerization. Many therapists call it emotional incest, but I prefer the other description. It is less sensationalist."

"And what's that?" he asked. It sounded horrible.

"It's when a parent replaces his or her spouse with the child for emotional support. In your case, your mother had—and appears still to have, from what you've told me—a host of unresolved traumas, which is completely understandable from her abandonment by her birth mother and her difficult life with her adoptive father. Your father, from your description, seems to have been an amiable, well-intentioned overgrown boy—especially when you were a child—who was not psychologically and emotionally capable of helping your mother see her troubles clearly and seek the professional help she desperately needed."

Robert had not heard of such a concept, but he thought it fit.

"The effect, for the child, is ... horrendous. Children aren't prepared, emotionally and psychologically, to bear the responsibility of easing a parent's sadness and trauma. But they also have no capacity to understand the situation or resist it. They feel the parent's pain, take on the burden of it, and adjust their behavior. They adapt, and they avoid all confrontation as much as they possibly can, so they don't add to the ill parent's pain. As adults, if this partnerized relationship with the parent endures throughout their childhood, in intimate relationships they are over-responsible, conflict avoidant, unable to communicate their feelings and needs, and have an insatiable desire for the independence they could never feel from the parent. Does that sound like anyone you know?"

Robert was stunned, and swept by another wave of relief, as he had been during their first session. "It does, indeed," he said.

"It appears to me to fit," she said, "but I must caution that identifying it only marks the beginning of a long, difficult road to recovery. It will require much determined, inner work. But I fully believe you can heal yourself if you want it."

Robert had not had the chance to consider the longer-term implications of her revelation. "I understand. But it still feels liberating to have some kind of explanation that makes sense. I'm forty-three years old, and I've never had the slightest understanding of why I feel and how I behave in relationships."

"I'm happy to hear you feel like that," Frau Frei said. "I would like to add one other thing, from a broader perspective."

"Please do," Robert said. The sessions were mentally, emotionally and physically exhausting, but they also flew by, and Robert felt he could stay another two hours.

"There is a lot of discussion in my field about intergenerational transmission of these traumas. Some people think they are passed along by parents' and grandparents' behavior, or genetically, or through the limbic system, or through the spirit or soul. I'm not convinced about any of them in particular, but I do believe it happens. And these traumas have a way of making themselves known, erupting in the lives of those who have inherited them. It is as if they want to be resolved, for some generation finally to address them and put them to rest, once and for all."

Robert did not see where she was going with this. Mysterious transmission of trauma across generations sounded flaky. But he liked and trusted Frau Frei, and he tried to keep an open mind as she continued.

"To me, what you are experiencing could be such a phenomenon. Your mother's partnerization explains your reactions and behavior, but the intensity of your feelings exceeds what I would expect. Indeed, what I have seen with many others in my practice. You have not only your abandoned mother in your history—searching for connection and identity—but also your biological grandmother, who must have been very bruised emotionally and psychologically to give away her children as you've described. And her trauma likely descended from your great-grandparents and great-great-grandparents, although you know so little about them. Only an intergenerational accretion of unresolved traumas, I believe, can account fully for what you feel."

Robert still thought it sounded a little crazy, but part of him also found it intriguing. "How would I even begin to sort that out?"

"Perhaps you should consider going to Spain," she said, "to the areas where your great-grandparents lived, and try to make some connection to your roots."

"But all I know are Barcelona, Galicia and Asturias," Robert said. "That's a pretty poorly defined target."

"It is, and I don't know whether it would help you at all. But to me, it seems like a way to begin. There is no way to predict what you will or won't find. One other thing," Frau Frei said. "I think your painfully strong aversion to having children also could be related to this rootlessness you feel, and that also could be partly from your mother and ancestors. Going there could perhaps help you crack that open, as well."

Chapter 36

September 2012

R obert and Marlene decided to make his journey to Spain their annual vacation. Like most Germans, she could take thirty days off work each year. Robert managed with some difficulty to get two weeks free from his U.S. employer.

They would spend three days root-hunting in Barcelona—where Robert's Aunt Pilar had told him Mercedes grew up—and three in Asturias—where she had said Antonio worked before going to America, and where he and Mercedes met. In between, Robert and Marlene would have a week of relaxation at the seaside Catalan village of Cadaqués, where Salvador Dali passed his summers. Antonio's homeland of Galicia was one province too far for such a brief trip.

"You won't believe what I just got!" Robert's mother Brenda told him on the telephone two weeks before his departure for Spain. "A few days ago, I found Debbie's sister on Facebook." Debbie was the unresponsive cousin who visited Spain in the 1970s. "And she has the letter Debbie sent her then, talking about her trip and the relatives she met!"

Brenda was right. Robert could not believe what he was hearing.

"And," she added with relish, "she emailed a copy to me today. I'll forward it to you."

"Oh, Mom, that's extraordinary," Robert said. "What does the letter say?"

"It's crazy. Mercedes was not from Barcelona, as Aunt Pilar always said."

"What?" Robert exclaimed. For thirty years, he had identified with the city. He learned everything he could about Barcelona and Catalan culture, believing that some of his roots lay there. He had even gotten a tattoo on his left shoulder of the seal of the medieval Catalan poetry contest called the *Jocs Florals*.

"No! She was from Asturias. That's where the family farm is. Debbie wrote that it's called Las Cepas, and it's close to that town where you're going. Debbie stayed in the same place."

Robert had picked Avilés as their destination in Asturias because *Lonely Planet* said it had a nicely restored medieval quarter; it was the hometown of St. Augustine, Florida, founder Pedro Menéndez; and it was close to a beach. He had no idea, when he was planning the trip, where in Asturias Antonio had lived before he emigrated across the Atlantic. Robert was dumbfounded by his mother's news.

"The letter even mentions the names of the three people she met, three old nieces of Mercedes," Brenda added. "Maybe you can find them!"

Robert was excited by the discovery, but that seemed impossible. "It was forty years ago," he said. "There's no way they're still alive."

"Debbie says the farm is near some village called Naveces," Brenda said, undeterred. "Maybe you could go there and ask somebody."

"Oh, Mom," Robert said. "It's not like we can just go there and start knocking on doors."

"I guess you're right," Brenda conceded reluctantly. "But it's good, isn't? That I found this information?"

"Oh, it's great, Mom," Robert said enthusiastically. He felt a little guilty about dashing her hopes of locating living relatives. "After all these years, it's a little hard to get my head around the fact that Mercedes is from Asturias and not Barcelona. But it's wonderful to know something concrete for a change. Thank you so much for tracking it down."

As soon as they got off the phone, Robert looked up Naveces on Google Earth. It was five miles from Avilés and less than one from the Cantabrian Sea. He zoomed in on the satellite image as much as he could and examined the bird's-eye view of the red-tile rooftops of houses and farms. One of them was his great-grandmother's home.

* * *

For three centuries after receiving its royal charter in 1155, the footprint of Avilés changed little. A sixteenth-century expansion outside the medieval defensive walls brought buildings like the Palacio de Ferrera and the municipal hall, as well as shops and houses along Calle Rivero—the old royal road to the Asturian capital of Oviedo—and Calle Galiana, which ran up the hill past the old Franciscan monastery of San Nicolás de Bari to the livestock market at the Plaza de Carbayedo.

In the nineteenth century, the town boomed again and it grew by half, with the addition of the Plaza Nuevo, where Mercedes and her brother came to the Monday market and old men pitched wooden rings into the iron frog's mouth at Café Colon. Shops and apartment buildings sprouted around the Parque de Muelle, on the filled-in old harbour, out Calle La Cámera, and between old Avilés and the medieval fishermen's village of Sabugo.

Still, only about 10,000 people lived in the town Mercedes and Antonio knew. In the late-1950s and 1960s, the slowly evolving world of Avilés turned upside down. Its population exploded from 10,000 to 100,000 after the Spanish dictator Francisco Franco decreed that steel mills and chemical factories would be constructed for miles along the Alvares River. Unemployed Castilians and Andalusians streamed north for work.

Asturiana de Zinc, the successor to the Real Compañía de Minas for which Antonio Primero and Antonio Segundo had labored, built one of the largest zinc smelters in the world in the village of San Juan de Nieva, at the mouth of the estuary two miles from Avilés. Modern buildings, with the apartments sold at generous subsidies to the workers, rose to meet the needs of the rapidly-expanding population. Scores of acres of farmland around the city filled with new development.

After Franco died in 1975, the same global market forces which devastated such mighty centers of heavy industry as the Ohio Valley in the U.S. and the Ruhr Valley in Germany descended on Avilés with the same lack of mercy.

* * *

Barcelona was magnificent. The unsettling revelation that he had no family ties to the city did not diminish the ardor Robert felt for it as they prowled the streets of the ancient Mediterranean capital.

Cadaqués, with its white-plastered medieval buildings clustered tightly between high, arid hills and the bright blue sea, was impossibly beautiful and peaceful. Robert wished they could stay there for a month.

As they approached Avilés, fourteen hours and two days by car from Cadaqués, Robert was appalled. Despite the nascent work he had begun with Frau Frei, he lapsed severely back into a frustration-fueled rage.

"I should have known anything associated with my family would be shit!" he ranted as they drove down the highway. The river valley was an industrial wasteland. The few sprawling, soot covered factories not shuttered and rotting were belching flames and smoke into the overcast sky. "Jesus Christ, look at that!" he shouted, pointing to a steel mill that could have been transplanted from 1960s Pittsburgh. "We'll have fucking cancer before we leave here."

Marlene thought it pretty awful as well, but she knew from experience that Robert's extreme reaction sprung from old issues. "It's okay, Hase. We're not here for the scenery, you know." Unless they were arguing, she always used this German term of endearment for him: rabbit.

"Okay? Okay?" he yelled. "It's a fucking nightmare. I'm so sorry I dragged you here on our vacation."

"Hase, it's fine," Marlene said tenderly. "Really. And it's only three days."

"Three fucking days in this," he muttered, gesturing to another smoke belching factory. At least he had stopped yelling. "It's like spending a long weekend in Nitro, West Virginia." Even as they approached the historic town center, most of the 1890s riverside buildings looked half-abandoned and were laden with decades of industrial grime.

When they turned up a narrow cobblestone street which led to the entrance of the subterranean municipal parking garage, Avilés became a different city. They passed brightly colored nineteenth-century apartment buildings and the richly carved seventeenth-century sandstone residential palace which housed the tourist information office. But Robert remained too agitated to notice the change.

Robert and Marlene dragged their suitcases from the rental car in the parking garage and took the elevator up to the hotel lobby. The doors opened, and they emerged into another world. Beige marble. Dark wood. High, painted ceilings. Regal red carpets. The Palacio de Ferrera—home to generations of the Marquises de Ferra from its construction in the 1630s until the late 1990s—had been skillfully converted into a five-star hotel.

"Oh, this is nice," Robert said. He felt immense relief and immediately snapped out of his frustration. Out the hotel's plate glass front door, he glimpsed the neoclassical municipal hall, with its eleven-arched arcade, pedimented clock face, and its central tower crowned with a fat bronze bell suspended in what looked like a Victorian iron birdcage. "Oh! Look at that," he said to Marlene, pointing out across the Plaza de España. His cheerfulness and boyish sense of wonder had returned.

They dropped their suitcases in the sleek, fashionable room in the hotel's modern wing and ventured out to explore the old quarter.

Robert was ashamed by his initial outburst. As he and Marlene meandered through the restored historic district, and the people they encountered were so pleasant and welcoming, he began to fall in love with the place. He could feel that his great-grandparents had walked these streets and seen these buildings, and the realization gave him a sense of belonging. He wished again, more intensely, that he could meet someone to whom he was related.

259

"Tomorrow," he declared to Marlene as they sauntered down the medieval blacksmiths' street of Calle La Ferrería, "I think ... I know it's probably useless ... but I think we should drive out to Naveces and just start asking people if they know Marina, Covadonga or Sagrario." They were the three nieces mentioned in the American cousin's letter.

"That's a great idea, Hase," Marlene said. She gripped his hand a little tighter. "And you know how these European villages are. Everybody knows everybody else."

"That's true," Robert said, though he had no confidence they would find anyone.

They went for dinner at Sidrería Tierra Astur, a festive cider bar across from the church of San Nicolás de Bari. They stuffed themselves with fabada, octopus, nutty Asturian ham and cold, acidic cider. Robert's first taste of Asturias. He could not remember enjoying a meal as much.

* * *

Robert slid a piece of paper across the reception desk to the hotel clerk. "Would you mind translating these phrases into Spanish for me?" he asked. "We are going out to my great-grandmother's village this afternoon, and I would like to ask around about my relatives."

"Of course," the raven-haired woman said.

Do you know Marina González Cueto? *Conoce Marina González Cueto?* My name is Robert Stevens, and my great-grandmother was Mercedes Gonzáles Conde. *Me llamo Robert Stevens, y mi bisabuela era Mercedes González Conde.* My great-grandmother was Marina's aunt. *Mi bisabuela era la tía de Marina.*

"That is all you need?" the hotel clerk asked.

"That should do it," Robert said, looking over what she had written. "Muchas gracias."

The woman smiled. "De nada, Mr. Stevens."

Robert ascended the Palacio's grand marble and oak staircase and went to the room to collect Marlene. As they passed the reception desk on their way to the elevator down to the parking garage, he waved the piece of paper with the translated phrases and said in jest to the clerk: "We're off to the village to find my family!"

* * *

Naveces was a fifteen-minute drive on the winding, rural road. The countryside was beautiful: sleepy villages and farmhouses, all plastered stone and red-tile roofs; steep hills covered in bright green pastures and capped by eucalyptus groves; sweeping vistas punctuated by glimpses of the Cantabrian Sea. Again, Robert was ashamed by his outburst the day before.

His heart swelled when they came around a bend in the road and he saw the simple black and white metal sign marking their arrival in Naveces. He insisted on stopping and having Marlene take a photo of him standing beside it. They drove a little farther, and he stopped the car beside the first commercial building he saw. An old woman was sitting in the sun on the tobacco shop's narrow terrace a yard off the road, a sweating glass of red vermouth over ice on the wine-cask table beside her. Marlene waited in the car.

Robert walked up to the old woman, smiled nervously, and said: "Hola, buenos días."

"Buenos días," the woman said.

"Conoce Marina González Cueto?" Robert asked. He did not know why he had chosen that name from the three that morning when he went down to the hotel desk.

The woman eyed him warily. "Por qué?" *Why?*

"Uh," Robert said, "uh, porque ella es la sobrina de mi bisabuela." *Because she is my great-grandmother's niece.* He had taken Spanish in high school, twenty-five years before, and the basics of it suddenly stirred in his brain.

"Pues, ciertamente se refiere a la hija Marina. La madre Marina es muerte," the woman said. *Well, certainly you mean the daughter Marina. The mother Marina is dead.* Robert was surprised he comprehended her, but his mind felt oddly receptive to the language.

"Sí! Sí!" he said, with an enthusiasm that appeared to amuse the old woman. He could not believe that the first person he asked knew one of his relatives.

The old woman called to the attendant inside the tobacco shop and asked her to find the telephone number for the daughter Marina. She lived in Avilés.

Robert thanked the old woman and returned to Marlene in the car. "The woman ... she knows the daughter, the daughter of Marina," he gushed. "The shop clerk gave me her number!"

"Oh, god, Hase, that's amazing! You have to call her, right now."

"I will," he said. "Oh, shit, I feel like I'm about to throw up. And what if she doesn't speak English? How can I talk to her? I don't speak any Spanish."

Marlene took his hand and kissed it. "It will be okay, Hase. You talked to that old woman well enough. Just ring her."

Robert entered the number in his cell phone. It rang four times.

"Digame," said a woman's voice on the phone. The standard Spanish telephone greeting: tell me.

"Hola," Robert said.

"Hola," the woman replied.

"Me llamo Robert Stevens y Mercedes González Conde era mi bisabuela y estoy en Naveces," he managed to get out of his cotton-dry mouth.

Silence on the other end of the line. And then, "Sacramento!" Marina exclaimed.

She spoke not a word of English, but enough Spanish swam up into Robert's consciousness that they arranged to meet at the Palacio de Ferrera. In an hour.

* * *

Robert and Marlene went down to the parlor off the hotel lobby fifteen minutes before Marina was to arrive. With its carved antique furniture, crystal chandelier, oil paintings and oak writing desk, it looked like the sort of room in which old-world diplomats would sign a treaty or conquistadors would unroll maps and plan their next campaign.

They sat on the hard, striped settee and waited. Robert was giddy and terrified. Overwhelmed. Completely unexpected events were unfolding at a bewildering pace.

When they had returned to the hotel, less than an hour after they left, Robert told the desk clerk: "I found them!"

"That certainly was quick," she said.

"But I have a problem," Robert told her. "My cousin speaks no English, and I have exhausted my Spanish already."

The young woman thought about it and asked him to wait. She disappeared into a side room and reemerged with an older woman who greeted Robert in Spanish. "Mi jefa," the young clerk began, "my, mmm, boss, says that you are welcome to use our intern for as long as you wish for translating. Her name is Fernanda. She is from Mexico and speaks English perfect. She is at lunch now but will be back soon and will come to you in the parlor."

As the bell atop the municipal hall across the Plaza de España gonged two, the glass door to the hotel slid open. In stormed a fashionably dressed, diminutive woman of about sixty with short grey hair. A tanned, balding, portly man trailed behind her. She came directly into the parlor with her arms extended, embraced Robert tightly and kissed him once on each cheek. "I knew it was you as soon as I walked in," Marina said in Spanish, and Fernanda translated. "You look like all the rest of us!"

Marina introduced them to her husband Arturo, and Robert introduced them to Marlene. They sat down on the nineteenth-century settee and flanking armchairs.

"How are you here?" Marina asked. "How did you find me?"

Robert recounted the events of the visit to Naveces and told her about the American cousin Debbie's letter.

"Ahhh, yes, I remember now, but I had forgotten until this minute," Marina said. "My mother told me then, back in the seventies, that she had met one of the North-American cousins briefly one afternoon when she came to see Las Cepas. Our house was just down the hill."

The hotel entrance slid open again, and a professorial, balding man with a bundle of papers and folders under his arm came breezing in.

They all stood, and Marina said: "This is our cousin, Antonio."

As he shook Robert's hand firmly and disgorged the pile of papers on the coffee table, Marina quickly relayed to him what Robert already had told her.

"Incredible. Incredible," Antonio said in Spanish, with Fernanda translating. He looked Robert up and down. "A hundred years we have waited for you, and you appear out of thin air!"

Antonio unrolled an extensively annotated family tree on the coffee table. "Bernardo and Casilda, your great-great grandparents," he said, pointing to their names near the top of the tree. "Antonio González Conde," he said, pointing at the name a rung lower flanked by the names Manuel, José, Ramón and Mercedes. Motioning toward Marina, he said: "Our grandfather, and the brother of your great-grandmother." He continued down the chart, increasingly dense with names, telling Robert about the descendants of Antonio González Conde, three more generations to the young children of the present day.

Robert counted twenty-five cousins of his mother's generation and forty-three of his own. It was more than his mind and heart could grasp.

Antonio passed his hand over a large blank space in the middle of the family tree. "This is where our American family belongs," he said, "but we have known so little about you."

He told Robert and Marlene what he knew about Mercedes' time in Asturias: her exile from Las Cepas after Casilda's death, and her return by Antonio González Conde; her life at the farm and Mondays at the market; how she met Antonio Rivas. He withdrew a heavy folder from his pile, opened it, and handed it to Robert. The folder contained a piece of fragile, faintly lined writing paper. It was yellowed with age and insect-eaten around one edge. But the spidery handwriting in slightly-faded black ink was clear.

"From your great-grandmother to our grandfather," Antonio said. He reached over and carefully turned the page over. Robert read at the bottom, in a full, nineteenth-century hand: "Mercedes González Conde." Beneath it was written a cramped but legible: "A Ribas."

"My father has had this for decades," Antonio told Robert. "I have looked at it many times but never translated it because the handwriting and the antiquated language are difficult to decipher. But I will do it for you tonight."

Then it was Robert's turn. He talked. Fernanda translated. He told them what he knew of Mercedes' life in the U.S.; the sad story of her daughter Julia; of his mother's abandonment, adoption and discovery of her family. He was choking back tears as he finished. Fernanda was unable to contain hers.

* * *

The next morning at ten, Antonio, Marina and Antonio's nephew collected Robert and Marlene at the hotel. The nephew was also named Antonio, and he spoke English. They drove to see Las Cepas, with its view down the little valley to the Cantabrian Sea. They visited San Román Church, where Mercedes was baptized, and Antonio told them of her marriage there by proxy. They went to a neighboring farm where Robert and Marlene met another granddaughter of Antonio González Conde and her large extended family. Three generations lived under the same roof.

The apartment Antonio shared with his sister and parents was the final stop on their tour. "El jefe del clan," Antonio said proudly as he presented his ninety-two-year-old father Manuel. The robust old man's eyes open wide as he gripped Robert's hand in both of his. "We are all so pleased you have come." His ninety-three-year-old wife África hugged Robert and kissed him on both cheeks. "It is a miracle," the stout old woman declared as she took a step back and looked him over, still holding both his hands.

They all gathered around the two Antonios after the older one had again retrieved the letter from Mercedes. He read, and his nephew translated for Robert and Marlene. "It specifies no year," the older Antonio said, "but we guess from the content that it must be from around 1930."

Anmoore
21 December

My dear sister-in-law and brother,

I have just received your letter in which I read that you are all well, which makes me very happy, That we all have work is everything, otherwise our lives will be as hard as the people who are suffering without relief from this endless Depression. It is as you used to say, Antonio. If I want to eat, I have to work, and God provides plenty where the people are not afraid of labor.

María, when your neighbor Tomás comes to Anmoore, please have him bring me the Asturian cabbage seeds and the jeans buttons you bought. Thank you very much for always sending me the things I need. These have been lean years.

Give my regards to all those who have asked about me, especially to Aunt Carmen and her family at La Siega. I send a strong hug to you and my nephews, and when you write to Ramón, tell him his aunt is thinking of him.

No more for today, and the same wishes from your brother-in-law.
Mercedes González Conde
A Ribas

Antonio returned the letter to a new thick envelope and handed it to Robert. "My father rescued this from the granary at Las Cepas after my grandfather died," Antonio explained. "I am sad to say, it is the only one we have. My grandfather had boxes and boxes of papers stored in the there, but some people, unfortunately, do not place much value on such things." He sighed and shook his head. "My father's cousins, who inherited the farm, had hauled much of my grandfather's archive away by the time my father heard what they were doing and dashed out to the house. He was able to save only this and a few other documents. We have held this letter, in trust as it were, for you and your family, and we agreed last night that you should have it."

Again, Robert was overwhelmed by a wave of emotions. He had lost count of how many times it had happened over the past twenty-four hours. His head felt as thick as a melon, but it seemed that his soul was expanding faster than the universe.

When they returned to the hotel, Marina had arranged for them to meet yet more relatives. Jorge and Loli were the great-grandchildren of Mercedes' brother Ramón, the one who had emigrated to St. Louis. His oldest daughter Sagrario, the grandmother of these cousins, married an Asturian immigrant to the U.S. in the 1930s, and they returned to Avilés to make their life there. Ramón's daughter and her husband had spun the Indiano story in the opposite direction: they had shown up in Avilés with a little money and made a fortune when the city boomed in the 1950s.

* * *

And then it was over. Part of Robert desperately wished they had more time in Avilés. But part of him was glad they did not. He was saturated. He could absorb no more experiences until it all had the time and space to settle.

When they passed those crumbling factories again, driving away from Avilés, Robert felt ashamed of his initial reaction for the third time. Even they looked beautiful to him now.

Years before, Robert had searched the Ellis Island database and found the ship manifest records for his great-grandparents. As he and Marlene drove back to Barcelona for their flight to Berlin, it occurred to him that they had come to Asturias one week before the hundredth anniversary of Antonio Rivas' departure for America.

Epilogue

R obert returned to Avilés six months after that initial arrival with Marlene. He spent two weeks visiting with his relatives, and meeting others he had missed the first time. He enjoyed getting to know them without the pressure of the original encounter. Then he went down to Oviedo, the capital of the modern Principality of Asturias—as it was of the medieval Asturian Kingdom—and he walked the Camino Primitivo, the original ninth-century Way of St. James.

Over two weeks and more than 200 miles, the Camino de Santiago carried Robert through the heart of Asturias and Galicia. When he set foot for the first time in the homeland of Antonio Rivas, on a gravel hillside trail in the rain, powerful sobs exploded from him unexpectedly. One second, he was merrily tromping up the trail, savoring the foggy, windy solitude. The next he was gasping and weeping with an intensity he had never experienced.

Robert placed a white stone for Antonio on the cairn marking the border. From his backpack, he pulled a plastic bottle he had filled with local red wine in the village where he had spent the night before. He raised the bottle and toasted his great-grandfather and Galicia. He suspected that under the stern exterior he had seen in the photos, Antonio would have been delighted. He hoped so anyway.

He returned to Berlin after the Camino, feeling as if he had closed the circle which opened a hundred years before with his great-grandparents' emigration. But he quickly grew restless again, and his thoughts drifted often to Asturias. Six months later, Robert moved to

Avilés, planning to live there for a year. He had to know this land and his family there better. His previous visits felt like they had only been an introduction.

Robert passed many carefree hours and days with his relatives, especially Antonio, Marina and Jorge. His cousins were happy to have him around, and they took him on frequent excursions to every part of Asturias. He grew closer to them than he imagined possible.

Every chance he got, Robert hiked the coastal trails alone, through the fragrant eucalyptus groves and along the high crags overlooking the sea. He went often to Arnao and stood in the sun and stiff wind on a bluff looking down at the castillete—which was now a museum of the Real Compañía mine—and across the small bay to the smelter where Antonios Primero and Segundo met and became friends.

He rented an apartment on Calle Rivero, where the street entered the Plaza de España. The Franciscan Brothers' was his parish church. Robert loved how its cut sandstone blocks were rounded unevenly at the edges and ridged horizontally—like a seaside escarpment—by the centuries of buffeting from ocean winds and rain.

Robert attended mass only occasionally, but he stopped in the church every time the door was open when he passed. He always knelt and said the same prayer, as he had at each church and chapel along the Camino de Santiago: "Thank you for this. For this day and this place. And for my family and for Marlene. Please keep them healthy and happy. Please help me always to listen. To know the way and to have the wisdom to follow it. And please keep me strong."

On a summery September day, a month after Robert moved to Avilés, he and Marina's son Arturo were strolling back toward Robert's apartment. They had spent the afternoon, in Asturian style, eating well and drinking well to celebrate the wedding anniversary of Marina and Arturo Sr., who had married six days before Robert was born.

"Let's get a beer over there, at Ochobre," Arturo said as they came across the Plaza de Carbayedo, where the old livestock market had been held until the 1940s. The compact, two-storey house in which the bar was located resembled a small fortress, with its thick walls of uncut stones, small windows and narrow wooden door. "This is one of my favorite spots in Avilés," Arturo said after they bought their bottles of Mahou and sat down in the sun on the elevated walk looking out over the grassy and treed square. "I think it was one of the first houses built on Carbayedo, back in the sixteenth century. The family who ran the livestock market lived there, and they used to sell beer and cider on hot days from the ground floor window."

Robert felt at home. "Thank you for inviting me today, Arturo. It meant a lot to be to be there."

"Of course we invite you," Arturo said, a bemused look on his face. "You're not just some American relative who dropped in for a visit. You're a member of the family."

Acknowledgments

I should like to thank Alex Myers for reading the first draft and for his suggestions which transformed the book. Michael Mirolla for agreeing to publish my debut novel, and Julie Roorda for her thoughtful editing. Ulrike-Luisa Eckhardt for helping me find my way. And Marina Iglesias González, Antonio González Díaz, and Jorge Rodriguez González for welcoming me into their lives and making Asturias home.

About the Author

SCOTT WALKER grew up in West Virginia and currently lives on the northwest coast of Spain. In between, he taught high school history, shilled for a Congressman, and has worked as a news analyst and editor while living in Virginia, Florida, New Orleans, Prague, and Berlin.

Printed in January 2018
by Gauvin Press,
Gatineau, Québec